# EVIL IN RETURN

# Evil in Return

## Weyman Jones

**FIVE STAR**
*A part of Gale, Cengage Learning*

GALE
CENGAGE Learning·

Farmington Hills, Mich • San Francisco • New York • Waterville, Maine
Meriden, Conn • Mason, Ohio • Chicago

LIBRARY OF CONGRESS CATALOGING-IN-PUBLICATION DATA

Jones, Weyman, 1928–
    Evil in return / by Weyman Jones. — First edition
        pages cm
    ISBN 978-1-4328-2911-7 (hardcover) — ISBN 1-4328-2911-4
(hardcover) — ISBN 978-1-4328-2908-7 (ebook)
    1. Cherokee Indians—Fiction. 2. Kidnapping—Fiction. 3.
Revenge—Fiction I. Title.
PS3560.O5584E95 2014
813'.54—dc23                                    2014014091

First Edition. First Printing: August 2014
Find us on Facebook– https://www.facebook.com/FiveStarCengage
Visit our website– http://www.gale.cengage.com/fivestar/
Contact Five Star™ Publishing at FiveStar@cengage.com

Printed in the United States of America
1 2 3 4 5 6 7 18 17 16 15 14

This book, about evils of the past, is dedicated to hope for the future:

Jason, Kelsey and Connor

# ACKNOWLEDGMENTS

My first readers offered thoughtful comments and suggestions, many of which are incorporated in this final version. Thank you, my Three M's—Mike Rodrigue, Marilynn Greenwald and Mike Plumer.

Those to whom evil is done
Do evil in return.

—W. H. Auden

# CHAPTER 1

"Three-quarters of the universe is dark energy, and most of the rest is dark matter, which means we know nothing about almost everything," Uncle Apple had said.

Why had he thought of that? As Ron selected the blue button-down shirt and navy windbreaker, he realized that he'd been thinking about Walt. Thinking that Walt didn't look like a real estate operator, more like Mr. Appler, back at Custis Academy. Mr. Appler knew the kids called him Uncle Apple. He even drew an apple under his name on the whiteboard at the beginning of each semester. Rumpled. Always needed a haircut. Not fat, but soft-looking. And the same way of smiling as he talked, as if he didn't want you to take what he was saying seriously. But it usually showed up on the quiz, and Walt usually came back to what he'd said in another conversation, as if checking to see whether you'd been paying attention.

As Ron changed into the button-down shirt and black jeans he remembered Uncle Apple saying, " 'Carpe diem,' boys. Seize the day. It never comes around again. Now, in the next ten minutes write a paragraph comparing and contrasting that with 'memento mori,' Remember that we are only mortal. It was written by the same Roman poet, Horace. Does it express the same idea?"

Ron laced the black and gray running shoes carefully and double-knotted them. With part of his head still back in Custis, years ago, he sang under his breath: "You can tell a Harvard man about a mile away, because he looks just like he'd blow away."

He found the can of talcum powder in the medicine cabinet and carried it downstairs to the garage, telling himself not to hurry. It's like foreplay. Savor each step along the way. "He always dresses with the greatest of care, he's got lace upon his underwear."

The box of vinyl gloves was waiting on the half-empty sack of driveway salt in the corner. "He always wears a pink chemise, he's got dimples on his rosy red knees."

The vinyl was flimsy, easy to rip, and so he blew up an extra pair. He sprinkled talcum powder on his hands and smoothed it. Like a baby's ass. Come to think of it, like Amy's ass.

Take your time. Feel the buzz. Live the moment. Carpe diem.

Walt had said he needed someone in the company who doesn't have to be told. Someone with initiative. "When you run a business, sometimes you need someone to take out the trash." What he hadn't said was, "Without getting your hands dirty." Ron shoved a pair of gloves into each jacket pocket.

He pulled the bag of salt back from the wall and fumbled behind it for the nine-inch butterfly knife. He snapped it open. Cheap, available and lethal. The kind of a blade an MS 13 gang kid would buy. No use for it in the plan, but it nestled in his palm as if it were custom crafted for him. He ran the blade along the pad of his left thumb, watching the red line welling behind it. He felt nothing. Razor sharp, but also he had a high pain threshold. He couldn't smell roses, either, or hear the difference between major and minor. He found a rag under the tool box and pressed it to the seeping wound as he shoved the knife into a hip pocket. Just in case. Contingency planning, that's the flip side of carpe diem.

"What I need is someone who sees opportunity," Walt had said. "I have lots of people, good people, who do exactly what they're told. But I need someone who thinks like me."

The can of purple spray paint was on what he called his workbench, the old dresser with blue paint showing through the chipped white enamel. He took the can out of the hardware-store plastic bag, uncapped it and tested the trigger. Firm. But he'd like to see the spray. He held it inside the bag for a squirt, but then hesitated. Maybe a tiny fleck of purple paint would land in his garage. Better to stop on the way and test it on the pavement. Maybe in the strip mall where Walt had slowed the Volvo to read the signs. "Bodega. I know what that is. Wetback grocery store. But what's a Hoy Delicatessen? Sauerkraut on the tamales? Chiles on the potato salad?"

Walt's Volvo had been a surprise. He'd expected a car that announced something. A Jag, or at least a Lexus. Now that he thought about it, maybe the Volvo *did* say something. Conservative. Nothing flashy, but quality. Understated. Man to be trusted.

He smiled at the thought. Yes, the strip mall would be the place to test the spray paint. He could paint a "13" territory marker.

"You know how many people there are in the world?" Walt had asked at the Depot Road light, watching an obviously pregnant woman push a twin-stroller across the intersection.

"Gotta be millions," Ron said. "Hundreds of millions."

The light changed and Walt eased forward, taking no chances. "Billions," he said. "Over seven billion people. All of 'em consuming and polluting. And a couple of hundred new ones every minute."

The milk crate he used for recycling was next to the bag of salt. Fishing through the empty soup and tuna cans and wine bottles, he selected the Meat Market Red bottle because when he'd emptied it he'd jammed its cork back in. He wiggled the cork out. Good tight seal. Thank you, Walter Taylor.

The gasoline can was in the far corner, with the plastic funnel waiting on top. He fitted the funnel into the neck, poured the bottle about three-quarters full, corked it, turned it upside down to make sure it didn't leak and sniffed his hands. He hadn't spilled a drop, but the fumes were clinging to him. Should have worn gloves.

The butane lighter was in the top left-hand drawer of the dresser, along with a jumble of mismatched nuts and bolts, wood screws, nails and rubber bands. He clicked the butane lighter on and off three times. Strong pencil of flame every time. He fished a rubber band out of the drawer, snapped the lighter into flame and stretched the rubber band from the thumb-press starter around the bottom. It held the flame on. He slipped the rubber band along the top until the flame snapped off but the band was still in place and then, careful not to move the band, slipped it into his shirt pocket.

He tore a rag from an old t-shirt in the box under the battered workbench-dresser and tied it around the neck of the bottle with about two inches dangling free. Thank you, Google, for the tutorial. He put the bottle and the gasoline can on the passenger-side floor of his VW Jetta. Common car on Long Island. Candy-apple red, which looked black at night. He hadn't bought it with that in mind, and he didn't believe that some invisible hand had guided his choice. Just luck of the draw, but he was lucky—that he believed.

He walked around to the rear. Take the bulb out of the light above the license plate? How to do that? And a missing light just might catch the eye of a patrol car. McVeigh had been caught because he didn't have a license plate. Rub dirt on the license plate? Probably wouldn't accomplish much. Should have thought about this earlier, made a plan.

Fuck it. Can't think of everything. And besides, safe isn't the point. Safe is no fun, and this job has to be bold and brash, the way a street punk would demonstrate his creds. An MS 13 job.

He went back inside and washed his hands at the kitchen sink with pot-scrubber cleanser. "Out, damned spot," he said, still thinking of Uncle Apple. "Young men should dream brave dreams," Appler had said. "But grown men should understand limits." Why not opportunity? You never understood opportunity, Uncle Apple. Not in your little chalk-dust world.

He held his palms to his face. Soapy but sweaty. Not a bad sign. Adrenaline sharpens perceptions, quickens reactions. Sweetens the risk. As he went back to the garage he yawned, and then he nodded. Reflexive response to excitement. His body telling him to relax. Get ready for action.

He stood by the driver's-side door of the Jetta as he went through a mental checklist. Molotov cocktail (where did that name come from?)—check. Gas can—check. Butane lighter—check. Gloves—check. Spray can—check. Balls, to savor risk—check. He hitched up the crotch of his black jeans and climbed under the wheel.

He backed out carefully—society survives because criminals make stupid mistakes—and turned onto Clay Pits Road. Where did that name come from? And East Rogues Path. Probably from back when rich guys like Walt wore powdered wigs.

Down Pulaski past the Dolan Medical Center, where no one is turned away, and the free preschool run by the Family Service League, he passed Patrician Drive and Stonehenge Circle. Pretentious names assigned by developers for families moving up from Queens and Brooklyn. Now they should be named Underwater Avenue and Foreclosure Court. In the headlights the oaks flashed glints of rust. The dogwoods were already wine-red but the maples were green and yellow. Halfway into fall. Walt would say halfway into *the* fall.

The moon, behind scudding clouds, was also in transition. Gibbon? Gibbous. A good word. Sounded bloody. A bloody moon in October. Best time of the year. Boot-camp weather.

San Diego comes to Long Island. Starlings are painting the sidewalks white, but at least they're moving on. Not like the damn geese that forgot how to migrate when they found the golf courses. Now even the environmental whackos agree that their nests have to be disrupted. For the good of the geese. Green fairways for geese are like welfare for wetbacks.

In the village of Huntington, couples waited on brick sidewalks for a table at Jonathon's, which reminded Ron of the guys standing around the hiring site in the barrio next to the train station. When Walt had stopped at the CVS parking lot light, half a dozen Latinos crowded up to the windows. "Job for me, boss?" "Yard work?" "Construction?"

"Poor devils," Walt had said, driving on. "Nobody with a payroll is going to hire illegals. Not since the ICE swept through here and grabbed a couple of contractors. Sooner these losers realize that and go back across the border, the better they'll be. The better we'll all be. And the neighborhood will have a chance."

He talked like Mr. Appler. Lectured. "You know what globalization is? A race to the bottom. Big competition to see who'll work for less. And the winners? Not Huntington, New York, USA. No chance. Mexico and Columbia and Pakistan will set the wage scale for everybody. Logic of capitalism. No way to stop it. But we can delay it a little. Maybe a generation or two. Your kids, my grandchildren. Enjoy the decadence of American empire. Golden age. Stem the tide, as long as we can."

The hiring site was deserted now, except for a huddled figure on the curb with a bottle in a paper bag beside him. Ron slowed, looking around the empty street, and stopped. "Hey, old man. You hungry?" No movement. Good. Eyes that do not see are better than no eyes at all. If the cops ask him what he'd seen, he'd seen nothing.

The strip mall with the bodega and deli was a block down

the street. He parked alongside three cars in front of La Hacienda Restaurant with the green awning that advertised "Especialidades: steak—marioscos pastas—sopas." Better to be one of four than a lone car in a parking area. He took a pair of the vinyl gloves from his jacket pocket and slid his powdered hands into them.

"Domenic's Hardware used to be in there," Walt had said. "And Smith's Stationery. When I bought into this community, roses were growing in the front yards and guys washed their cars in the driveways on Saturday afternoons. White guys."

Ron looked around as he took the spray can from the passenger-side floor, shook it four times and then slid out from under the wheel. A salsa guitar thrummed from an open window somewhere. Homesick music. Holding the can knee high, he squirted a solid purple stream onto the concrete. Side-stepping, he sprayed a tilted "13" across the entire lined-off parking space. He looked around again—no one—and got back into the Jetta. He set the spray can upright on the passenger-side floor, twisted the key with a gloved hand and backed out of the strip mall.

"That house," Walt had said, slowing the Volvo to point, "the one on the corner with a strip of siding missing? When I bought it, that was what we called a 'starter home.' Something a young couple could afford. Some paint and wallpaper and maybe some new foundation planting—it was a house where you started a family. A life." He shook his head. "Now look at it."

Ron turned on Depot Road, twisting his head left and right to check the sidewalks and cramped front yards. No one.

"Now I'm stuck with it," Walt had said. "And I can't legally rent it for enough to cover the carrying costs. Just the insurance, a neighborhood like this . . . ," he shook his head again. "I have to get fifteen hundred a month, which doesn't even provide for depreciation, and the only tenant who'll pay that is a wetback who is subletting to three illegal families for probably eight hundred apiece. They hang up blankets to make rooms and cook on hotplates. Place is a bonfire, just waiting for a spark. And the basement—who knows how many wetbacks he crowds in there, at maybe $500 a head? These people prey on their own. Trash preying on trash. And I'm providing the house." He raised both hands to show innocently empty palms. "I hate it, but I'm trapped. Just like they are."

Ron stopped across the street from the corner house with the missing siding strip. Lights showed in upstairs windows and, sure enough, spilled out of a basement window onto the litter in the bare dirt yard. The gibbous moon burned through a gauzy layer of cloud to create momentary graveyard shadows. Time to disrupt the nest.

He drove on, paying close attention to the accelerated thump of his heart. This was it. His hands were steady on the wheel. Control and confidence. Out here on the edge is where you feel life. Without risk, life is just . . . drift. The choice is to drift it or live it.

Ron parked at the intersection where he had four escape routes: north and south on New York Avenue, east and west on Depot Road. The butane lighter was in the right-hand pocket of his jeans. He looked around. No cars. He got out, walked around, opened the passenger door, lifted out the gasoline can and set it on the pavement. The wine bottle had fallen onto its side, but when he ran his fingers around the cork he could feel no seepage. He put the bottle on the pavement between his feet. Carefully, he opened the can and dribbled gasoline onto the rag wrapped around the neck of the bottle. An astringent smell like cleanser. Taking out the trash.

He screwed the cap back onto the can and lifted it with his left hand. Maybe half a gallon. He picked up the spray can from the floor and slipped it into his jacket pocket. He grabbed the bottle with his right hand and kicked the car door shut. Walking toward the house with the missing siding strip, he listened to his heart. *Thump-thump, thump-thump.* Alive. On the edge. He didn't hurry.

He stopped in front of the house. What was that music? Some kind of a jiggling beat for a Spanish falsetto. Not anything American. He checked both ways. No one. The moon obligingly hid behind orbital cotton. He took a deep breath, fumbled the spray can from his jacket and scrawled "13" on the sidewalk. Not as elegantly tilted as his work in the strip mall parking lot, but good enough for gang penmanship.

He took the butane lighter from his other jacket pocket and thumbed a flame. Everything was working. Don't get complacent. Expect something unexpected. The soaked rag started with a cracking flash. Holding it at arm's length, he took another deep breath, chewing his cheeks, trying to taste the moment. Risk and control.

He tossed the bottle, watching its flaring arc into the litter. A perfect, simple shape against the clutter of corruption.

Nothing happened. Had he heard a crash of glass? He thought so. He tossed the gasoline can and then the lighter into the yard and walked on. A cat darted through the milky light on the sidewalk and disappeared.

Whoof!

He stopped and looked back. Flame sprouted around the trash.

He realized he was rooted to the sidewalk—how long?—watching the hypnotic flames licking along the foundation toward the siding. He wrenched himself around. Street was still empty. He walked back to the intersection, listening to the rhythm of his heels on the concrete. Brisk. Not like a man escaping, just a man with somewhere to go.

As he opened the door of the Jetta he allowed himself a look. Upstairs in the burning house a light was on. Those wetbacks in the basement, their backs better still be sopping wet. How long would it take the fire department? Hook-and-ladder trucks, guys in clumsy boots and those antique-looking helmets dragging hoses and climbing around the roof to chop holes. Ambulances, stretchers, police cars, whirling red lights. He could stand right here and watch.

No. Don't get sucked in. He slid under the wheel and started the car. As he drove away his rearview mirror bloomed orange.

This was too easy. There should have been some danger, some surprise to provide that shot of adrenalin. He held the speed at thirty-two as he cruised past the La Hacienda strip mall. He slowed at the hiring site. The homeless man was still there, nodding over his bottle in the paper bag. Ron slowed and slipped the shift lever into neutral, leaning forward to reach the butterfly knife in his hip pocket. His adrenalin was buzzing again. He flipped the blade open and tested the point on the ball of his thumb. He felt the tiny prick. His skin had come alive. Every follicle spoke to its hair. He caught a whiff of greasy onion cooking from La Hacienda and, from some distant speaker, the thud of a bass guitar that seemed to be synched to the suddenly-felt beat of his heart. Had the clouds broken apart? The moon shone a stage light on the huddled figure. His mouth went dry.

He saw it in his mind's eye: Stop far enough from the curb to open the door. Slip the gear into park and step out. Left hand grabs the tangle of gray hair as the right flips the blade open. Jerk the head up. Bend over to look into the bleary eyes. "Hey, old man. Memento mori." Record the moment. Watch the face while swiping the blade across the throat.

Would the eyes widen and bug? Would the old piece of trash try to say something? Would there be wheezing and kicking and a lot of blood? Yes, of course there would. Blood all over. After he'd been so careful with the spray paint and the gloves. Control and confidence.

He tossed the knife out the window. Gang weapon for the cops to find. He hesitated before he shifted into drive. Leaving this place, this moment, was like going from Technicolor to black and white. Once underway he drove a little faster. Get into the traffic on Jericho and then he was home free. Behind and to his left he heard a siren wind up its wail. Volunteer firemen on the way from Huntington. Now he had ears like an antelope. It would be fun to watch them, but that's a sucker play. For poor schmucks who can't help themselves. He could turn away. Control and confidence.

He sang to the passing street lights and big-box stores and car dealers: "Fair Harvard, thy sons to thy jubilee throng, and with blessings surrender thee o'er." As he turned east on Jericho he laughed and sang, "Surrender thee whore."

★ ★ ★ ★ ★

# Two Weeks Later

★ ★ ★ ★ ★

The trouble with Eichmann was precisely that so many were like him, and that the many were neither perverted nor sadistic, that they were, and still are, terribly and terrifyingly normal.

—Hannah Arendt

# CHAPTER 2

"Your website says you know how to squeeze money out of the privileged class." His telephone voice sounded young, and not from here on Long Island.

"It does?" she floundered, aware that she was being tweaked, but not ready with a comeback. "I thought it said I manage fundraisers."

"Same thing, isn't it?" The voice was definitely young, and not local. Not even New York. And testing her.

"No. I help people use money to create human value." And then, to stop playing defense, "I didn't catch your name."

"Because I didn't toss it. Have you heard of the de Dendermonde mansion?"

Another test? "No. Should I?"

"No, and that's the point. Nobody has. We're not open yet, and we need to make a splash when we do." Flat intonations. Some flat place. Indiana, or Kansas, maybe.

"What is it?

"*Newsday* calls it a Gilded Age mansion. Truth is, it missed the top of the arc. But there was lots of gelt left over. One of our trustees calls it the Gelt Age."

She laughed. Then, going carefully because a first impression can turn a prospect into a client: "That period was all about gelt, for sure, but 'gelt age'? I don't think that sings as a slogan."

"Do you know what 'gelt' comes from?" Not waiting for an answer: "Geld. You know what that means?"

Test question—can she play with the guys? She answered, "Cutting off the balls." His laugh sounded like she'd passed and so she went on: "What's that got to do with money?"

"I don't know. Matter of fact, I don't know a lot about money, which is why I called you. I'm told you can get gelt out of a gala." She wondered who'd recommended her but didn't ask, as if another recommendation were no big deal. "I've had good luck with fundraisers." Set a business tone: "Are you a five-oh-one-C-three?"

"Not yet, but the paperwork's done. We're not open yet, and we need to make a splash when we do. When can you come over? Case the joint and talk about how you might be able to help us?"

She waited a strategic few seconds before she said, "I could come by on Friday afternoon around four, if you're free." As if Wednesday and Thursday from dawn to dark weren't also wide open on her calendar.

The directions she got off the Internet took her along the spine of a peninsula that separated Centerport and Northport Harbors. Brown-skinned crews raked leaves out of sculptured beds of impatiens, rhododendrons and azaleas. From the road she could see that the faded and weary de Dendermonde mansion looked across both harbors and down on an architectural—what would she call it? Mishmash. Maybe a 1950s development morphing into the twenty-first century. Ranches and splits were now being razed, one at a time, to make room for so-called colonials with wraparound porches and Victorians with turrets wearing witches'-hat roofs. A sky blue BMW was parked in front of a three-car garage, probably waiting for a thirty-something sporting a Caribbean tan who drove with the top down and the air conditioner at full blast. Young families on their way up and eager to show it. The kind of neighbors who could raise plenty of political hell about a gala, with its deejay spinning amplified rock. And where are the paying guests going to park? Issues to raise when she has a contract in hand.

The driveway was announced by squat pillars that might have been copied from a Greek temple, supporting a hip-sprung cast-iron gate that could never be closed again. Okay, we're talking 1910 here. Flappers and bathtub gin. So the gate is a ruin. Didn't the Gatsby people ruin everything they touched? But can she pump herself up for another bash with Charleston contests and art deco favors? The idea brought a smile. With her credit card maxed out—you damn betcha.

Crunching up the curving, gravel drive past overgrown forsythias into a plaza, or piazza—some kind of a pretentious waste of space—she passed a marble nymph supporting a five-foot urn. Must have once been a bubble fountain feeding that crumbling reflecting pool on the lower terrace. She parked her Camry, fresh from the car wash but showing its age, right in front of the entrance. Let him check it out. Cheap wheels, but believe me, I've got a rich rolodex.

She flipped down the visor mirror, added just a touch of lipstick and fluffed her boring brown hair, thinking, for the umpteenth time, that if she wasn't ready to change the color, what about some highlights? She straightened the skirt of her navy suit so as not to show too much leg getting out of the car. Long legs that Ron had said go all the way to heaven. The bastard.

When she stepped out, she could see the weary sag of the mansion's roofline. It was some sort of Mediterranean architecture, maybe Spanish Colonial, with deep windows protected by wrought iron that echoed the ruined gate. The white plastered walls were streaked and stained. Some of the red tiles on the roof were broken. Suppose that means leaks? Wobbling a little on the Belgian blocks, probably the real deal brought over as ballast in the holds of merchant ships and not the imitations that lined the driveways she'd passed on the way here, she decided that this was a great place to break a heel. Have to build a boardwalk for the gala. So much to do before this place could be ready for a fundraiser. Even then, another restored North Shore mansion competing with the Phipps and the Marshall Fields and the Goulds and all the others—what kind of a crowd would another gala draw? And would the yield even cover the renovation cost? Another post-contract discussion.

Skinny marble dogs—greyhounds, maybe, or whippets—guarded the landing above the three wide steps. Just below the keystone a block was missing. Imagining herself arriving at a fundraiser, she thought maybe she could turn that touch of decadence into fun. Maybe something out of the *Son of Frankenstein* movie. The studded door was recessed under an arch like a church's entrance. Or a prison door out of Dickens. That had possibilities. Before she had to decide whether to knock, the door opened.

A young man in jeans and a yellow cotton sweater, hiked up past his elbows to reveal forearms as bare as a girl's, offered his hand, saying, "Welcome to my humble abode." As she took his hand—firm grip but delicate bones—he went on: "I'm Andrew but I go by Charley. You're Samantha. How do you feel about Sam?" His hair fell halfway to his shoulders in a surfer's bob, but it was thick and black instead of sun-streaked blond.

"Sam is okay with me. How do you get from Andrew to Charley?" She noticed that he was only an inch or so taller than her five feet six but that somehow he occupied a lot of space. The angle of his eyes and set of his cheekbones suggested Polish, but his skin was dark. Eurasian? A touch of something exotic. She thought of a term she'd learned in a rose garden fundraiser: hybrid beauty.

"Long story. I'll tell you sometime." His hand was firm on

her elbow as he steered her into a dark entrance hall. She noticed a terrazzo floor in a geometric pattern and a chandelier that made her think of "Phantom of the Opera" suspended from a dim fresco of clouds and cherubs. "But first I want to show you around Plaisance. You want coffee? Tea? Diet Coke? Boilermaker?"

"Maybe a coke later. What is Plaisance?" His jeans were pressed. He probably rolled the toothpaste up from the bottom and made his bed before breakfast.

"That's what she called the place. Countess de Dendermonde. It seems to mean 'pleasure' with some kind of a nautical flavor. I know that 'bateaux de plaisance' means 'pleasure boat,' and she loved her yacht. Even had some yacht speaker tubes installed in the house." He took her attaché case. "I'll stash this in the drawing room while we're walking around the place."

Through the door he opened she glimpsed a gold-and-white room with leggy furniture and what looked like a carved white-marble fireplace that had never known a speck of soot. When he came back she followed him into another dark room where the drapes were drawn to protect what might be Aubusson rugs and damask-upholstered chairs. Not a place for a crowd to stand around with drinks and hors d'oevres. "She was a countess?"

"I think she was probably an adventurer. Brooklyn girl went to Belgium and bagged a count." He shoved open a heavy door that revealed a shadowy room where bearded men peered out of gilt frames into narrow shafts of light admitted through drawn drapes. "What I said about the gelt age on the phone, remember? The proper name is 'La Belle Époque.' Beautiful clothes and luxury."

"And this is the time to sell that," she said, drawing on last night's Wikipedia research. "In tough times, people crave glamour. The Golden Age of Hollywood was the Depression."

"I hadn't thought of it like that," he said, "but yes—that's what we're bringing back. Glamour. Divine right of wealth." He ducked his head a little and grinned, like a little boy caught showing off. "Maybe we could put some theater into our gala. Actors playing some of the famous guests that were entertained here."

"Hey, that's an idea," she said. "There must be a dozen amateur theater groups on Long Island. Who were the famous guests?"

"I looked through some scrapbooks, but didn't really study them. I remember that Caruso sang here at least once." He pushed open a door into a ballroom with a parquet floor and flocked scarlet paper, which she associated with western movie whorehouses. Another crystal chandelier, this one caught in a beam of light from the arched windows that revealed a festoon of cobwebs. Cleaning service would need ladders. "Right here, in this room." He pointed. "And Pearl Buck and Howard Hughes were sitting right here, listening."

She wondered who Pearl Buck was, but didn't ask as he led her into an echoing, white-tiled kitchen. She noticed his tight butt, like a compressed spring propelling a high-energy walk. Butcher-block counters bigger than her dining room table. Good. Caterers could deploy an army of waiters from here. He swept a gesture. "This is a Warren and Wetmore house. Vanderbilt's architects. The same guys that designed Grand Central Station."

She nodded, as if recognizing the name, and then stopped, looking at a black cast iron structure crouching against the far wall. "What is *that*?"

He laughed. "Welcome to the age of the beautiful people. All those dazzling dinners were prepared by Irish women bending over coal stoves down here. First thing I did when I took this job was to install propane burners and tanks outside the window there." He opened one of the walk-in refrigerators. "Let's have that Coke in here. Where the help hung out. My kind of people."

"The curator is help?" she said, pulling a stool from under the triple sink up to the cutting table in the center of the kitchen.

Over his shoulder, with his head in the refrigerator: "I don't have a museum to curate yet. If we get there . . ." he stood and managed to shrug, turning around with bottles in his hand and elbowing the refrigerator door closed. "But for the time being, my job description says 'estate manager.' Truth is, I'm the caretaker. Glass?"

When she shook her head he dragged a stool to a place across the table from her. "Get free rent from the Historical Society to keep the place from being vandalized. I keep thinking I ought to learn to cook." He swept a big gesture. "All this equipment. But I keep ordering Chinese and pizza. You're wondering where I get my gelt, aren't you?"

She nodded, not saying that what she was really wondering was what kind of a fee the budget of the Historical Society might support. "I'm a day trader," he said. "My Belle Epoch alarm goes off at five every morning."

"Your what?"

"It's a beautiful old brass clock that I found in Countess D's bedroom. Still keeps time. Anyway . . . I fire up my laptop two hours before the bell and read the posts of a bunch of people who play half a point, up or down, on the opening quote of a dozen stocks. I'm usually zeroed out by noon. Plenty of time left for what I like to call my curatorial duties."

"What are those?"

He waved a dismissive gesture with his bottle. "I Google the furniture and art of the period, looking for something we might like to acquire. And I try to plan some fundraising, which I've come to realize I don't know from Sanskrit."

He tossed his hair back in what seemed a feminine gesture.

She asked, "But you *do* know the period?"

He smiled, considering his answer, and then opened his hand on the table. A hand that could reach an octave. The thought of his hands on a keyboard pulsed a watch-your-step warning: she had an eye for a man's hands the way some women notice a tight butt. Come to think, she'd also noticed his butt. "Not really," he said. "Did you ever see that t-shirt, 'You must have mistaken me for someone who gives a shit?' That's me. The job was posted on Craigslist. I can write a dynamite resumé, and nobody checks references. Especially if you're willing to work cheap."

Those bottomless brown eyes held her a moment before she answered: "No, but I'd like to know why you wanted this job."

"I'll tell you that, but first—aren't you curious about your own job? Who referred you to me?"

"One of my satisfied clients, right?"

"Wrong. I found Langshan Public Relations on the Web. When I called, I expected to get somebody named Ron Langshan."

She managed a smile and a nod to say she wasn't surprised. "My husband. We were in business together, but special events aren't his bag."

"You *were* in business together?"

"We were. Now we're separated. Divorce in the works." She wasn't going to mention the pending order of protection. "I didn't change the name of the agency but I narrowed the focus to special events. You must have gotten that from the website."

He nodded. "Why I called you. We need to run a fundraiser."

On familiar ground now, she leaned forward: "Let's talk about that. Get you from caretaker to curator."

He drained his bottle and stood. "Okay. First, we need to talk about a narrative. A storyline that differentiates Plaisance from all the other Gold Coast relics. Something that skillful PR can turn into gelt." He motioned to her. "I'm going to show you the most interesting room in the place. The scene of the drama."

Drama. He was giving her a one-man show. So find a way to applaud. He opened the door to what looked like service stairs and fumbled along the wall for the light switch. "Right now, this is the new age of entitlement, y'know? And behind every great fortune is a great crime."

"That's an interesting idea."

"It's not original," he said with a dismissive wave. "Did you know that Brookville is the richest zip code in America?"

She nodded. "I saw that."

"So we're going to invite all of today's Long Island entitled— with all their ill-gotten gelt—to come visit America's original entitlement class. Hang onto the banister, these steps are steep."

As she followed him down the threadbare carpeted stairs he kept talking over his shoulder: "But Countess D wasn't just a party girl. She had a heart, even though she kept it hidden down here. We've got to figure out how to spring this on our guests. You know, get the most mileage out of it, because this is more interesting than all that period stuff upstairs."

Pointing down the windowless hall with four wooden doors, he said, "Those are storage closets. Two of them are cedar-lined for woolens. That door at the end goes into the furnace room, which has a coal chute from outside. There's also a humongous pump with cast-iron pipes that brought water up from the harbor into her pool behind the back patio. She had a pretty little private beach, but I guess she thought a salt water pool had more class." He turned to open a door opposite the stairs and stood aside for her to enter a square, yellow room with a big sun woven into an oval rag rug that might have come from a craft fair. "Here's the heart of our narrative."

Four miniature chairs were drawn up to a knee-high table in the center of the room. On the left was a child-size bed under a shelf where two lead-soldier armies menaced each other. At the far end was a wing chair covered in purple brocade with gold threads that seemed out of place on the rag rug among the miniature furniture and toys. Next to it was an end table with what looked like a portrait clipped from a magazine of a dark man in a turban. Overhead, a flared brass fixture was missing a bulb. Beyond the chair was another door.

"She called this the nursery," he said. "And apparently it was, literally." With a gesture toward the wing chair: "There was always a nurse on duty." He stepped in and closed the door, gesturing toward the child's bed. "Eric had a bed, but I guess the nurse had to spend the nights dozing in that chair. Their meals must have been sent down from the kitchen. I think Eric might have been autistic, but I'm just guessing. The historical record is almost silent. We only know that he was 'touched,' which was something that Countess D felt she had to hide. But she hid it with constant attention."

Sam studied the collection of framed drawings over the little table: Alice holding a bottle labeled "Drink Me," the white rabbit in ascot and waistcoat looking at a watch on a chain, Alice dancing with a weeping tortoise and a menacing gryphon, the grinning Cheshire cat disappearing into the foliage of a tree and a scowling Queen of Hearts. Sam said, "It's a nice room. A little claustrophobic, but I feel a mother in here."

He nodded. "I think Countess D was a real mother. But she also soundproofed this room, as best she could in those days. Eric must have been a handful at times."

Sam hugged her arms under her breasts, suddenly feeling a basement chill. "Noise? Is that how you come up with the idea that he was probably autistic?"

He shook his head. "We've located a few of her letters. Not many, but one described Eric as flapping his arms. He seemed to be constantly in motion and easily frustrated." He pointed.

"And that's obviously Eric's table. See what's on it?"

She took another step into the room. "A chess set?"

Smiling, he nodded. "With a game in progress. I don't know if that's a real game—hard to believe that nobody's touched the pieces in all this time—but a chess set for a kid who was only about six? I think maybe he was a savant."

"What became of him?"

"More silent history. Countess D went back to Europe. She entertained Hemingway and Gertrude Stein, and she bought a Picasso napkin drawing that's now probably worth more than I'll earn in a lifetime. But we don't know what happened to Eric. My guess? He was lobotomized into a vegetable. That was the preferred treatment for those who are different in ways we don't understand."

Sam looked around, thinking about how to tell this story to potential donors. Compassionate mother, doing her best in the ignorance of her time. Sam noticed the top paper on the end table by the wing chair: a color print, a portrait, of a dark man in some kind of a turban. "Who's that?" she asked.

He took a step back, into the doorway. "A man who was different in ways people didn't understand. I want his difference in this room." He took another step and closed the door.

Click.

Sam stood in the center of the little room, waiting for the door to open. This must be some sort of a demonstration. Giving her a taste of life in this claustrophobic nursery. Soundproof, he'd said. She realized that she was breathing rapidly as the silence sucked the air out of this windowless little room. She went to the door, twisted the knob and tugged. Not even a rattle.

How long would he let this demonstration—or joke or whatever the hell it was—go on? He was going to get an earful. Is this your idea of getting me into that *narrative* you were talking about? Well grow up. Get me the hell out of here and then you're on your own with a gala that was never going to get off the ground anyway.

Her right hand twitched, reaching for the smartphone to call 911. Then she remembered: he took her attaché case: "I'll stash it in the drawing room while we're walking around her house." The attaché case had her smartphone, purse and laptop.

She hammered her fists against the door. Kicked it. Took off one of her black pumps and used the heel as a hammer. This whole gala idea, it never rang true. She should have smelled something fishy. Should never have followed him down here alone. But she was in business, wasn't she? What was she supposed to do, hire a bodyguard for prospect calls? Somehow this would turn out to be Ron's work. Hadn't the guy said he'd been looking for Ron? Somehow, Ron had gotten her into this.

How long had she been in here? She glanced at her watch: two thirty-five. The appointment had been at two. She'd been five minutes late to avoid seeming eager, so she'd been locked in here for what, ten minutes? Seemed like . . . she couldn't put a number on it.

Could he have locked her in by mistake? Was there any other possible explanation? Yes, a fairly obvious one, but she didn't want to think about it. Deep breath. Do something. Keep the panic down.

She slipped her shoe back on and went over to the little table. She picked up a child's chair and turned it over to grasp two of the legs. Walking back to the door she swung the chair as if throwing snow out of a shovel, finding a natural motion. She planted her feet, took a practice half-swing and then whacked the door alongside the knob. Satisfying impact, all the way to her shoulders.

She listened. He must have heard that. Then she widened her stance, took a full back swing and hit it again. One upright

36

chair strut shattered. Fragments bounced off the rag rug, and the back sagged crazily. She swiped a wrist shot into the door that broke off the chair back. Now, with the back at her feet and just the seat and legs in her hands, she faced the door and pounded with an overhead stroke. Found a rhythm. Hear this, you Craigslist phony. Playtime is over.

There was no echo. The sound of every blow seemed to die inside this airless room, but she was producing a satisfying mosaic of scars on the white paint. She paused. Did those marks organize themselves into a constellation? Orion? The letter *A*? Amy would be getting up from her nap soon, asking for Mommy.

The lights went out.

Absolute darkness. Darkness that clung to her face. Compressed her chest.

And silence. Only the sound of her breath.

She reached out, found the door and felt her way to a corner. She put her hands on the solid two walls and focused her mind on deep, regular breaths.

"All right," she said aloud to defeat the silence. "He's messing with my head." To push back, she tried to remember what she'd read about captives. Two women from some third-world place—the Philippines? Indonesia?—enslaved here on Long Island for years. And that monster in Europe who kept his daughter locked in the basement for years, raping her. This guy's a little dramatic, but a monster? No. All right, maybe. Maybe monsters come with soft brown eyes and big white smiles and a patter about Belle Epoque. If this is all about some sex fantasy . . . then what? Play along. Don't miss the main chance.

Her mind skipped a track. "I'm not going to miss the main chance," Ron had said when Walt hired him away from the PR agency. "PR is all about images and impressions. Real estate is about assets. Money."

What else did she know about captives? Something Scandinavian. Oslo? Maybe Stockholm. For some reason, perhaps just to claim a place in this black void, she said out loud: "He thinks scaring the shit out of me will make me his pal. So my job is to fake it. Play along until I can catch him off guard."

She pushed off from the wall, groping for the wing chair. To press back the silence she recited a school assignment: "If you can keep your head when all about you are losing theirs and blaming it on you . . ." There—the back of the wing chair. She fumbled around it and sat. Fuck you, Charley-not-Andrew. Out loud: "If you can trust yourself when all men doubt you, but make allowance for their doubting too."

The main chance idea had brought Ron into her mind. What had Charley said about Ron? When he called Langshan PR he'd expected to get Ron. Would he have brought Ron down here? Was *down here* the plan, or was he just making this up as he went along? That banter on the phone about gelt, was that scripted? Hadn't sounded like it. But so what? None of this was getting anywhere. She crossed her legs and closed her eyes against the pressing dark. "If you can wait but not be tired of waiting . . . I can wait you out, Charley-not-Andrew."

# CHAPTER 3

Charley climbed back to the kitchen, went across to the entrance hall and up the sweeping stairs supported by Ionic columns to the rose bedroom. That blossoming wallpaper was gaudy, but he had decided that it didn't overpower a big room with massive furniture. The mahogany sleigh-bed concealed a brass tube that sprouted through the floor in the corner. He shouldn't have told Sam that Countess D installed yacht speaker tubes in the house, but maybe Sam won't remember. He took his shoes off and stretched out on the bed. The albums and scrapbooks contained no evidence of a Count de Dendermonde, and Charley wondered if the Countess might have entertained some of those celebrity guests in this lumpy bed. Leaning over, the way she must have leaned to check on Eric and the nurse, he quietly twisted the butterfly latch and eased back the cover of the speaker tube.

"... the next part, something about dreaming and thinking, and then there's the bit about 'If you can meet with triumph and disaster, And treat those two imposters just the same.' Two imposters, that's pretty good. And somewhere in there is, 'If you can make one heap of all your winnings and risk it on one turn of pitch-and' "—pause—"pitch-and-something-or-other, 'And lose, and start again at your beginnings, And never breathe a word about your loss . . .' "

A sigh came up the brass tube. "Like being a loser is something to be proud of. Samantha, you were born to lose with men. Or maybe you were trained that way. Daddy wasn't all that bad, I guess, but he was no winner. Especially when he fell into the bottle, which got to be pretty often. Paul, he was crazy about me, but he gave off a whiff of the wimp, y'know?"

Charley propped his head on his fist. Should have a tape recorder so he could play this back to her. Down the tube. Her own voice coming to her out of the ceiling—that would be a nice effect.

"Cassie never said it but I could tell—she never thought Ron would work out. She didn't even buy the Harvard thing. Tried to get me to check him out. But I couldn't see anything but the cool way he wore his class necktie for a belt on his jeans because real Harvard men don't take it seriously, and those beautiful square fingers and all that bullshit he talked about Miles Davis and Mozart and why red wine goes with fresh tuna, which, of course, must be cooked black and blue . . . God, how long is he going to leave me down here in the dark, talking to myself?"

Charley raised his head off his fist to look at his watch. No hurry. She doesn't go for wimps. Likes her men with cojones. Maybe she'll talk some more about Ron.

"Don't lose it," echoed up from below. "Probably what he wants. Get me scared shitless so he can . . . whatever. Don't think about that. Keep talking. Four score and seven years ago, our forefathers brought forth . . ."

The silence lasted so long that he lay back with his hands behind his head. When the voice came up the tube again it was fainter. Maybe she'd moved, or put a hand to her face, weeping. He sat up again and leaned closer. ". . . is no wimp. Maybe a terminal case of cool, but plenty sexy. And doesn't everybody like him? Men and women both. Successful, smooth . . . I was ready for something permanent and . . . Was I just too stars-in-my-eyes to pick up the clues? I can't believe I'm a natural-born victim." Pause. "Whatever. Now I have Amy . . ."

A quick breath, almost a gasp. Her voice hit a higher pitch: "Oh-my-god . . . could . . . He was looking for Ron. Could this Charley-not-Andrew be . . . How long will it take Ron to figure out that I've got her at Cassie's? We need some time. Cassie's working on it, but we need . . ." A moan. "Oh-my-god. Oh please . . ."

Time to interrupt this. She's no use if she gets hysterical. Keep the pressure on, but change the subject. He put his mouth to the tube and spoke, just above a whisper: "Let there be light."

# CHAPTER 4

He was in the room. Right next to her, in the dark? Charley's voice carried an echo inside it. Ghostly.

Slowly, she reached a hand toward his voice. Touched nothing. Reached the other hand. Nothing. How did he get in? "Where . . ." she began, but her voice quavered. She forced a dry swallow. "Is that you, Charley?"

"This is the Nunnehi."

She turned her head, trying to locate him. "The what?"

"Did you ever hear of the ghost dancers?"

"No," turning her head to the other side. His voice seemed to come from everywhere.

"The Nunnehi are spirit people. They can go anywhere. Be anywhere. Shoot around corners. See in the dark. But you can't do that, can you Samantha?"

"No."

"Do you believe that there are special people in the world, Sam?"

"What do you mean?"

"People who have a past and a destiny. People who are here to do something important."

He wasn't here in the room. It must be wired, somehow. Play along. "I don't know. I suppose so."

"That's not good enough, Sam."

"Good enough?" Whatever has to be said, or done . . .

"Special people find special people. That's the way it works.

Now, I have to find out if you are my special person."

His? What does that mean? She realized that she was groping around in the dark as if she might touch him. "What do I have to—how will you know?"

"Oh, I'll know, when I know a lot more about you. In the meantime, would you like some light?"

"Yes."

Silence.

"Yes I would, please."

"Is the autistic outburst over?"

"What do you mean?"

"I mean, will you not break any more furniture?"

"Yes." She tried to swallow the quaver out of her voice. "I mean no. Yes, it's over and no, I won't break any more furniture."

"Remember, the Nunnehi are with you. They give the light and take it away."

"I understand." Is he crazy? Am I caught in some loonie fantasy?

A tiny metallic scrape. Not a ghost noise, and not something electronic. More silence. Finally: "Charley? Are you still here?" She counted to ten and stood. She took a step and waved her arms back and forth. Another step, more waving, and she knew she was alone. How could he have gotten in and out of this little room? He couldn't. Is this just a terrified imagination running off the edge?

With both hands behind her she stepped back and found the wing chair again. She fumbled to find the arms and sat, gripping her hands in her lap. Play along with this craziness. Whatever it is. Find a way to get out, and keep Amy safe. Whatever it takes.

# CHAPTER 5

Charley took his time going back down the stairs into the front hall, past the ballroom and through the kitchen to the row of switches at the top of the back stairs. He paused and then flipped one. Just the bathroom now. Save the other light for another reward. Let her percolate a while. Appreciate a little light. Understand dependency. Like gentling a horse. First, feel the empty saddle, learn to answer the tug of the hackamore. Riding comes later, when you're broke. When you're mine.

He went back to the drawing room and sat at what, according to the inventory, was a Regency table. Sam's attaché case looked awkward and out of place on the rosewood marquetry. The case had locks with keyholes, but the latches snapped open without a key. He extracted a small black purse with a shoulder strap, laptop with a plug-in charger, cell phone, roll of breath mints, blank pad of lined yellow paper and a manila file folder with a single sheet headed "EVENT MANAGEMENT AGREEMENT." The first paragraph stated, "This agreement is effective between Samantha Langshan and _____, referred to hereinafter as 'the client.' " After that were numbered paragraphs headed "Employment," "Services/Form of Work" and other contract boilerplate.

No calendar or address book. Probably in the laptop. He took that out and booted up, predicting that it wouldn't be password protected. While he waited, he snapped open the purse: wallet with forty-two dollars, coins in the change pocket, driver's license and four credit cards; Kleenex, lipstick, compact and tampon. Better let her have the purse. He closed the purse and dropped it back into the attaché.

The computer opened a desktop of Amy snapshots: blowing out a birthday cake, learning the tricycle, feeding ducks in a park. No threesome with loving parents. He tried to open "Documents." Surprise: she had her files protected. He tried "samantha." Tried it backward. Opened her wallet again, found her birth date and tried that. Found her Social Security number and tried that. Found her checkbook and tried the account number. Nothing worked. So she's cautious and methodical. Could be a good sign. He shut down the computer, found a socket and plugged in the charger.

He opened her cell and found the speed dial screen. The first number was for "Cassie." Next was "School" and then "Howard," "Anna," "Ron," "Phyllis" and "Arnold." He punched "Howard." A female voice answered, "Hairstyles by Howard." He punched off and tried "Cassie," got an answering machine and punched off. For no reason he skipped "Anna," hesitated at "Ron" but went on to "Phyllis," which turned out to be a nail salon. "Arnold" was a law office. He remembered that she'd said she was separated with a divorce in the works.

He went back up to the speaker tube in the bedroom, eased the lid up and sat on the bed, listening. After perhaps a minute he heard a rustle of movement followed by more silence. He leaned over and spoke into the tube in a conversational tone, "I'm glad the tantrum is over, Sam. But I was enjoying the recitation, and the discussion of the men in your life. And Amy."

"What do you want?"

"You sound defiant, Sam. That's really the wrong attitude. You see, I'm not another superficial guy in your life. I don't know which wine goes with what, but I'm a man on a mission."

"What's your mission?"

"We'll get into that later. Right now, all you have to understand is that nothing will stand in my way."

"All right. So what do you want with me?"

"At the moment, all I want is your computer password."

Silence.

"Sam, you're not a natural-born victim at all. You're an independent businesswoman. You know how to separate people from their money and make them feel good about it. That means you're smart. And Ron doesn't know you've hidden Amy at Cassie's. But he'll figure that out, right?"

Silence.

He let that soak in a while before he went on: "Sam, this can all work out just fine. If you do the smart thing, you can be out of here and taking care of Amy. But first I need a little co-operation. Okay?"

After a pause, she began, "This mission . . ."

"It won't interfere with what you need to do with Amy. Not if you don't waste a lot of time deciding to cooperate a little."

Now she came back in a solid, made-up-my-mind voice: "Okay. The password is mary-liz-twelve-fourteen. One word. Twelve-fourteen is numerals."

"Thank you, Sam. We're getting somewhere now. Who are they?"

"Who?"

"Mary and Liz."

"Why do you need to know?"

"I don't, but telling me would be an expression of trust. Trust is important, Sam."

She hesitated. "It's one name. I mean, one person. Mary Elizabeth. My mother."

"Interesting. And the twelve-fourteen?"

A longer hesitation indicated that he was getting too close to something. "Just a number. Passwords are supposed to have letters and numbers."

"I see." She was lying. December 14? She wouldn't use her own birthday, but maybe her daughter's? Let it go for now. He tried, "Are you close to your mother?"

"No. She's been gone a long time."

Gone could mean dead, or just gone. "I'm sorry." And then, making it a statement: "Using her name as a password, that's kind of keeping in touch, isn't it?"

"Look, you said you wanted the password and I gave it to you, okay?"

He sat back, thinking about what they had covered. Enough for now. "Yes," he said. "Thank you for the trust. I'll close the voice tube now to give you some privacy."

He closed the lid with a click she might hear and twisted the butterfly nut home. Then he went down the hall to his bedroom, which may have been the butler's. Comfortable, with a scratchy, overstuffed chair and a narrow bed. Good enough. Helps keep the discipline. The focus.

# CHAPTER 6

He took the deerskin pouch from the walnut armoire. No closets for the help in these old houses. The pouch felt like suede to his fingers, but he knew that long ago a woman had chewed this hide into supple leather. "Old mother," he said, "you live with me in spirit, as perhaps her mother lives in her computer."

He went back down to the drawing room, opened her laptop and logged in with "maryliz1214." When her email opened he felt a furtive pulse that reminded him of skulking along side streets when he was twelve or thirteen, looking for lighted bedroom windows. Rummaging through her outbox he thought about her talking out loud in the dark, whistling past the graveyard. Something about a sexy man. Has to be her ex, Ronald. Heavy sexual politics going on there. And it involves Amy, who has to be her daughter. Theirs? No obvious clue in her mail.

He looked through "Documents" and found her calendar. Business isn't booming. Nothing scheduled tomorrow. "Arnold" at ten on Friday. Hairdresser? No, lawyer. Probably cancel that with an email. "Alice" was at three. New name. Probably figure out who she is from the saved email, but give Sam a chance to volunteer it. See if the saddle fits.

He shut down the computer, picked up the pouch and went down the hall past the ballroom, glancing at the French doors that opened onto the brick terrace in back. He'd never tried those doors, just as he'd never pulled the drapes in the drawing room or searched for the source of the damp stains on the wall of the maid's room. A Wikipedia knowledge of the place was all he needed. He went back through the kitchen, paused to flip the switch for the main nursery light and let himself out into the gathering dusk.

Walking past the garage he wondered where Countess D's chauffeur had driven her. No expressway then. Long before Robert Moses and his parkways. The Vanderbilt automobile race course, perhaps? A frost-heaved brick walk took him into the remains of the rose garden, past scattered metal markers for Iceberg, Don Juan, Blaze and Fourth of July, but now only a few frowzy Paul Scarlets survived among the weeds.

Past the rose garden was one of his favorite places: Countess D's maze, copied from the eighteenth-century Villa Pisani in Stra. Charley paused at the entrance, remembering how he had followed the diagram in her album to clip the boxwood into the original narrow aisles. The Plaisance Foundation had approved his time sheets because they saw the maze as a prime attraction for donors first, and then for tourists. But it meant more than giggling kids blundering through the labyrinth. It meant mystery. This maze, and others like it, were the Stonehenge of the Belle Epoque.

He'd piled the prunings into a frowzy stack alongside the path because he couldn't think of an easy way to dispose of them. Couldn't burn in this neighborhood. Orgies and coke parties might go unnoticed but a wisp of smoke would bring the cops.

Farther down, the path was increasingly gap-toothed with lost bricks as it wound into the swamp maples, cedars and mulberries that had claimed the neglected slope. Back in Oklahoma the trees would be scrub oak and persimmon and bois d'arc, but the same waning moon would be rising. The same dying moon that must have watched Old Tenkiller meet his obligation. A night when the owl cast no shadow.

Before he could see the water, the Northport stacks blinked their red aircraft-warning lights through the dead leaves that clung to the oaks, resisting the approach of winter. Countess D would never have tolerated those ugly, blinking lights and red-and-white stacks. If necessary, she'd have bought all of Northport to preserve her view and to keep her air free of those tons of carbon and God knows what other chemicals.

He shouldered past a rampant stand of bamboo. At certain times, when the wind gusted off the water, they became giant reeds that moaned a basso profundo. Tonight they were silent. Everything waited.

He thought the quarter-timber boathouse looked vaguely Swiss, or Bavarian, like a whimsical afterthought down here out of sight from all the Mediterranean pomp above. He went through the unlocked door into the launch crew's combined kitchen and living room with its permanent low-tide smell onto the porch that looked across Northport Harbor. Standing on the wide, stained floorboards, he thought about the crew watching for the *Bateau Sans Souci* from here. Long before she'd hove to, they'd be below, muscling the launch out of its davits and into the little channel dredged under the porch. By the time she'd changed into her shore clothes—he imagined her in a white linen suit and a floppy straw hat—the launch would be bobbing alongside.

The whine of a jet turning onto LaGuardia distracted him, but the splash of bluefish slaughtering bunker in the harbor brought him back. The crew had fished from this porch, staining the planks with bait and fish blood along with engine oil and probably some Belle Epoque semen. Preparing the site for him. Everything kept coming together for him, ever since he had begun to understand who he was and what he was meant to do. That little channel under the porch was perfect. Complete with a blue crab colony that would collect to a feast and polish the bones as thoroughly as the beetles had prepared the possum skull for him.

At the beach club across the harbor, kayaks and canoes leaned against the timbered seawall. He thought of Dragging Canoe, the warrior who had killed Davey Crockett's grandfather. Davey hadn't held that against the Principal People. He'd fought Jackson over the Indian Removal Act, but Jackson had won.

He turned to the west, toward Tahlequah. The direction of death. The sun perched on Lloyd Neck, smearing a bloody stain across Huntington Bay. Shading his eyes, he could make out the eroding concrete remains of Sand City, which locals said had been a mine for the towers of Wall Street. Dropping his hand he looked across the bay to the slender umbilicus the dredges had left to connect Eatons Neck with the mainland potato fields. Land drenched with pesticide, on which were built the ranch houses and schools of America's first suburb. Now the capital of smug. Home of people like the Langshans.

As twilight gathered, he undressed and stacked his clothes under the boathouse window. Holding the deerskin pouch, he checked the nanny-cam under the eaves, an electronic eye that never forgot what it saw. He stood naked at the railing, breathing the damp exhalation of the harbor and projecting his mind into the flow of time. Traveling upstream into the past.

From the pouch he took four dry wisps of wild onion tops. Without raising them to his nose he knew they were odorless. No longer a flavoring for soups and stews, but a reminder that the Principal People were careful to cut the tops and not to pull the bulbs, which held the new year's life. He pinned the wisps on the railing under the possum skull against the breeze off the water.

Next he extracted the clay disk that had consecrated his old, new name, Tsali. A name the whites had pronounced "Charley."

He fingered the tracing of this name that he had baked into the damp clay, using the Sequoyah alphabet, a system of writing designed by one man, illiterate in every other language. Why was he not studied like Copernicus, or Shakespeare? The characters looked like CP with flourishes.

With his eyes on the possum skull he listened for the past. The first sound was often running water. When he heard that, he thought he could sometimes identify the Mississippi by the smell of rotting leaves, and Sallisaw Creek by a whiff of sulfur from a hot spring somewhere. The next sound was always the crying of children and the keening of women. But today the possum skull didn't lead him back.

After a few minutes he broke his concentration because he knew that he either got back quickly or not at all. He took out the knife. He had ground a mill file into two sharp edges and then rammed its pointed handle into a buck horn he'd found in the woods. There was no record or memory of what kind of knife Tsali had carried. It could have been a broad frontier blade exchanged for a pinch of yellow dust at the trading post, but it could have been something fashioned from a worn-out tool such as the file. Grinding the edges of this one on a treadle-operated stone had made him feel confident of its purpose.

Now, he went to the wall where his clothes were stacked. He stood on tiptoe to reach under the eaves for the nanny-cam, checked to make sure it had been watching and reset it. He went back to the rail and, standing naked in the clotting dusk, he held the knife up to the east. "You are the Principal People. Awake to that understanding."

# CHAPTER 7

*. . . under its market value and you are now faced with the threat of foreclosure. I am pleased to tell you that I represent a firm that has purchased your mortgage from the bank for less than its original value, and that this firm is willing to share the discount with you.*

Kurt looked away from the screen, thinking about how to say that the name of the generous firm must remain a secret, although it is a well-capitalized investment company in a lawful business. The sound of the door made him look around.

The three other brokers' desks were black shadows beyond the globe of light around his computer. A silhouette figure stood in the refracted street light at the door. Kurt always left that door unlocked. Every broker in the Hersch agency knew the story of the walk-in who'd bought a three and a half million-dollar colonial on Lloyd Neck. But this walk-in took a step across the threshold with what seemed to be an embarrassed open-palms gesture and said, "Excuse me, please?" making it a question in the Hispanic way.

Kurt asked, "Help you?"

The silhouette—the voice was on the low edge of contralto, but something about the way he took another step announced a man—said, "I was passing by. Saw your light?" He kept his hands open, as if to show they were empty.

A burst of laughter from a group of after-work drinkers leaving Lois and Len's across the street reminded Kurt that no one knew where he was, but there was nothing threatening about the short, slight man with the choirboy's voice. "I'm afraid we're closed."

"Just have a question?" He moved to the client's chair next to Kurt's desk but remained standing. Kurt could see a barrio uniform: black hoodie, shapeless gray cargo pants and loose-laced black sneakers. How old is this guy? Twenty? They look young—probably twenty-five. The man said, "You collect rent?"

"I don't, no. Some of our brokers—what is it you want?"

Another of those open gestures brought his left hand into the light on Kurt's computer desk. "One of your brokers collects on Depot Road?"

The hand had a small tattoo in the fork of thumb and forefinger. "I don't know," Kurt said. "No, I don't think so. I'm afraid I can't help you."

The man shrugged. "You know about the fire?"

"Of course. It was terrible." In spite of himself, he glanced down at the tattoo. It was "13."

"Yes, terrible. Friends of mine."

"I'm sorry. All those people . . . but we don't handle any of those properties."

The man nodded, as if expecting that answer. "But you're in the business? So maybe you know who does?"

"Usually they have a manager. Someone who lives in one of the apartments and collects the rent."

"But that manager, he pays someone?"

"Usually the owner." Kurt started to add, "In this case, it's a corporation," but he held up. The less said the better.

"And who is this owner?"

"Why do you need to know?"

"Like I said, my friends . . . You don't want to tell me, do you?"

"I don't really know. Who owns it, I mean. I don't know for a fact."

"But you—" a dismissive gesture "—you gotta idea." When Kurt didn't answer, he went on: "So, you don't want to tell me who, maybe how I can find out?"

"The owners would be listed at City Hall."

The man flashed a white smile. "Oh, I'll just drop into City Hall and say 'Hey, man, I want the name of the white man who's collecting the insurance on that fire.' That's all I have to do?"

"It's public record. Anybody can see it."

"Anybody? You mean, like, any legal citizen? C'mon, man. It's no skin off your ass."

Kurt's eyes slid to the telephone on the corner of his desk. Police station was less than a mile away. But first he'd have to pick up the phone and press 911. "Sorry. I really don't—"

"Whoever started that fire," the man leaned slightly forward and held the "13" tattoo under the light, "he wanted the police to think that friends of mine . . ."

Kurt hesitated. He could just say, "Wallace Enterprises" and this would be all over. Wallace is not even a client. What duty does he have to the local slum lord? "I understand. I'd like to help, but . . ."

"Really? C'mon man, not asking much. Just a name. Like you say, anybody can get it."

"But I don't . . . Look, I'm not the Hall of Records."

Slowly, as if the plastic business card holder on Kurt's desk were fragile, the man extracted a single card and leaned forward to study it in the light of the desk lamp. "Hersch Agency top producer" he read out loud. "Congratulations."

Kurt didn't answer.

"Business phone number, fax number, voice mail number and email address. You got no home address?"

Kurt didn't answer.

"I'll bet you're listed in the white pages. Your business, you wouldn't want an unlisted phone. You have a wife, Kurt? Kids?" He made a show of slipping the card into a thigh pocket of his cargo pants. "You think about helping me just a little. Just a name. I'll give *you* a name, make it a trade."

He took another card from the holder and a ballpoint pen from the collection in the Starbucks mug on the edge of the desk. "Maybe you'll remember something on the way home to your nice wife." He jotted on the back of the card and handed it to Kurt. "You think of something, you call this number." He dropped the pen back into the mug with a *cling*. "It's just a little bodega. Guy sells groceries, beer, lotto tickets. You ask for Pedro Loco. Got that?"

Kurt didn't say anything.

The guy stepped back so that just his feet and lower legs remained in the puddle of lamplight. "Guy on the phone will say, he don't know anybody with a name like that. You say, okay, wrong number." Another step back, and now he was completely in shadow. "I'll call you in ten minutes."

Kurt watched him turn and go to the door. He paused, looking up and down the street. He fished a pack of cigarettes and a book of matches out of a side pocket and tapped a cigarette out. "All you have to say is a name and I won't be hangin' around your neighborhood." He lit the cigarette and dropped the match, still burning, onto the floor as he went out.

# CHAPTER 8

The bathroom light spilled across the rag carpet and up the wall where two armies of lead soldiers faced each other on a shelf. Sam walked from wall to wall, counting. The room was six paces long and four wide. One of her paces was probably a little less than a yard, so the room was about twelve by fifteen. Holiday Inn size? Seemed smaller, but maybe that was claustrophobia. Six paces from the hall door to the bathroom door, right face, four paces behind the full-size chair to the wall with the little table and chairs, about face, one pace away from the wall to clear the table, left face, six paces to the corridor wall, right face, two paces to the wall with the bed under the two armies on the shelf, right face and start again.

Along the way she kicked one of the fragments of broken chair back into the corner. So much for raising a ruckus. Do the smart thing, he'd said. A little cooperation. What did that mean? Play along and find out.

Bathroom was definitely smaller than a Holiday's. No shower or tub. Hot water, though. Thanks for small favors. Back and forth: six paces, four paces, two paces out and six paces again. To estimate elapsed time, she counted laps.

In the dim light from the bathroom, pacing toward the little table she studied the collection of *Alice in Wonderland* drawings framed over it. Old-fashioned line drawings, with cross-hatched shadings. Not cartoons, but not realistic, either. Alice dancing with a weeping tortoise, the white rabbit in ascot and waistcoat looking at a watch on a chain, Alice holding a bottle labeled "Drink Me," the grinning Cheshire cat disappearing into the foliage of a tree and a scowling Queen of Hearts.

Sam paused at the Queen, trying to remember the story. Hearts didn't mean love. She remembered "Off with their heads!" The Queen was always angry.

"Your mother doesn't want to live with us anymore," Sam's father had said when Sam was old enough to ask, Why? she'd wondered. Had they done something, she and her father, to make her mother mad? It wasn't until she was in junior high that her father finally said, in an offhanded way, that "it was another man." She didn't have to be told that any further discussion was out of bounds.

Sam had outgrown her dolls by then, but Barbie and Ken still had a place in the corner of her closet along with the baby doll from an earlier time. That night she took the baby doll to bed and whispered to her in the dark, "Mommie will never leave you. Not for any reason. Not ever."

Their Bayshore ranch house had no pictures of her mother. In the mirror over her spool dresser, Sam had studied her own face: wide-set hazel eyes, a little too much chin and ears that would stick out if she dared to cut her hair short. Would her mother have that same full mouth and that hint of a dimple in the left cheek when she smiled? And the other man . . . Sam imagined him in a tuxedo. Perhaps her mother was elegant, too fine for her father's plodding, Postal Service personality. She had vague memory of loud voices and doors slamming, which caused her to associate her mother with anger. Queen of Hearts.

Pacing past the little bed with its overhang of lead-soldier armies, she imagined that she caught a lingering scent of the Gold Coast. Something faint and delicate. Floral. Perhaps lavender. She studied the sun woven into the rag rug. Along with the yellow walls, had the Countess tried to introduce light into this windowless basement room? She studied the Wonderland illustrations over the bed. The white rabbit emerged from his hole wearing an immaculate ascot and waistcoat. When Caruso sang here the men probably wore dinner jackets. And the women? Sam imagined gowns that displayed white shoulders and diamonds that celebrated cleavage.

She imagined Countess de Dendermonde—what does that name mean? A region? From the Dendermonde? Whatever. She imagined the countess in a dinner dress, something elegantly simple set off by lustrous pearls, having slipped away from her guests to sit on the edge of this little bed and talk to her son. Perhaps she told him about the world down the rabbit hole. A world where the unexpected is ordinary. Where caterpillars smoke pipes and cats disappear and croquet mallets are live flamingos. Perhaps she told him that he had his own rabbit hole down here, where he could create his own world of the unexpected.

After thirty-five laps—ten minutes?—she paused and sat in the brocade wing-chair. Did the walls close in on that troubled little boy the way they closed in on her now? Did the Countess turn off his lights to control his outbursts? Did he understand why he was imprisoned down here?

She looked at the interrupted chess game. Charley had said the boy was what? Six? A couple of years older than Amy. What a different room this was from hers, with the Dora the Explorer posters on the walls and the IKEA dresser they had painted pink and white, with the picture of Sam in its stand-up frame. It was her wedding picture, which would have to do until she found a reason for another studio shot because her daughter was not going to be without a picture of her mother.

And what was this picture on the end table next to her? A dark, brooding face with a blade of a nose. That turban of some rich-looking, satiny stuff. An Arab? And that long, skinny pipe in his hand. Opium? No, he didn't look Chinese. Hash, maybe. Gentle eyes. Were they the same cast, slightly tilted, and color as Charley's? What had he said? Something about a man people didn't understand. Well, you could bet that Charley would turn out to be one of those sad, misunderstood men.

She stood again and began lap thirty-six. Keep moving. Don't give in to claustrophobia. Play the game. But what the hell *is* the game? Probably some kind of softening up. For what?

One, two, three, four, five, six paces and turn. What was that captive thing she read about? Long time ago, but newspapers still referred to it when there was a hostage story. Some rich kid kidnapped by terrorists who ended up liking them. Worked with them. Probably slept with one of them. They probably kept her locked up in a dark room too. So scared and isolated she'd latched onto the first kindness to come along.

Three, four and turn. Was this some kind of a kinky thing? Was there something odd . . . One, two—maybe something feminine about him?—three, four, five, six. Lap thirty-seven. Not the shoulder-length hair. Something about the hands.

One, two—no hair. Come to think of it, none on the forearms, either. Three, four and turn. Some sort of Asian blood? They aren't hairy, are they? One, two—wispy, Fu Manchu beards. She paused at the picture of the man with the pipe. Not a photograph. Some kind of a print. Not Chinese, but maybe some kind of Asian.

She paced on. Okay, suppose this is some kind of a sicko sex game. Maybe he can't get it up until the woman is, what? Submissive? Dependent on him. Ooh, you're so big and strong. And look at that. Is it all for me? Five, six and turn.

So if this is all about something like that, it starts with some kind of a submission dance. He takes a step forward and I take a step back. Instead of a pace, she shuffled a dance step. He steps forward again and maybe I take a side step. Keep him coming but not getting there. Find out what he needs. And along the way—

Click.

She turned to face the door. It didn't open. If this was the step forward, what was her step back? Was he outside, waiting for her to come to the door? That's not submission. She stood in the middle of the room, waiting.

The door opened a crack. "Where are you, Sam?"

Instead of, "Where the hell do you think I am?" she answered, "Right here."

"I mean, where are you in the room? Over by the big chair?"

"No, I'm kind of in the center."

"I want you to go sit down in one of those little chairs at the table. The one that you didn't bust up. Will you do that, Sam?"

What is this, some kind of a playroom fetish? Is he going to want me in a pinafore? But she said, "All right," and squeezed into the remaining chair, squirming to get her skirt down with her knees in the air.

"Are you sitting down?"

He steps forward, I step back. "Yes. Just like you said."

The door swung open. "Good. I have some things for you." He came in, carrying two brown paper bags. "I didn't want you to be tempted to try to dash out while I'm serving dinner." Flashing the same charming smile that had greeted her at the front door, he set the bags on the foot of the bed and carefully moved the chess game, without disturbing the pieces, onto the floor under the table. "I tried sitting in one of those little chairs once and so I know you wouldn't be able to leap right into action." He picked up the bags and set them on the table. "Hungry?"

She considered how to answer and settled for, "Actually, that wasn't my first concern." Sounded petulant, she realized. Not playing the game.

He turned his hand over as if to show he was hiding nothing. "I know. I'll explain everything." Bending over the table he opened one of the sacks and took out her black Hobo clutch purse. "First, you'll want this back. Girl needs her lipstick, right? I confess that I looked inside, but I didn't take anything."

She took it from his hand but put it in her lap without opening it.

"I doubt that you're a Big Mac girl—right?—so I brought a Caesar salad from the deli, some iced tea and—" spreading Styrofoam cartons around the table "—do you like rice pudding? Comfort food, I thought."

She answered an inadequate, "Rice pudding isn't going to do it for me."

He sat in the nurse's wing-chair beside the door. "I know. But first there's something I want you to do for me."

Here it comes. Time for the side step. "And then you'll let me out of here?"

"Sure. Soon enough." Another open-hand gesture. "But first we have something to accomplish together."

"Accomplish? What is that?"

"It's a little complicated, but I'll explain it all. I promise."

"Okay, good. I'm listening."

"It'll take a little time. Try your salad."

She managed a smile. "I'm not all that hungry right now. Why don't you just explain things?" Holding the smile and adding a little nod that she tried to make encouraging. "I'm pretty understanding."

He nodded agreement. "I could tell that, even on the phone. You pick up an idea right away. You're a special person. We both are. That's why I know this is going to work out just fine." He leaned to one side of the chair to dig into the paper bag again. "But first I have to ask you to do a couple of things." He came out with her cell phone.

"Whatever gets me out of here."

He smiled and nodded. "Mary Liz twelve-fourteen let me into your computer, just like you said. Good start. And your Google calendar shows an appointment tomorrow with Alice at three." He raised his brows and cocked his head in a question.

"Hairdresser."

Still smiling and nodding, he handed her the cell. "Don't think you're going to be able to keep that. Why don't you just call and cancel?"

She scrolled down to the number and entered it. "She'll ask me when to reschedule," she said.

"Just tell her you'll call in a couple of days."

As she talked to Alice—"Hate to do this but there's a business thing I just can't postpone"—he opened Styrofoam containers and distributed napkins and plastic forks. When she clicked off he said, "Good job. Now, how about Arnold on Friday?"

"Friday? How long are you going to . . . ?"

He served himself some salad on a paper plate. "You may be able to keep that appointment. I won't keep you a minute longer than necessary. Depends on how fast we can get everything together. But just to be on the safe side, why don't you put it off?" He went into the other paper bag and came out with her laptop. "An email is probably good enough, isn't it?"

Without saying anything, she handed the cell back and took the laptop. She logged on and, waiting for it to boot, said, "What do you mean about getting everything together?"

Poking at the salad he said, "They always put on too much dressing, don't they? I'll lay everything out for you, I promise. It'll take a little time, and so first—" he gestured toward the laptop "—let's get the preliminaries out of the way."

She drafted an email saying she was sorry but that something had come up to make a meeting Friday morning impossible

63

and she'd call his office for another appointment. She twisted the computer around so he could read the screen. "Good," he said.

She twisted it back, clicked "send" and logged off. "Now will you tell me what's going on?"

"Just one more thing," he said, returning the laptop to the paper bag. "I need you to call Cassie."

"Cassie?"

He laughed at the expression on her face. "No big deal. Not a ransom demand or anything like that. Just tell her to take care of Amy a little while longer."

Her hands clenched involuntarily. "Amy? What's she—what do you mean? What do you know about Amy?"

He put down his plastic fork and raised an open palm in a "wait a minute" gesture. "Just what you told me." He pointed an index finger toward the ceiling.

"I didn't . . ." She followed his gesture to the empty brass fixture in the ceiling. Now she could see that there was no socket for a bulb. "What's that?"

He flashed that smile. "It's a brass ear."

She studied it. It looked like the mouth of a trombone. "You were . . ." she pointed up.

"I told you that Countess D had her own nanny-cam system. Nineteenth-century version. Speaking tubes from her bedroom down to the nursery, so she could hear what was going on with her Eric. She must have adapted it from what she found on her yacht." He cupped his left hand around his mouth and leaned forward, as if calling down a tube. "Bridge to engine room, stand by the anchor windlass."

Sam said, "It sounded like you were right here in the room."

He gestured toward the ceiling. "Something to do with the shape of that thing, I suppose, and the acoustics of this room. In one of her letters, Countess D says it's like the whispering

64

gallery in the Senate Building."

"I didn't understand what you said. Something about none high."

"I'll explain all that." He stood and offered her cell. "But first, call Cassie."

"Why Cassie?" she said, trying to remember what she had blurted out loud to control her panic in the dark.

"Amy's at your friend Cassie's and Ron doesn't know that yet." He paused. "But I do."

A fist tightened inside her. "What are you saying?"

He shrugged. "Your car have a GPS? With directions to Cassie's programmed into it?"

"No," she lied.

He waved a dismissive gesture. "Not necessary. Her address is probably in your computer. Even if it's not, her phone number is in your cell and I can get her address with that."

"What do you want with her address?"

"Nothing, if you and I can work together a little."

She tried to read his face. Was that just the color of an October tan? He seemed to have no shadow of a beard. She forced herself to hold the stare into those midnight eyes that never seemed to blink.

When he finally spoke she felt that she had waited him out. Good moment, but scoring points isn't the way to play this. "Those are nice snapshots of Amy on your computer's desktop," he said. "I don't think you want me to pick her up on the way to what? Nursery school? Or the park, or wherever they go. You think Cassie's going to stop me?"

Sam took a deep breath. Submission was her job. "What do you want me to do?"

He raised the cell phone but didn't hand it to her. "I'm going to ring Cassie and hold the phone for you. First, you tell me when you have something to tell her that she'll buy. Something to explain why you won't be coming around for a few days. But tell her you'll keep in touch by phone, so she's not to worry."

"She'll ask where I am."

He nodded and flashed a smile indicating they were on the same page. "Of course she will. But you're both big girls, right? You know how to tell her that it's none of her damn business." He gestured with the phone. "Think about it, and let me know when you're ready."

Play the game. Dominance. Garter belt, nurse's cap—whatever it takes. Keep Amy in the clear. She twisted in the awkward child's chair and grimaced as she stretched a leg from under the little table as if to head off a cramp, letting her skirt ride up. She said, "You know the first rule of public relations?"

He shook his head.

"The best story is usually the simple truth. I'll tell her I met an interesting man." His eyes widened. Okay, that worked. Push a little: "Cassie'll want to know how long." When he didn't answer, apparently still assimilating what she had said, she explained: "How much longer she's going to have to take care of Amy."

He nodded. "Keep it open. Tell her it won't be long."

She reached for the phone, but he held it back.

"We're going to work together, Sam. So we have to trust each other. When you talk to Cassie, I'm going to trust you not to do something stupid."

"Stupid?"

"Stupid, like blurting out something before I can ring off. Or talking in some kind of a girl code."

He waited for her to nod understanding. Then he pressed a speed dial code and held the cell to her face, leaning over to share the earpiece. "I trust you, Sam."

Involuntarily, Sam pulled away—wrong move—and glanced at her watch to cover. "Her office is closed, but an executive coach never misses a call. It'll roll over to her home number."

Cassie picked up on the third ring. "Hello, Sam—Mike and I are enjoying Amy so much we're going to hold her for ransom."

Ransom? Sam avoided Charley's eyes as she hesitated, getting past that idea, to say, "I suppose you're spoiling her rotten."

"She does seem happy with us. And before you ask, yes, she's been practicing her numbers and letters."

"She's not getting in the way? What about when you have a client?"

"I had a couple of long phone sessions yesterday afternoon and so I just left her at the computer. When I hung up she was learning two-syllable words in ABC Mouse."

"She doesn't seem sullen? Withdrawn?"

"Maybe a little quiet. We don't put any pressure on her."

Sam glanced at Charley—his face was over her shoulder so close that she could smell his faintly minty breath—and said, "Cassie, I hate to ask you this, but could you possibly keep her another couple of days?"

In the surprised pause, Sam raised an I-can-handle-this gesture to Charley as she went on: "If this is an imposition, please tell me, but something's come up and, well, I really would like a couple of days on my own."

"A couple of—ooh my." Cassie giggled. "I hope . . . No, I'm not going to say another word. Of course we can keep her for another couple of days. Matter of fact, it might be good for her. She knows her creepy father doesn't know she's here." A pause to shift her tone of voice. "And I hope it turns out to be good for you too, Sam."

"Don't jump to any conclusions, Cassie."

"Kiddo, I'd just like to see you catch a break. You're way overdue."

"Could I speak to Amy?"

"She's at preschool now."

Sam looked at her watch. "Of course. Tell her Mommie loves her and I'll be back in a couple of days."

"Enjoy your weekend, Sam, and don't worry about Amy."

Looking at Charley, she said, "Tell her I'll call her tonight," and he nodded.

When she punched off the cell he took it from her and straightened up. "Your hair is the color of a lion's mane," he said.

Startled, she stammered: "My—I—" She took a breath and said, "I call it nondescript brown. I keep telling myself to do something about it."

Going to the door, he said, "It's complicated. Full of subtle tones. I think you should leave it as it is. Now I'll get out and maybe you can try the salad and the rice pudding."

"When are you going to tell me what's going on?"

"Later. We have a lot to talk about. In the meantime, I'll turn on the lights. I hope that little bed won't be too uncomfortable."

When he closed the door she heard the lock click. As she struggled out of the tiny chair she was thinking, a lion's mane? Was that some kind of a pass? And the mention of the bed, was that suggestive? As she'd told Cassie, don't jump to any conclusions.

# CHAPTER 9

After Sam had eaten half the salad and all the rice pudding she put the remains with the deli cartons and the plastic fork and spoon in the one paper bag he'd left, rolled it tight and put it by the door. Keeping house like a good little captive.

She went back to the chair. To keep her mind off Amy she studied the two armies of lead soldiers on the shelf. Some pointed long-barreled rifles at each other and others brandished swords. Officers, probably. The officers on the right wore blue jackets and the left wore red. Not Union and Confederate. Napoleon and Wellington? Appropriate for the son of a countess. Sam thought she saw something about pride and principle in the stance of the soldiers. Did the Countess tell him stories about honor and courage to help him face his own inadequacy? Whatever, if little Eric could handle this cell, so could she. She imagined a lonely little boy creating an imaginary world in this locked-up place, but that brought her back to Amy.

Control. Don't get fluttery.

She picked up the picture of the man in the turban from the end table. He had brown skin, darker than Charley's, but a high-bridged nose like the profile on a Roman coin. Charley's nose was understated, as if it didn't want to compete with those velvet brown eyes. A man who was different, Charley had said. Like the autistic child. Different in ways that people didn't understand. Well, Charley's different, that's for sure. Is he asking for understanding? He'd said we're both special people.

Instead of some kind of kinky thrill, is he looking for a momma? Or maybe both, in the same package?

She put the picture back on the table and looked at the collection of prints framed along the back wall. Alice with the "Drink Me" bottle—she'd found that right after she'd fallen down the rabbit hole into Wonderland. Was this room supposed to be some kind of a fantasy world? Don't overanalyze.

The white rabbit with his watch and chain—that was early in the story too. But the Cheshire cat didn't appear and then disappear until Alice had learned to accept the impossible. Was this little room with the brass ear and the chess game without an opponent some kind of alternate reality? By the time Alice was dancing with the weeping tortoise—

The lock clicked. The door opened a crack. "Where are you, Sam?"

"In the grown-up chair. And I don't want to squeeze into Eric's chair again."

In the silence that followed she realized that she was holding her breath. Finally, he said, "All right. But I don't want you just inside the door. Go sit on the little bed."

She smiled and nodded. A little push-back. When she was settled on the low bed with the pillow against the wall, she said, "Okay, it's safe to come in."

He peered around the door, closed and locked it before he took the chair with what she thought might be an apologetic smile. He held up the cell. "You promised to call Amy. It's seven-fifteen. When does she go to bed?"

"Nine. Nine-thirty sometimes, but mostly just in the summer."

He slipped the cell into the pocket of his jeans and crossed his legs. "Then we have time for a little conversation."

Still trying to push back, she said, "Time for you to tell me what's going on."

He nodded. "We can get started, at least." He raised a forefinger. "First, let me set your mind at rest about one thing. When you were talking in the dark you wondered if I might be working with Ron. I'm certainly not. Actually, you and I are on the same side of that issue."

"What issue?"

"The Ron issue. Tell me, Sam, what did Cassie mean about Amy's creepy father?"

She shrugged. "You have to know Cassie. If she likes you, nothing's too good, but if she doesn't, everything's bad."

He nodded, smiling. "I'm glad you understand that kind of a person. I'm like that too."

"What did I do to get on your bad side?"

"Nothing, Sam. This isn't about you at all."

"So, what's it about?"

He looked away, as if studying the Alice prints, or something beyond them. "When you were on your way here, driving along Little Neck Road, did you notice the stacks? The smoke stacks on the other side of the harbor?"

She shook her head.

"Most people don't," he said. "We just turn on our lights and our TVs and our microwaves without thinking about all those tons of carbon going into the atmosphere. Oh, we're aware of it, and we may think it's a big problem, but it's not my personal problem, or yours. Not the way Ron is your problem."

"You said you're on a mission," she said. "Is it some ecological thing?"

He thought about that. "Yes," he said. "At one level it is. It involves respect for the earth and the spirits that dwell in all natural things. But just like you, I can't make every problem mine. I choose my issues."

"What issues did you choose?"

He hitched forward in the chair. "Do you know Gauguin?

71

The artist?"

"Sort of, I guess. He went to Tahiti."

Charley spread his hands to open a lot of space. "He found *everything* in Tahiti. Simple people, living in harmony with the sea and the forest and each other. He tried to express it on canvas, so we could understand. Do you know what he said?" Without waiting for her to shake her head he answered: " 'Life being what it is, one dreams of revenge.' " Charley gestured toward her. "Now, Sam, how's that for a mission?"

"Revenge?"

"Beats the hell out of love and reconciliation, don't you think? Much more practical."

"Revenge on who?"

"I'll explain that. But first, Sam, you must understand that I am a fanatic. I have found the shelter of religion. Like the God-fearing Christians who exterminated the people they found in this country and the Allah-fearing Muslims who want to exterminate those Christian descendants. Religion makes me dangerous. Do you understand?"

Sam folded her arms, pulling herself closer. "I think so."

"Good. Now you must tell me about Ron. What is it about you and him and Amy and the sex offenders?" He fished her cell out of his pocket. "You're dealing with a fanatic, Sam. This is a moment of truth. If you want to talk to Amy, talk to me first."

"You couldn't . . ."

"Keep you from keeping your promise to Amy?" He snorted a little laugh. "I'll show you what I could do." He looked at his watch. "But we don't have time now before Amy's bedtime. By the way, does Amy play computer games?"

Sam hesitated. Why does he keep talking about Amy? "No, she doesn't. But what do you mean about the moment of truth?"

"I thought not," he said. "Most games aren't designed for

girls. I wonder if that's one reason girls are doing better than boys in school. They don't waste so much of their learning years blowing up cartoons on a tube."

"The moment of truth, Charley. What's that all about?"

He leaned forward in the chair. "What that's all about is, where are your values? Your loyalties?"

"My . . . loyalties?"

He tossed a little gesture. "Amy or Ron. That's your choice, Sam. One or the other."

"What . . ." she tried to swallow the tremor out of her voice. "I don't know what you're asking me."

"Make your choice."

"There's nothing I wouldn't do for Amy. Nothing."

He nodded. "And her creepy father doesn't know she's at Cassie's. You two are hiding her from him?" When she didn't answer, he went on: "He's not somebody you'd protect at her expense, right?"

"I told you—there's nothing I wouldn't do for Amy."

"Good. You have a purpose. So do I. Something we can't be distracted from."

"I don't understand . . ."

"I know this is all very confusing, but once you see how our purposes"—he held up two parallel forefingers—"are aligned, then we'll have a good partnership. You and I."

She managed a smile. "Sorry, but this doesn't feel like a partnership, Charley."

"Of course not. Not yet. Do you tell Amy bedtime stories?"

He's talking about Amy again. "Yes. She has favorites. She's so bright she corrects me if I change something."

"I see. Then she must be, what? Four?"

When Sam didn't answer he waved the question away. "No matter. While we wait until it's time for you to call her, I could tell you a little story. Would you like to hear it?"

Another story. He'd brought her down here to talk about a story. Some kind of a PR narrative about this big old house. She asked, "Is it going to be about our . . . partnership?"

He smiled and nodded. "In a way, yes it is." He sat back in the wing chair and opened both hands. "Once upon a time there was a sorcerer who had a secret house in the deep woods where he conjured magical charms. People came from all over the kingdom to buy his charms, and so he became rich."

He paused and glanced at the ceiling. Sam felt sure that he was working off some kind of a script. Something he'd rehearsed. He went on: "But the sorcerer was born with a curse. Just as the magical ability had been passed down to him from his father, and from his father before him, so had the family curse been passed down. That's the way curses work. You don't know you have one until . . . The sorcerer found out about his curse one day in the Thrift Way parking lot."

He laughed at her reaction. "A bedtime story doesn't have to be far away and long ago, does it? Well, our story takes place on a little island called Vashon, which is a twenty-minute ferry trip from Seattle. The Douglas firs are deep and dark and there are more deer than people. Houses hide behind privacy fences that support jungles of blackberry vines. There's one movie theater across the street from the Thrift Way, which is where our story begins. The sorcerer leaves the store with two paper bags containing a dozen eggs, a pound of freshly ground coffee, a baguette, a sirloin, a small sack of Idaho potatoes, a salad he'd assembled at the fresh bar and a Châteauneuf-du-Pape that the store manager had stocked at his request.

"He puts his bags on the back seat of his Lexus, climbs behind the wheel and glances into the mirror. Some sort of a circular has been pasted onto his rear window, obstructing the view. He mutters 'shit' and gets out and pulls it off, leaving the key in the ignition. When he slides back inside he discovers a man in the passenger seat with a serious-looking pistol."

Charley glanced at his watch. "The rest of the story takes place in this hideaway house in the woods, but now I think it's time for you to call Amy." He fished the cell out of the pocket of his jeans. As he handed it to her he said, not making it a question: "And you're not going to say anything foolish that might put her at risk."

She shook her head as she took the phone. "The curse . . . is that about revenge? The Gauguin thing?"

"Let's not get ahead of the story, Sam."

She opened the phone but didn't press the speed dial. "Okay, but Amy and I—are we cursed?"

His brows went up in surprise. "Oh no. You don't have to worry about that. The curse goes down the male line, clansman to clansman. What you have to worry about is me. Right now, all you have to do is cooperate a little. Are you ready?"

"I guess so. What do I have to do?"

"Just call Amy and reassure her. You can promise to keep in touch." He cocked his head, studying her face. "Did I say something wrong? Something about touching?"

She shook her head and punched the speed dial. Cassie picked up with, "So how's the adventure working out?"

Charley smiled, watching her find an answer: "Uh . . . a little too early to tell. How's Amy?"

"A little quiet. She's fine, but I think she needs to talk to you. She's right here."

"Mommy?" Amy sounded far away, and needy.

"Hello, love. How are you getting along with Aunt Cassie and Uncle Mike?"

"They aren't really my aunt and uncle."

"No, but they love you just the same."

"I know that, but . . . Mommy, are you mad?"

Blinking back sudden tears, Sam said, "No, of course not. I

just have—there's something I have to do, that's all. Did I say
something to make you think . . ."

"I guess not."

"Amy, I'll never be mad at you. Not really mad. Whatever
happens, I'll always love you. Do you know that?"

"I guess so."

"Then what is it?"

"Nothing."

Now the tears overflowed down her cheeks. "Amy, I know
something's worrying you. I don't want you to tell me what it is
unless you want to, but when you do I'll understand. I promise.
Okay?"

"Okay. When are you coming home?"

Sam looked at Charley as she repeated, "Coming home?"

He held up two fingers.

She said, "A couple of days. Will you be okay with Aunt—
with Cassie and Mike for a couple of days?"

"Yeah. I guess so. Sure."

Wiping her cheeks with the back of her left hand, Sam said,
"That's my big girl. And Amy, do you remember when we went
to the Air and Space Museum and you couldn't understand
how those big metal machines could fly up in the air?"

"Yeah."

"I told you you'd understand when you're a little older. And
you will, I promise."

"Okay."

"And what's worrying you now, Amy. You'll understand that
too when you're a little older. I promise. Just try not to let it
upset you now."

"Mommie, when are you coming home?"

Sam swallowed her voice back into control. "Just a couple of
days. And I'll be thinking of you the whole time, because I love
you. You know I'll never leave you, don't you?"

"Okay. Yeah."

"Goodbye dear. I'll call you tomorrow."

Amy hung up without saying goodbye. Sam clicked the cell off, dropped it on the floor and sank her face into her hands, sobbing. Charley picked up the cell and touched her arm with just the tips of his fingers. "Good job," he said.

Between gasps, she said, "Fuck you."

"What you're promising that she'll understand, it has something to do with Ron, doesn't it?"

"You goddam betcha," she said, her shoulders shuddering. "She said he takes—took—showers with her."

He waited for the gale of tears to subside before he said, "Well, he's her father, isn't he?"

She banged both fists on the little bed. "What's that got to do with—what do you know about him?"

"More than you might suppose. But tell me, why is the shower such a big deal?"

"Because I was his wife. I know what he likes to do in the shower. With a female human being."

Charley stirred in the chair. "I see. So that's why you've hidden her with Cassie."

"The goddam judge won't suspend his visitation rights. Not unless Amy says something—definitive. And I'm not going to make her do that."

Charley reached toward her with both hands and then pulled back, closing them into fists. When he spoke his voice had found a lower pitch. "A man that abuses his own daughter doesn't deserve to live."

"Tell that to the judge." Sam sat back on the little bed and looked around, centering herself back into the moment. Why had she blurted out that stuff about the shower? Is she buying that partnership bullshit? No, just a weak moment. Whatever, it doesn't matter. All that matters is that she has to get out of here and back to Amy. Whatever it takes.

Charley leaned forward, elbows on knees. "Sam, I know something about abuse. There's only one major ethnic group in the world that never discovered alcohol—d'you know that? Only one. Indians. What's now called Native Americans."

So that's what he is, she realized. Not Polish or Eurasian. Indian.

"They had tobacco," he went on, "and peyote and jimson weed, but alcohol—the whites brought that, along with measles and smallpox and some other blessings. You've heard that Indians can't handle alcohol?" He waited for her to nod before he said, "Well, there's some truth in that. My father, he never was a cuddle guy. He said there're two kinds of men, the doers and the done to and I didn't act much like a doer. But he never batted me around except when he came home from the Nineteenth Hole, and then mother and I both had to keep out of his way."

"Why are you telling me this?"

"So you can understand that I know something about abusers. Not like Ron. Dad wasn't a beast, he was just a mean drunk and a bully. But he made me feel weak and worthless. That's what abuse does."

"Okay, you understand abuse and so you know that Amy needs me. That I have to get back to her."

He stood up. "Yes you do. But first you need to do something about Ron."

"Ron? How am I going to . . ." she circled a little gesture to take in the little room.

He went to the door. "I'll show you." He smiled. "Wait here for me."

Wait here. Charley's idea of a joke. She said, "What did you mean about religion? Your religion—what is it?"

He paused, hand on the knob. "It's called animism. It's a big idea. Not just the Principal People—a lot of people discovered it. A long time ago."

"What does it—animism—what does that mean?"

"Do you believe that everything is electricity?"

She tried to read his face. Aren't they supposed to be impassive—Indians? She said, "You mean, like electrons and protons? I guess so. Yeah, I suppose I believe that."

"And you understand it?"

She shook her head. "Haven't the first."

He nodded. "We're talking about the biggest—" he threw up both hands "—the deepest questions of all. At the end of those questions there are no answers. We all have to take something on faith. Walking on water, virgin birth, matter that's just energy and particles that exist in two places at the same instant—none of that makes sense, right? And yet," he rapped his knuckle against the door, "none of this makes sense either, without something else."

He took a half step toward her and opened both hands. "Sam, I've found my something else. I'm not trying to recruit you to that. I think you have to find your own."

She squirmed into a new position on the little bed. "Why do I have to find it in here?"

He smiled. Benevolently, as if speaking to a child. "You can accept the idea that everything is electricity, without the first idea what that really means. In the same way, we believe that everything is spirit. Maybe the two words mean the same thing."

He sounded like a school teacher. No, someone making a show of learning. A self-taught man. She said, "But that doesn't sound—you said religion makes you dangerous."

"Religion imposes obligations." He opened the door. "Sam, what you believe isn't really important. Believing, that's what's important. I'll be back in a few minutes. With answers."

# CHAPTER 10

"Terrible tragedy," Walt said, shaking his head. The ragged gray hair—he must use the three-dollar barber in Northport—fell over his forehead. "What happens when we create an environment for gangs."

Ron waited on the tired leather couch, glancing over the photographs framed above the scuffed oak desk: Walt with the Police Athletic League team wearing Wallace Enterprises jerseys, Walt squeezed into a tuxedo to accept a man-of-the-year award from the Hope Foundation and Walt posing as Cradle of Aviation Museum Gala Honoree in front of the wood-and-canvas Lindberg Jenny. When Walt didn't go on, Ron asked, "How many houses were lost?"

Walt waved a little dismissive gesture. "Two. Firemen saved two others but they're so damaged . . ." he shrugged. "Not important. The sad thing is the people. All crowded in . . . three people couldn't get out. Another one badly burned, trying to get to his little boy."

"Illegal people," Ron said. "Living in illegal apartments."

Walt nodded. "That's the root problem. Only solution is to change the conditions that created this tragedy."

"Does this create the opportunity—"

"Don't talk like that. Don't even think it. This was a cruel tragedy."

Ron controlled the impulse to smile. "Of course. All the houses—were they ours?"

"Three of the four."

"So, are we going to rebuild?"

Walt raised a palm that said, "stop." He waited a beat, and then: "You mean, more little ticky-tacky fire traps? Would that be socially responsible?"

Still keeping a straight face as he shook his head, Ron said, "Worst thing that could happen." Pause, selecting his words: "But with the right vision, that area could become a vibrant community. Solid people, upscale shops . . ."

Another rueful shake of that shaggy gray head. "Town Board doesn't have that kind of vision. They're going to insist on affordable housing. And then here we go again."

An adrenalin jolt told Ron this was the moment. Careful not to overplay it, he said, "That's a public relations problem."

"Kind of problem I brought you into the firm to handle. Maybe you could work up a plan."

Ron took a breath. He looked at the framed, handwritten letter on the wall with love-me photos. It wasn't legible from here, but Ron knew it was signed by the mother of a nine-year-old leukemia victim thanking him for the World Series her son had watched in the Wallace box. The man was all heart.

Ron said, "That kind of a campaign would be expensive."

"I understand. Suppose I establish a discretionary fund. Say, a hundred thousand for openers. Keep it separate. Auditors won't be looking over your shoulder every time you need to take a Councilman to lunch."

Ron considered that, cautious about the adrenalin buzz. Playing poker with a pro. "That's the right concept, but . . ." he shook his head. "Let's make that two hundred thousand."

Walt cocked an eyebrow. He let the silence settle between them until Ron went on, turning over a palm: "We were talking about initiative, Walt. How you needed somebody who didn't have to be told."

Walt nodded. "That's right. Don't want to cramp initiative." He looked away, considering his words. "Where did you say you went to school?"

"School?" Ron repeated, in spite of himself. Where did that come from? He answered, "Custis Academy." Walt's brows seemed to raise a question, and Ron added: "In Virginia. Dad was stationed down there."

"I meant college. Where did you go to college, Ron?"

"Harvard." He didn't say, like I told you. He waited to see another card.

Walt nodded again, as if remembering. "Right. And if I asked you to bring me a diploma?"

Ron sat back and managed a smile, walking up to the edge. "You wouldn't do that. You and I are about vision."

Walt smiled, still nodding, as if he'd expected an answer like this. "The Registrar doesn't seem to know you."

Ron considered that. Time to double down. "Did you check Custis Academy too?"

"Didn't bother. What happened there?"

"A little hazing trouble. Custis called it 'bullying.' Dad said it was kid stuff. Nothing compared to what went on at Annapolis when he was there."

"Tell me about it."

"The Naval Academy?"

Walt gave him that kindly-uncle smile. "No. Tell me about your little hazing trouble. If it's not too painful to remember."

Ron returned the smile to show he got the sarcasm. "There was this nerdy guy at Custis. Name was Alan. Everybody knew he was a fruitcake. I mean, he never came on to anybody, far as I know, but the hair down to his shoulders and way he walked, and those flippy little gestures, you know?"

Walt nodded. "That kind of thing can be very threatening to teenage boys."

Ron shook his head. "What we did . . . it was just boarding-school pranks. Kid stuff. We short-sheeted his bed. One night after he'd gone to sleep we put his hand in warm water to make him pee. Didn't work. Just woke him up."

"That was all?" still with that kindly-uncle smile.

Ron doubled down. "No. It did get a little out of hand. One night we trimmed his pageboy into a buzz cut." Ron smiled, remembering. He decided not to mention the "Cunt" painted between Alan's shoulder blades, with an arrow down his back. "You wouldn't think . . ." Ron said, "I mean, wouldn't you think he'd be too embarrassed to complain?"

Walt prompted: "I would. But I guess he wasn't. What happened?"

Ron said, "No damage done. Alan went on to Harvard."

"But you didn't."

"Not me. I should have. My grades were better than his. And my character—I was a Custis all-star. Instead, I saw the world."

Without looking, Wallace tapped the file on his desk. "You volunteered into the Navy. Like your father."

"Not hardly. He was an officer. A fighter pilot. Golden boy. I was a white hat."

"But you got to see the world."

"Not really. Got to see the inside of a steel ant hill. Couldn't wait to get out and draw a deep breath."

Walt looked away at something beyond Ron's head. "So when you came out you wanted to get a taste of the good life, is that it?"

Ron considered that. "I came out understanding what makes the world turn." Now, betting all-in, he said, "Two hundred and fifty would be better."

Walt looked back and smiled. "You're not shy, are you, Ron? Catch you in a lie, and you just raise your price."

"Rather have somebody who backs off?" And then, leaning

forward: "It's working in Owens Falls, right? And now it'll work here in Huntington."

Walt sat back as if slapped. "Owens Falls? What are you talking about?"

Ron waited a beat, savoring control of the moment. "I'm talking about a fire that erased a row of junk houses. Now Owens Falls—as soon as they can get their political act together with our PR help—Owens Falls gets upscale shops and restaurants and the whole package."

Walt's jaw sagged open and he shook his head slowly as if denying what he was hearing.

"Come on, Walt. You explained it to me, remember? Seven billion people and couple of hundred new ones every—"

"Stop!" Walt held up his hand. "I don't want to hear this."

"It's just seven billion minus three, Walt. No big—"

Walt interrupted in a voice pitched higher than Ron had ever heard it. "No." He moved his hand back and forth in front of his face. "I don't want to hear any more." He closed his eyes a moment, collecting himself, and then he cleared his throat and said, in his usual controlled tone, "You know what's the worst thing that can happen to a rental property owner?" When Ron didn't answer, he went on: "Fire."

"But Owens Falls—"

Walt raised a hand to stop him again. "Owens Falls was a kitchen fire. Grease in a skillet. Well documented. Four witnesses. Even so, the insurance company . . ." His eyes drifted away again, and when he came back he hitched forward in the chair. "But Huntington was arson."

"Gang bangers," Ron said. "You said it—these people prey on their own. Trash preying on trash. And their tag—"

"I know. Right there on the sidewalk. Probably good enough for the police, because that fits into their frame of reference.

84

But you know the frame of reference of an insurance investigator? I'll tell you. He sees two fires in one year, and now one of them was arson."

Ron thought about that. "But if there's no evidence . . ."

"It's still a problem."

Ron put on his client smile. "Public relations problem."

Walt pulled an expression as if tasting something sour. "You might say . . . Tell me, Ron—who are you? I mean, really."

"I'm trying to work that out, Walt. I mean, aren't we all? But what I know is, PR, that's my schtick. This Huntington problem—I'll think of some way to handle it. I always do."

Walt tented his fingers into a little barricade on the desk. "Yeah, Ron, you always do. But whatever you come up with, you bring it to me first, understand?"

"Sure."

"And nothing in writing, Ron. On your computer, or anywhere. Understand?"

"Sure, Walt. I'll call you and we'll talk." He stood and took a step toward the door.

"And Ron, when you figure out who you are . . ."

Ron paused at the door, on top of the conversation now. "You know Lady Gaga, Walt?"

Walt shook his head.

"She sings about that. What you said. Why you own those fire traps in Owens Falls and Huntington, and why I do what I do."

"What does she say?"

"I can't sing it, but what she says is, 'You were born this way, baby.' "

Walt cocked his head. "What way is that?"

Ron looked past him, listening to the song in memory. "What she's singing about is flippy. She's singing about a guy who was born flippy, like my old friend Alan." When he looked back he smiled. "But it works for us too, doesn't it, Walt? I mean, the way we are, we were born our way too."

He touched his forehead with a slow, sarcastic salute on his way out.

# CHAPTER 11

She waited half a dozen breaths before pushing up out of the little bed and going to the door. Locked, but worth a check. Check everything. Replay everything. Listen to what he says, and doesn't say. Find the way into him. That's the way out of here.

She sat in the wing chair and tried to sort out what she had learned. He's an Indian. Cherokee. What does that mean—tepees and scalps? Whatever, he's into it. All that stuff about electricity and spirit. Spooky. But he seems so . . . sane. Maybe a lot of wackos do. What was it he said about his father? The doer. So Charley's the doer and I'm the done to. Like the abused child, vulnerable and ready to bond with the strong adult to survive. Bullshit.

What else? He knows something about abuse. When I was talking to Cassie, he picked up on the word "touching." His Cherokee father—wonder if his mother is Indian too? What difference might that make? Whatever, his father made him feel weak and worthless. And he said Ron doesn't deserve to live. Is he just playing a sympathy card? Telling me that he knows abuse and so he's on my side? Ron is a beast—Charley's word—and we're partners. Just how? Explanation to come in his own sweet time. Probably in one of his damn stories. Wait here, he says with that little smile. Telling me that he's the strong one.

Self-important. Narcissistic—that's what Cassie calls Ron. Uses other people. Can't understand what others feel. Is there something about me that attracts narcissistic men? No, the woods are probably full of them.

Play the game. Find a way into him and out of here, for Amy. Charley, you are important. Your ideas shine. Your dick inspires awe.

She felt a vibration through the rag rug before she heard the trundling sound in the hall. Again, he cracked the door and said, "Where are you, Sam?"

"I'm right here in the nurse's chair." She stood. "But now I'm going back to Eric's little bed." She sat down and propped the pillow against the wall for her back.

He came in with his arms full. "Brought you some soap and towels." He dropped them onto the wing chair. "Countess D didn't install a shower down here, but—oh yes, I even found a new toothbrush for you." Then he reached into one of the brown paper bags. "And I brought this. Also, for your night wear . . ." He unfolded a gray sweatshirt and held it up. Then he dropped the shirt and purse on the chair and shook out a baggy pair of warm-up pants with "PINK" printed in white across the seat. "Old Navy's latest fashion statement. Had to guess your size. Medium okay?"

As he moved the things over to the little table under the Alice prints, he went on, like a host to a house guest: "There's no cable connection down here and I'm afraid the rabbit ears wouldn't pick up much. But if you tell me what you like to read—I have a small library of paperbacks. But my taste in bedtime reading—" he shrugged "—might not be yours."

Submission is the name of the game. "Anything that would help me understand what you were saying about electricity, and spirit and all that—I'd like to read it."

That stopped him. "Really?" he said, brows pulling his eyes wide. He went to the wing chair. "I have a book about second lives. All the people who can remember another life back in history. Would you like to read that?"

"If you believe in that, sure I would. Do you?"

He opened his hands in that familiar "would I lie?" gesture. "Genetic memory? Why not? Birds don't learn migration maps, do they? Of course not. They're hatched with that knowledge in their genes. The monarch butterfly gets from Canada to Mexico with the route in that pin head—and it takes them three generations to get there. So why not genetic memory in people?"

He paused, giving her a chance to answer. "Do you believe that an ancient Jew built a boat that saved all the animal species in the whole world from a terrible flood?"

Something about the way he asked made her smile. "No. That would have been a big boat."

He nodded. "But I believe it. I believe what that story *means*. Do you know that at the rate things are going, half of all the species now on Earth will be extinct in a hundred years?" He waited for her to shake her head before he went on: "We're causing the flood. Habitat destruction. Trawlers strip-mining the fisheries. Acres of rain forest chopped down every day. Ice caps melting and oceans rising over the shores. Someone has to start building a big boat. A political boat. That's what the bible story means."

Play the game. "I didn't realize—is that what you mean about the none such?"

"Nunnihi. They're a little more complicated, but yes, I believe that all religions are probably true. We just have to figure out what they mean." He smiled and raised a lecturer's index finger. "Do you believe in fate?"

"I don't know, but this doesn't seem like my fate." She circled a little gesture at the pictures on the wall. "Not here in Wonderland."

He flashed that quick smile. "I don't think so either. Your fate is bigger than this place. It's grander. You are going to help an entire people discover themselves."

She held up her hands. "Not me. I'm just interested in my little girl."

He stood up and took a step toward the door. "We don't choose our parents or our fate."

"You've given me a lot to think about."

"Think about this: We live in angry times. People just need a focus for their fury."

He waited for a reaction and then chuckled at what he saw. "Maybe that's too much to think about all at once. For you to read, maybe I should just look for a good Agatha Christie."

She shook her head. "I've already got more mystery than I need. You said you were going to answer all my questions."

He took the other step to the door. "At least I'll make a start." And then, with that annoying ironic smile, "Wait right there."

He left the door ajar as he went out. She could be waiting behind it when he came back in. This hard mattress under her— was it spread on bed slats? Could she bring herself to club Charley? Even when he gave her that sweet smile? Damn right.

She was on her feet with the corner of the mattress pulled up—solid wood of some sort underneath—when she heard a thump on the door. She dropped the mattress and sat down, a corner of her mind thinking about a time of rage, just as Charley pushed the door wide open and rolled into the room a two-wheeled trolley that might have been designed for motels. On top was a TV; on a rack underneath was a DVD and CD player. A set of tubular steel niches on the bottom stored cords and adapters.

He unwound the power cord from a fixture on the side and began searching the baseboard, saying: "After Countess D passed on to that great gold coast in the sky, this aristocratic old house was rented to Mary Pickford and Douglas—here it is." He plugged it into a socket behind the door. "They rewired the place, but it wouldn't meet code today."

He retrieved a DVD from the top of the player, saying: "When we left our story, our hero had discovered a passenger in his SUV. A passenger with a weapon. Do you remember?"

Sam couldn't contain a sarcastic: "Vividly."

He nodded as he inserted the DVD. "While our hero and the sorcerer are driving to his house in the dark woods, remember? They talked about, what was your word? Deep. They talked about deep things. But nothing recorded them, and so we just have my recollection."

"Yours? You're the guy with the gun?"

He pressed the power key and the screen filled with snow. "Come on, Sam, you knew that, didn't you?" A scene popped onto the screen. Black and white, with the back of a man moving away from the camera. "Okay, it works," Charley said. He punched off the player and took the wing chair.

"You must wonder why I call him 'the sorcerer'?" When she nodded encouragement he went on: "Because he created stunning illusions. Whole worlds—" his voice dropped into a stage timbre "—populated with creatures he invented." He swept a gesture. "Creatures as fantastic as these *Alice in Wonderland* animals, but able to move in front of our eyes and react to us— make us a part of their adventures. Isn't that sorcery?" He paused a dramatic beat, enjoying the moment. "We call them computer games." He sat back with a smile, waiting for her reaction.

She fed him what he seemed to want: "Computer games? Okay, I guess they *are* a kind of magic show."

"More than that. They are as addictive as heroin. They dope the imagination. I know. When I was in high school, Phantasy Star was my reality. The only place where I had any control. Everything in the real world made me feel like nothing, but in Phantasy Star I was . . ." He thrust his elbows out to strike a pose. "I had power. Purpose."

He dropped his hands back into his lap with a dismissive flip. "I didn't kick that addiction until . . . well, that's another story. The point of this one is, the sorcerer was a game designer."

He *was* a game designer, she noticed. Past tense.

Charley hitched forward again. "Actually, he was more than that. He owned a design company. With animators and editors and sound engineers and"—another big gesture—"I don't know what all. But he was the concept guy. On the way out to his house on Tramp Harbor, the sorcerer—let's call him The Designer, shall we? He tried to ignore the pistol. It was just a Beretta pellet gun I'd ordered on the Web, but it looked like the real nine millimeter. Especially to a guy who spent most of his time in a cyber world of devastating weapons. He tried to engage me in conversation, which, you may have noticed, is not difficult."

Still offering what he seemed to want, she said, "No, I'd say you're a conversationalist."

Now his smile reminded her of Ron. In control, always thinking about something beyond the moment. He went on: "Along the way The Designer explained that he was working on a"—he drew quotation marks in the air—"mega concept. I didn't follow all of it, but I remember he said that computer gamers now spend a couple of hundred million hours on some warcraft game every week. I asked him to repeat that, and yes—two hundred million hours every *week*. So, the idea is, make something like a stock market game that's really fun to play and you could learn how bubbles and panics occur and maybe what to do about them. Or a virtual city—you could throw disasters at it and learn how to organize the response. You could test all kinds of big policy issues as long as you make the games realistic and fun. All those players, now they're also lab rats. Pretty sneaky, don't you think?"

She decided to push back a little. "So now we're going to play a computer game?"

He laughed out loud. "No, this is going to be reality TV. But first, I need a little more set-up."

He waited for her to shrug and nod before he went on: "You see, The Designer owned a studio in LA, but he worked out his concepts on Vashon Island. Out in Puget Sound, away from everyone."

Charley dipped a mock bow. "Except me. I found him. And I had a great idea for a computer game. Just because I chose to pitch it at gunpoint, well, he was used to dealing with creative, unconventional people. One time a guy sent him an email—he told me this in the car. The guy said 'I have your dog. If you want to see him again, read the attached concept pitch.' " Charley shook his head and chuckled. "The Designer didn't even own a dog, but the email was so ballsy that he had to read the attachment. I asked him if this was the first time anyone had held a gun on him to make him listen, and he said, yes it was, and my pitch better be damn good.

"By the time we got to his cedar-plank house looking across the bay at the dock—he said eagles hang out there on the pilings in the mornings and his neighbor claimed that one of them grabbed his cat. On the way he was like a tour guide. Pointed out a big cedar stump that he said had been left when they logged the island a hundred and fifty years ago. Stump had a slot in it for what he called a spring board, where a guy could stand and work a buck saw. Anyway, by the time we got there, I liked the guy. I mean, I could spot a charm offensive, but"—he shrugged—"what the hell. Charm works."

He raised his brows and opened a little gesture to say that she and he both knew that this is a charm offensive too. She nodded—what the hell, let him think it works. "We're almost ready for the TV show," he went on. "You have to understand, the production values aren't like . . ." he paused, coming up with an example. "*Law and Order.* The show wasn't—when I asked if you believe in fate? Well, sometimes things just happen to me. Important things."

"What do you mean?"

"The first time was—remember what I told you about my game addiction? That was the only time I had any purpose? Well, one day I stumbled onto something. Something that was waiting for me at just the moment I needed to find it. I don't think I can explain it, but right then I knew I had a . . . I had something to do. I didn't know what it was. Took a little time to figure that out. As I worked on it, other things happened to me. Things I could never have planned. Things that tell me I'm on the right track. You're one of those things, Sam."

"Me?"

He stood and went to the TV trolley. "You weren't in my plan. I mean, I didn't realize you were. It was your husband I called, remember? Not you."

She nodded.

"Sam, The Designer's name is Langshan."

"Langshan?" she repeated.

He nodded. "Your name. Actually, your husband's."

She closed her eyes and took a deep breath. I should have known. Ron never gave me anything good except Amy, and he's doing his best to ruin that. I should have known this was all about him.

Charley had just paused for a dramatic beat—the man should be on the stage—and now he was going on: "It's not a common name. There are only eleven Langshans in the United States, and six are women. Google makes this kind of stuff easy to find out, and when you know that much, the Mormons will cough up family tree connections." He waved a gesture. "All us religious zealots work together. So I knew that The Designer is what the cops on TV call a 'person of interest.' And so is your beloved Ron."

"I don't understand."

"You will when you've seen the TV show. That was another thing that just came along. Too perfect to be planned."

"I thought you said it's not so hot."

"I said it's not a production. It's not even a documentary. Just a tad better than a home movie. You see, The Designer had installed a kind of a studio in that house. A lot of games use live actors that are mixed into animation, somehow, and so he had a video camera on a tripod and some mannequins and cardboard figures and a bunch of other props. He could set up a scene and then push the props around with a closet pole to work out his game ideas on camera. Then he'd play the DVD as he drafted the script. And I just lucked into that setup."

She almost asked, "And me—am I another setup you lucked into?" but decided to play along in silence.

He fiddled with the controls as he spoke over his shoulder: "Now, the show begins after The Designer and I have arrived and gone inside."

The screen filled with static and snow. "He's showed me the little studio—he was proud of that—and I'd felt fate patting me on the back. A video record—I'd never thought of that. When I said I wanted to make my pitch on camera he didn't like the idea, but rather than argue with my mean-looking Beretta he fired up the lights and the camera."

With an audible pop the black-and-white image of a man's back appears on the screen. Charley takes his seat as the man walks away from the camera, saying, ". . . over here. I use these chairs for stage furniture, but if you want to be on camera, have a seat."

Charley walks into the frame, saying, "You're sure it's on?"

The Designer turns to take one of the two straight-back

wooden chairs. "Yes, we're rolling." Sam realized she'd been expecting a slender, artistic-looking man, but this designer had shoulders like a dock worker. "Now put that gun away and let's hear your pitch," he says.

Charley puts what looks like a gym bag on the floor as he sits down. He holds up the gun for the camera—it *did* look lethal— and then puts it in his lap. "The player's mission is to avenge an ancient wrong. The game's back story is about a brave people with a culture based on honor who were driven out of their land by a high-tech conqueror."

"I don't know," The Designer says. "Sounds like another war game."

"This is just the back story. We haven't gotten to the game yet."

"Okay, let's get there."

On the screen, Charley adopts his stage voice. "These people had to walk a thousand miles. In the winter. Barefoot in the snow, a lot of them. Mothers carrying their babies. Old men slipping into the creeks at night to drown rather than be a burden to the group. They walked west, which they believed was the direction of death. And that's what it was, for hundreds of them."

The Designer squirms on the wooden chair. "This is a lot of back story."

"We're almost ready to start the game. A few of these people refused to face west and leave their land. It wasn't a matter of property, but principle. They lived by principles. Their land was a part of them, as they were a part of it. The earth does not belong to man, but man belongs to the earth. Those who refused to leave were led by a man named Tsali. 'Charley' is the way the conquerors pronounced it."

Sam glanced at Charley, but he kept his eyes on the screen.

"Come on," The Designer says, "is this a game or a history lesson?"

"I promise you, the game will be exciting. The conquerors captured Tsali and executed him. The commander of the firing squad was a young officer, just months out of West Point. Second lieutenant Hiram Langshan."

The Designer's mouth opens as if to speak, but he seems to reconsider.

Charley nods. "Yes. Your name. Your ancestor." He picks up the gym bag, zips it open and drops the pellet gun inside. "And now the game begins."

The Designer stands. "None of that has anything to do with me. And I'm not interested in your game."

Charley draws out of the bag an unusual blade, long as a carving knife but thick, with what looks like two cutting edges. "Oh, but you will be. This is the most exciting game you've ever played." He stands, looking like a boy as he faces the bulked-up designer, and holds out the blade, turning it back and forth to catch the light. "Tell me, is it true that one is never more alive than when facing death?"

The Designer grabs his chair and holds it in front of him with the legs pointing toward Charley. "Are you crazy?"

Charley gives the blade a little toss into his left hand as he circles into the middle of the room, his back to the camera now. "I'd put it a little differently. I'd say I'm driven by a powerful idea. A principle. But as far as you're concerned it comes to the same thing."

Circling to keep the chair legs toward Charley, The Designer says, "I didn't have anything to do with—whatever you're talking about."

As Charley's hands come back into view he is hefting the blade in his left hand, as if estimating its weight. "True," he says in a conversational tone. "But beside the point." When he tosses the blade back into his right hand, Sam could see that the handle was white and curved. A piece of bone?

"The point?" The Designer says, thrusting the chair forward a little. He takes a step toward Charley, who crouches slightly, making him look even smaller. "There's a point to this craziness?" There is a tiny quaver in The Designer's voice.

Charley takes two quick, shuffling steps, keeping his weight on the balls of his feet like a boxer, slaps backhand at a chair leg and feints a slash at The Designer's left knee. When The Designer jumps back, Charley laughs. "Yes, there is a point. The point of this knife must have blood on it. The blood of the man who executed old Tsali is in you, and so the knife is thirsty for your blood." With his eyes on The Designer, he tosses the blade back and forth, left hand to right, showing how well his hands know it.

"Why?" The quaver is gone now. The Designer shifts his grip on the chair back, holding now with just his left hand. The legs of the chair don't tremble. "What have I ever done to you?"

"Nothing. And afterward I will ask for your pardon, as we asked for the pardon of the deer, and the bear. Especially the bear. We ask the pardon of everything we must kill."

Sam said, "I don't want to see any more of this," but she kept watching the screen as The Designer shifts his grip again to hold the chair with both hands.

Without looking away from the television, Charley said, "You want to understand what you must do, don't you? What you must do for Amy?"

On the screen, The Designer swings the chair back and forth in a small arc, testing it as a club. In his big hands it looks as light as a nine iron. "Well, fuck you," he says. "I don't pardon you, or your crazy ideas. Primitive ideas. This isn't the fucking stone age."

"No, this is now," Charley says, tossing the blade from hand to hand. "Honor killings happen now. Every day. The Afghanis, the Arabs, the Kurds, even the Turks. Wherever people live by principle instead of profit."

Charley feints with the blade in his left hand, swiping it close to The Designer's arm. The Designer pulls back, slowed by the weight of the chair, and raises it to swing. Charley shuffles back into his crouch, blade at belt level, thumb on top. The Designer returns to the chair to legs-out defense. "Not in this let's-make-a-deal society," Charley says. "A society of fact with no meaning. For all of human history, most people have lived by principle and purpose. As we are living now. You and I."

"What the hell does that mean?"

"It does not mean love thy neighbor. It means—" he feints an upward thrust and kicks The Designer in the groin. The chair legs come down as the designer staggers back with an explosive grunt. Charley shoves past the chair and slices the blade across The Designer's left forearm. The Designer releases his left hand and the chair swings aside. Charley takes another step and thrusts the blade just below The Designer's armpit. It seems to penetrate only an inch.

Sam covered her eyes. "Don't make me watch this."

"I don't have to," Charley said. "You can't look away."

She couldn't.

On the screen, Charley kicks The Designer's left heel as he probes the blade. The Designer coughs as the blade finds a place between the ribs and slides in until the end of Charley's thumb disappears. The Designer drops the chair. Slowly, like one of the Douglas firs outside, he sags onto Charley's knife hand. Charley pulls back. The Designer's knees buckle. As he crumples to the floor, his left leg doubles under and his right splays out, Charley holds the dripping blade up to the camera. The Designer reaches under his arm as if to discover what had happened and coughs again, spraying blood.

"We were talking about honor," Charley says. "You're a man of character. Not principle, but character. I'd like you to understand your death in time to understand your life, but I don't think we have a lot of time." The Designer is breathing red froth from his mouth. "You see, God is the enemy of honor. One God, that is the curse of Abraham. It gave us Judaism, Christianity and Islam. The father God teaches that anyone who disagrees is a heathen, or a pagan or a heretic—take your pick. Are you still with me, Designer?"

Another bloody cough. The discovering hand drops.

"Good. I don't want you to leave too soon. When we had many gods we lived closer to reality. To nature. And we accepted the obligations of honor. If you kill my clansman, I must kill a clansman of yours." Charley takes a step closer and slowly folds into his left hand the crown of The Designer's hair. The Designer's eyes widen, looking up at Charley.

"You understand that this is not personal," Charley says. "Personally, I like you. I like the idea of using computer gamers as lab rats. But this is a matter of honor. I beg your pardon for what I must do now." He bends closer to look into The Designer's eyes, and then he sweeps the blade across the stretched throat and steps back.

A gout of blood pulses half an arm's-length in front and then upward as The Designer kicks both feet forward and slides onto his back, hands clutching his throat. With blood dripping off his elbows and painting his face, he writhes and gasps a strange bleat that rises into a falsetto wail.

Sam said, "Oh my god," but she kept watching. After a long, squirming and kicking time, the fountain diminished and the scream collapsed into gurgling. One leg began twitching. First his left hand, and then his right dropped to the floor. His mouth worked, but now there was no noise. The twitching slowed and stopped. The eyes widened and the mouth went slack above the gaping throat.

Charley hitched forward in the chair to pause the DVD and then turned to look at her. "There was no dignity in his death," he said. "Maybe I should have given him that, do you think?" When she didn't answer he went on: "But I had to use a traditional weapon. And he died much easier than my people did."

"But he didn't have . . ." Sam started over: "But when you were watching that . . ."

"What did I feel?" he said, looking at his own face frozen on the screen as if to recall the moment. "I remembered."

Making it a question, she repeated: "You remembered?"

Now he looked at her. "What's the biggest thing—the biggest memory in your life?"

Without hesitation she said, "When the nurse handed me Amy."

He smiled. "It wasn't like that, but it was big. It was like . . ." he raised both hands around an invisible globe. ". . . like my whole life had been heading to this moment and I'd finally found my way." He keyed the remote to restart the DVD.

On screen, Charley turns to face the camera. "My Cherokee clansmen," he said. "You know me as Andrew. My parents are modern people and so they did not realize that they were giving me the same name as the President who uprooted us. But I have studied our history, and I have taken the name of Tsali, who faced death to protect the values of the Principal People. Our values."

He holds the bloody blade up to the camera. "Before the whites, with their measles and their smallpox and their cruel god and their idea of property"—he seemed to be reciting a memorized statement—"we lived in harmony with all around us and in honor with each other. But honor requires retribution. Without honor, there is no order. My clansmen, today I meet our obligation of blood vengeance to recall our other values. We are a powerful and spiritual people. Clansmen, claim our identity."

The screen went to snow and Charley stood to punch it off.

"That was awful," Sam said.

He nodded. "Awful, yes. Inspiring awe. And some part of you thrilled to it. You couldn't look away. That tells me it'll work for a TV audience."

"What are you talking about?"

Charley sat in the wing chair. "Maybe it's a little too bloody. The Designer was a big man and so he had to pump a gallon of blood. Probably more. But we could edit some of that." He smiled at what he saw in her face. "What I said about just lucking into a setup that was too perfect to be planned—who would have expected to find a TV studio? But as soon as he told me, I realized I had been guided to him."

Sam looked away, trying to find something real to escape this craziness, but her eye fell on the drawing of the Cheshire cat dissolving into the leaves.

"Charley, you . . ."

Charley nodded. "Stuck him like a pig, on camera. After he bled out I dropped him off the pier where the eagles watch for salmon. There's a good tide in there and so . . ." he shrugged and continued as if talking about a day at the beach: "Probably depends on the crabs. The eastern blue crabs would feast on him, but I don't know about the Pacific." He crossed his legs and continued in that conversational tone: "My face was on camera, too. Which is where you come in."

"Me?" She sat forward on the little bed. "What's this got to do with me?"

"For openers, you married the right name. Or the wrong one. Langshan. Same as The Designer's, and the Lieutenant's. Unusual name. If the firing squad had been commanded by

Lieutenant Smith or Johnson, I'd have a different problem."

"You mean, a different victim?" Her own voice seemed to match his tone, as if it were coming from some detached person she didn't know. Is this conversation really happening?

Charley nodded. "I think of it as a target. A duty to my blood. My target of choice would be a descendant of Andrew Jackson. The old Indian fighter. He drove the Cherokee out of the Great Smokies. But he and Rachel had no children, and vengeance follows blood." He waved a little gesture, as if clearing smoke. "There're too many Jacksons anyway. Langshan was preserved for me, just like The Designer's studio was set up for me. And you. Sam, you're in PR—what do you know about YouTube?"

She sat back on the little bed. Where was this going? "Not a whole lot," she hedged. "It's kind of an amateur night on the Web."

"How about LiveLink?"

She shook her head. "Never heard of it."

He smiled. "I appreciate your honesty. D'you know—how does something get on YouTube?"

"It's not difficult. Starts out with a blog, or . . . I'm not sure. Maybe just an email address."

Charley gestured toward the TV. "So we could put our show of The Designer's last game on YouTube?"

"That?" She shook her head. "That's too gory. They'd never permit that."

Charley cocked his head, considering that, or perhaps studying her. "Who wouldn't?"

"There's some kind of a boss, or administrators—whatever they're called. They can take down anything that they decide is offensive."

"Take down? You mean, they'd let it on, and then take it down?"

Sam thought about that. This is all about Amy. Submission.

Going along. "There's no preliminary screening, if that's what you mean. And there's such a load . . . I don't know exactly, but every minute, hours of content must get added to YouTube. There's no way they could prescreen it, even if they wanted to. Which they don't. They're open source."

"You mean crowd source?" The way he smiled said he'd known this all along. Testing her. When she nodded he went on: "So, after something's up on YouTube, how do they decide what's offensive?"

Play the game. "When someone complains, I suppose," she said.

Charley swept a wide gesture. "Which means it's already been seen by . . . how many people, would you say?"

She hesitated. Careful. Another test question. "No way to know."

"Hundreds? Thousands?"

"Only if it catches on. Most YouTubes—" she shrugged and shook her head.

"And what makes a YouTube catch on?"

"Charley, if we knew that we'd be rich."

"How about promotion? Doesn't that help?"

"Sure. You can get some clicks with a hot promotion."

"And that's something you know how to do, isn't it? Isn't that something you do for a gala?"

"Charley, you don't need me to promote a YouTube. Blasting an email is simple if you have the addresses, but why—"

He interrupted: "And then each one of those people can send it on to their own set of contacts, right?"

She nodded. "That can happen. That's going viral."

He nodded and made a "go on" gesture. Something in his eyes, the momentary twist of his mouth, told her that he knew all about YouTube. This was just another test. Okay, play the game. "Once something catches on," she said, "trying to suppress it is like trying to take pee out of a swimming pool. Worse than that. It's like advertising a place to pee in. People copy the stuff"—Sam wiggled her fingers on an imaginary keyboard—"and send it to friends who copy and send it. It's an Internet epidemic."

"An epidemic," he repeated, pointing as if to pin the phrase in the air. "That's what we want. A vendetta virus. It'll spread through the Cherokee nation like smallpox did. And measles. But this virus will restore health. Moral health."

Sam shook her head. "That video . . . it's a nightmare."

He nodded. "Exactly. It'll turn some people off. But everyone'll be fascinated. Just like you were. Plus or minus, it doesn't matter much. Get the idea out there. Some hate it, others buy it. They all respond to it. Care about something. Ready to act on conviction."

"Charley, what possible good could this"—she gestured toward the blank TV screen—"violence porn do anyone?"

He stiffened, and she realized she'd gone too far.

"Porn?" he repeated. He dropped both feet on the floor and leaned toward her. "That wasn't porn, it was purpose. Purpose creating meaning." He swept another broad gesture. "Porn is politics supported by corporate greed. Permanent war economies. Economies that poison societies as they poison the environment."

He pushed off his knees and stood. "Sam, that's the real porn. Now, I'm going to give you a little privacy."

He followed her glance up at the horn that connected this room to the upstairs. "I sleep in the servants' quarters." he said. "The voice tube is in Madam D's bedroom and the lid is buttoned down. The Nunnehi won't speak to you tonight. I'm going to bring you coffee around eight in the morning. And a bagel—cream cheese, okay?" When she nodded he went on: "I hope you get some sleep. And I hope you also think about how we're going to make sure that no harm comes to Amy."

She sat forward. "Amy? Harm to Amy? What do you want, Charley?"

He opened the door and paused. "I want Langshan here. At Plaisance. On camera. Under the knife."

# CHAPTER 12

Sam undressed, shook out her skirt, blouse and jacket and spread them across the wing chair. "Even a Holiday Inn provides a pressing iron," she said to the overhead horn, in case he might be listening. She took the sweats and towels into the little bathroom, managed to get first one foot and then the other into the sink as she sponged a haphazard bath. She pulled on the sweats, welcoming the cotton against her skin, washed out her bra and pantyhose and draped them over the sink. She padded barefoot to the other room for her purse, extracted the comb and went back to the mirror.

As she studied the wreck of her hair, which she wore in what she thought was a cross between Cher and a schoolgirl-bob with the severity of the bangs softened by ends that curled under at the shoulder, she remembered what Charley had said: the color of a lion's mane. Damn nondescript lion. That brought back Charley's rant. All that porn and politics stuff, and getting on YouTube—that's puffery. The boy who got no respect, can't deal with the world—now he's after guys who made it big. And he needs the world to know. The loner is a closet performer.

But he's not just performing. Goosebumps pebbled her arms as she remembered the video, with blood geysering over the collapsing designer to spill down his arms and drip off his elbows into the growing puddle on the floor. In her mind's ear she heard Charley: "And I hope you also think about how we're going to make sure that no harm comes to Amy."

A faint noise. Door slamming? She grabbed the sink and held her breath, listening. The silence seemed to hum. This place spooked the senses. If that was the front door, was she alone? What if this old wiring started a fire? She looked through the open bathroom door at the brass ear in the ceiling. "You there, Charley?" What had he said about a lid over his end of the tube?

She took a step into the doorway. "Charley, if you're there— I'm feeling kind of panicky. Like I'm buried alive. I'd like to talk some more. I didn't understand everything you told me about the Cherokee and . . . your duty and . . . all that." She waited. Nothing from the ceiling. She realized that her fists were clenched at her sides. She took a deep breath, shook her hands out and stepped back into the bathroom.

Keep your eye on the ball, Sam. This guy isn't your pal. He's the warden. And he's threatening Amy too. Think about the beautiful things in the world.

Breakers creaming along Robert Moses Beach. Sandpipers skittering after the receding water. Some kind of larger bird probing the wet sand with a beak that drooped as if the bird had run into a wall. Beyond the bulge of forming breakers, gulls screaming and circling over a patch of disturbed water. Amy furiously erecting a wall around her castle against the rising tide.

The primrose path and rose garden at Westbury Manor. Under the arbor. Shifting patterns of sunlight filtered through the wisteria. Amy following a black swallowtail butterfly from blossom to blossom. Her mouth forming a silent O as it momentarily lands on her arm, like a blessing.

The clarinet opening "Rhapsody in Blue." Lonely, frail, ascending and seeking, summoning the orchestra to announce the melody. Amy dancing herself dizzy in circles until she falls giggling onto the carpet.

Everything beautiful had Amy in it. But now Amy was sullen. Confused. Maybe ashamed.

Get centered. Think about something beautiful and calm. Something before Amy. That snowflake. Sam was what? Fourth grade, maybe. Miss Krebbs walked around the playground in the snowfall during recess with a magnifying glass. When it was Sam's turn she saw an impossibly complicated, five-pointed arrangement of tiny diamonds sparkling on the midnight blue of her jacket sleeve. That reminded her of Amy playing in the snowfall, trying to catch flakes on her tongue. Everything beautiful led back to Amy.

Sam looked at her face in the mirror over the sink. Scared eyes with a mouth pressed to hold back sobs. So hang in. Don't let this loony con you into his world. Just play along. If he wants Ron, serve him Ron on a platter. Like whoever it was that served up the head of John the Baptist.

She ran some water and washed her face. Now the mirror said that she could use some eyeliner and mascara. But maybe scrubbed and vulnerable was the strategic look. What was it he'd said about the CIA? Out of all the spooky newspaper and magazine features she'd read about the CIA, what could she remember about manipulating captives? Waterboarding was part of it, but so was dependency and humiliation. Hunger, sleep deprivation, loud music, cramped positions. By CIA standards, Charley had been generous. So far.

Lack of stimulus dulls minds. So what does that say? Keep thinking. Keep reciting whatever comes to mind, even if he's eavesdropping upstairs. Don't let him zombie you.

What else could she remember? Every small contact with the captors comes to be appreciated. A smile or a kind word is a big deal. So be careful. You've already followed one man into deep shit. Come to think of it, that was part of that man's magic. He was so on top of everything. He didn't lock her up or anything like that, but he was always in control. Did Charley perhaps sense something dependent in her? That she is drawn to controlling men? Had it all started, maybe, when her father—

The door clicked open.

"I have something to show you," Charley said, standing in the door naked.

"Not much, you don't," she said, grabbing both sides of the door frame for balance as she shifted her weight to her left foot to kick with her right. So that's why he wanted her into these pull-down sweats. "Get out of here."

He laughed. "I come and go as I choose, Sam." He stepped into the room and closed the door behind him. The lock clicked.

She noticed that what he had to show wasn't ready for action. Did he need something from her? Some kind of a reaction? Fear? Submission, that was the game. Play along. She dropped her hands from the door frame. "Charley, if we're going to be partners—aren't we going to be partners?"

"That's the idea," he said. He took another step into the room but didn't hide behind the wing chair. He had a swimmer's body, smooth-muscled and hairless, but there was nothing feminine about his equipment. "And that's why I need to show you something. Do you remember that I said I'm a fanatic? That I have a mission? 'Life being what it is, one dreams of revenge.' Remember?"

She nodded, keeping her eyes on his face. "Does that mean you're a terrorist?"

He made a "yes!" gesture with his fist. "Absolutely. Do you remember how I know that I have a mission for my people? That I have been chosen?"

"You said you stumbled onto something." She glanced away, recalling. "Something that was waiting for you to find it. You didn't say what it was."

"You were listening." He tossed a little gesture. "Doesn't

110

matter what it was. It was just a little animal relic, something to start me thinking about how fragile life is. That started me reading about climate change and extinction, and then one day"—he snapped his fingers—"I realized that I understood Noah's ark. That we're all in the same boat. And if you know how to listen, then animals speak to us. But never mind, what matters is what it meant to me. At that moment. It confirmed this."

He turned around, revealing a spine valley shaped by feline muscles ending in a tight butt. "Do you see the Mongol stain?"

"What?"

He reached back and touched the base of his spine. "That birthmark."

She could see a bluish splash across his lower back and right buttock. "Yes," she said. "It's very faint."

When he turned to face her his member was not so inert. "But it's there. The Cherokee—all the Indians—we came from Asia. Over the narrow land bridge during the ice age. We were Mongols."

He spread his hands in a global gesture. "Genghis Khan's warriors created the greatest empire in history. Made the Romans and the British look like amateurs. A lot of Cherokee are born with the stain but they lose it by the time they're two or three. Mine is permanent. It says that I do not outgrow my heritage."

"Your what?"

He took another step into the room. "The Mongols torched cities and slaughtered the citizens." He paused. "After they raped the women and the young girls."

She could see that he was ready for action now.

He went on: "But not the Cherokee. We honor our dead, and I honor them with revenge." He turned and went to the door, his member flopping. "I hope you can sleep in that little bed, or in that chair, like Eric's nurse." He paused, looking at the pieces of the broken child's chair in the corner. "We're beyond this," he said, gathering them up. "I'll see you in the morning."

The door clicked shut. She relaxed her arms one at a time and thumbed her cramped biceps. What was that all about? Sexy. Coming in nude, and talking about rape. And he was obviously getting into the idea at the end. But then that stuff about honor and revenge. And he had walked away without making a move on her.

Didn't turn him on? Looked like he was ready, but was there something he needed? Can I—is it possible that I'm a little frustrated? Disappointed? Is it possible that I'm a little damp?

# CHAPTER 13

Kurt stared at the business card under his desk lamp without touching it.

*Kurt Cavanagh*

*Licensed Associate Broker*

*Top producer since 2008*

*Hersch Real Estate*

Somewhere a bass guitar throbbed a night pulse. A limb from the yellow maple in the law offices next door scratched the outer wall behind the file cabinets. The sound was familiar, but now he started and looked around the shadowy office. When he finally reached for the card his fingers trembled. He slid it to the edge of his desk, got his thumb under it and, glancing again at the door, turned it over.

There was just a scrawled number: 757-0230.

A little bodega, the man had said. Kurt tried to remember the Huntington barrio. He'd driven through it so many times, paying so little attention. Vaguely, he recalled a green awning and boxes of produce stacked on the sidewalk. Around the corner was the hiring site where guys stood in the street to stop passing cars, pleading for a day's work. Friendly faces, without a trace of menace. Could he have passed Crazy Peter without noting him?

He could call right now. Wouldn't even need to ask for Pedro Loco. Just say, "Tell Pedro Loco the company he wants"—no, say, "the name he was asking about is Wallace." Then he'd never have to see Crazy Peter again.

Or would that perhaps just open the door? Like paying the first blackmail demand. Now we're in this together. And did he really know that Wallace owned the place? Sure, every realtor knew that Wallace owned the ticky-tacky faux Capes along Depot and paid the inspectors to ignore the multiple satellite dishes and trash cans that advertised illegal occupancy. From the town's point of view, what's the practical alternative? Homeless families on the street would just be a bigger problem. Kurt knew all that, just as he knew—not firsthand, but common knowledge knew—that the vulture fund designed for "sophisticated investors who understand the Huntington real estate market" was somehow connected to Wallace too.

But before he loaded someone into the gun, perhaps he could establish that this common knowledge was a fact. He Googled "wallace huntington ny," expecting dozens of site listings, but only two came up. The Walter Wallace Foundation had a vague mission to support suburban youth programs. The other, Wallace Enterprises, Inc., opened a thicket of subsidiary corporations, each with directors and officers, balance sheets and legal-accounting mumbo-jumbo. Obfuscation by over-information.

He opened www.hoovers.com, entered "wallace enterprises" and clicked on "news." Half a dozen headlines came up: "Developer Proposes Planned Community," "Nassau Planning Commission Holds Meeting on Condo Project," "Is Canoe Landing Inn a Historic Structure?" and then, "Town Vetoes Development." He clicked on that and got a three-inch story from *The Owens Falls Daily News* last year.

An application to construct twenty-three condos, to be priced at a million to four million dollars each, in a planned community featuring shops, restaurants and entertainment within walking distance, was rejected by the Town Board.

"Applicant failed to adequately address community concerns about increased traffic, utility and school impacts," said Board Chairman Jonathon Britz. "Further, the Owens Falls master plan requires provision for affordable housing in development projects, which applicant insists would render the project not economically feasible," Wallace spokesman Ron Langshan said . . .

Kurt leaned toward the screen, eyes stuck on that name. Shouldn't have been a surprise—he knew Amy's father was working for Wallace. But Owens Falls? He read on:

"Owens Falls is turning its back on an opportunity to convert a tragic fire into a smart-growth community that contributes to the economy and the quality of life of the entire area."

When asked if the developer will now sell the property for another purpose, Langshan said, "No. We have a commitment to the Owens Falls community. We hope to see the election of a new Board with more balanced values."

Kurt looked away from the screen. Where *was* Owens Falls, anyway? Somewhere up in the chilly breath of Canada. He had a vague idea, probably from some real estate magazine article, of one of those riverbank mill towns that had died when manufacturing moved south and was now gentrifying into craft shops and organic food markets with an outlet mall.

He went to the *Newsday* site, accessed the archives, entered "immigrant home fire" and got a screen full of references. Shopping through them, he found an item identifying the Depot Road landlord as Island Fair Rentals. He went back to Wallace Enterprises and found Island Fair Rentals among the third-tier subsidiaries. Wallace was having a run of bad luck.

So, if Crazy Peter knew that Wallace enterprises was the Depot Road landlord, what would he do? Presumably, he could mobilize the MS-13. Then what? Try to exact some kind of revenge on Wallace himself? Not easy. Guy like that must have personal protection. Go after the entire corporation? Probably impossible.

Kurt's eyes went from the card to the phone. He imagined himself trying to describe Crazy Peter to a cop. Hispanic. Average height and build. Dark hoodie and cargo pants. A "13" tattoo on his left hand. Like maybe a couple of dozen guys on the street tonight. Cops might want Kurt to call the number and try to set up Crazy Peter. Probably wouldn't be easy, but suppose it worked. What law had he broken? The most a cop could do would be to warn him, maybe push him around a little. And what would that accomplish? An angry Crazy Peter, more dangerous than before.

# CHAPTER 14

Sam squirmed into the little bed. The shelf holding the two toy armies was so close to her face that she knew she could reach up and touch it, but she suppressed the impulse. Don't confirm the claustrophobia. Instead, stretch out and get into zen or whatever you call a little distance from the moment. She closed her eyes and tried to empty her mind, but it kept drifting back to Charley.

What does he want? A gory DVD on YouTube. Not hard to do. Not enough to require this kidnapping, or capture, or whatever it was. What does she know about him? She tried to remember what he had said on the video about the Cherokee. A lot about honor and nature. Something about second lives and the way birds and butterflies know how to migrate. What does that mean? And religion. Religious zealots. But his exact words were washed out by remembered images of spouting blood. Maybe it didn't matter. All she had to understand was that he had this crazy idea about paying off old debts and, somehow, he thought he needed her to help.

And that business about the birthmark. He wasn't showing her his butt just to prove that he had warrior blood. All that stuff about torching cities and raping the women, that wasn't just a history lesson. When he walked away, she could see what he was thinking. But why hadn't he just come on to her, like any other obviously horny and reasonably attractive male? Actually, more than reasonably attractive. It was not just his hands,

with square workman's fingers and nails clean as a surgeon's—
Sam knew she had a thing about nails—but also the way he occupied space. When he was in the room, he filled it up.

Thinking about him now, the cast of the eyes and the slant of
the cheekbones that she had associated with Poland but now
understood was Cherokee, she remembered the term that had
come into her head when she first met him: hybrid beauty. A
pretty boy. That opened a new speculation. Had he not come
onto her because he wasn't sure of himself? Could all this warrior stuff be trying to get to be a man? Male?

Nothing wrong with the equipment. Compared to Ron he
had—was she really thinking about this? Damn right. Whatever
is going on, she has to try to figure it out. Does an impressive
set of equipment—at least compared to Ron's, which, not counting high school glimpses, was her only basis for comparison—
was that enough to establish a secure male orientation? Probably not. Some male ballet dancers made impressive statements
in those tights, and surely some of them were gay. So, just suppose this macho preening is compensation. Then what's her
strategy?

Perhaps the understanding older woman who can make him
competent. Older woman—that made her smile. But she'd had
a lifetime of sex education with Ron. She knew positions that
would make a Cherokee warrior blush through his Mongol
stain.

Positions. Get him into Eric's little bed under the armies and
then change the negotiating positions. Could she do that for
Amy? Damn right. Fake passion? Sure. Thinking about it now,
she realized that she might not have to.

Never mind. The job now is to figure out how to do it. Create intimacy. Coming on to him won't work. Not if he's the
warrior, the avenger. "I come and go as I choose, Sam." He has
to make the move. But he clearly needs her, for something. An

audience? Confirmation? Maybe, but he seems to have every-thing worked out in his head. Isn't that the way crazies operate? They get everything worked out so airtight that nothing so trivial as a fact can get in the way.

So go along. What had he said about computer games? Ad-dictive as heroin. When he was in high school, some game was the only place where he had control. So now she was his control game. Her job was to give him that heroin high. Open up, put her in his power. Tell him about a father who never abused her, just diminished her. And Ron, who saw her potential, courted her with grace and consideration, gave her a beautiful child but then . . .

Could she confess all that? For Amy, damn right.

Something was happening. Something she didn't recognize, couldn't identify. The air seemed to thicken, congealing like gelatin. She sat up in the little bed and bumped her head on the lead soldier shelf. The *clunk!* made her realize that she had been listening to silence, for the first time in her life. Absolute, mine-shaft silence. No electronic hum, no scrape of branch across the roof, no wind-click of window against the frame, no insect whirr, no distant traffic mutter, no neighbor's television. The silence sat on her chest, a physical, weight-bearing presence.

Keeping her head down she crawled out of bed, creating a rustle to dissolve the silence. She went to the bathroom and flushed, just to hear the familiar sound. Coming back out, she looked at the brass ear in the ceiling. He said he wouldn't listen tonight, but could she believe him? She needed noise, but instead of saying something he might hear and try to analyze she hummed "Dreamlover" as she threaded her way around the wing chair back to the bed.

She paused at the shelf of toy soldiers, imagining the Countess and her autistic child playing with them. The soldiers were French and English. Did the Countess reenact Waterloo?

Ron had talked about Napoleon. He was always talking about winners and losers, that success happens to some just like blue eyes or big feet. The difference is it happens in their heads. Successes grow up without a concept of defeat. They just never let it into their lives. Accidents happen to accident-prones and success to success-prones. Thinking about that now she wondered, wouldn't growing up without a concept of defeat be like one of those strange children who grow up without a sense of pain? A terrible handicap; the child is apt to cripple himself. Isolation breeds delusions.

She paused and picked up one of the soldiers. It looked French, maybe a cavalry officer, wearing a cylindrical hat and brandishing a curved saber. When she touched the saber, it bent. "Sorry, Eric," she murmured, bending it back in place. She noticed how soft it was, and then how heavy it felt in her palm. Lead.

She picked up two red-coated riflemen, probably British foot soldiers. She cradled them in her hand and then slowly closed it, watching their rifles collapse into their bodies. She weighed the three damaged toys in her hand. Melted down, they would be smaller than a golf ball, but they must be heavier than a baseball. She picked up a French drummer boy and squeezed him into the others as she went into the bathroom, thinking about the afternoon when she was twelve and a neighbor boy had flattened her with a baseball. She hadn't been knocked out, but he hadn't been trying to hit her, just tossing the ball for her to catch. Still squeezing the four soldiers to compact them, she looked around. A towel might work. Panty hose drying on the towel bar—that would be better, if the mesh was strong enough.

She pulled the hose off and dropped the ruined soldiers into one toe. She held it in place with a knot and wadded the rest of the hose into a tight lump that she could hold in her left hand. She went into the outer room and swung the lead over her shoulder onto the bed. *Thwunk!* A satisfying sound, like an exclamation point. She tried it again, and then checked the toe of the hose: two strands broken—nylon or spandex or whatever—but her pantyhose weapon was still ready for action. Like a blackjack.

She studied the lump of lead in the hose, thinking: a blackjack is a one-hand weapon. She held up the hose, letting the lead stretch out the leg. Everything below the knee on that leg was superfluous. Actually, it was in the way.

She needed a sharp edge to cut off the surplus. She looked around the room: bed, Alice prints, wing chair, rag rug, bathroom door, floor lamp, chessboard and pieces under the table, ceiling speaker horn. No tool in sight. She stretched the fabric and chewed the strands, but they fled between her teeth and reappeared intact. Synthetics. Better living through chemistry.

She went to the wing chair where he'd dropped her purse and rummaged through it, looking for a nail file, a credit card, even a key. Nothing sharp. She went back to the bed, pulled the mattress away from the springs and felt along the frame. Smooth, rounded edges. She went to the TV trolley, ran her fingers along all the tubular frames and tested the bolts. Two seemed to have little burrs of metal, but even if she could get one loose she'd need a week to saw through the pantyhose with it.

She sat on the bed and looked at the TV. She could break the tube and get a shard of glass. But when he saw that . . .

Maybe she could clean up the room and clobber him before he noticed. But she was only going to have one shot. As soon as he comes in, *whack!* and then bolt out the door. But if that's the plan, she doesn't need the broken glass. She could hold the pantyhose all wadded up and swing two-handed. More force, but probably not as much accuracy. She thought about the cautious way he had come into the room, making her answer and then just opening the door wide enough to look around to be sure she's seated where he can see her. She'd never get him on the way in.

She hid the blackjack under her pillow, trying to play a scenario in her mind's eye in which he was in the chair and she was on the bed. Perhaps she could ask him something about the Alice prints. What did she remember from the book? Starts out with a rabbit hole and then Alice drinks something that makes her tiny. After that . . . a keyhole. Something seen through the keyhole.

Sam imagined Charley coming back into the room. Cautiously, looking around from the door and then taking the chair. She'd point to one of the pictures—the Mad Hatter in the top row—and say, "Do you remember, Charley, is that what Alice saw through the keyhole?" and when he looked up—

Now she reached under the pillow, grabbed the blackjack as she stood and took one step toward the chair. Holding the legs of the pantyhose she swung the lead into the back of the chair. Not hard, just enough force to test her aim. Close to dead center, but only close. If she hits his shoulder, or if he reacts in time to raise an arm . . .

Too risky. So, what's plan B? Obviously, get him out of his pants and into bed. Which means another hiding place for the blackjack. It might squeeze between the cushion and back of the wing chair, but getting it out would be a fumble. No place else in this bare little room.

She went into the bathroom. Toilet tank? When she lifted the lid it clanked hollowly. Maybe if she practiced she could learn to lift it without a clank, but she'd still have to set it down silently and fish out the blackjack. Too complicated.

Wrap it in a towel? Might work. She draped the pantyhose back over the towel bar and spread the towel across the basin.

She paused. The pantyhose were springing back to their approximate shape. She arranged them on the bar with the stretched-out and knotted leg in the back, against the wall. They looked like they were just spread out to dry.

He wouldn't follow her into the bathroom. She'd have time to take the hose off the bar, wad the excess into her left hand, grab the knot with her right, shove the door open and . . .

Would the collapsed soldiers make that same exclamation point sound against his head? Don't think about that. Think about Amy. Do what must be done. Whatever that is.

She went back to the bed. The silence still filled the room but it no longer sat on her chest. Hands behind her head, looking up at the brass horn connected to the de Dendermonde bedroom, she thought about what must be done. There was another way to do it. What he seemed to want was to use her to lure Ron into Plaisance. "I want Langshan here," he'd said. "At Plaisance. On camera. Under the knife."

Why not? What did she owe Ron, except grief? Not entirely true. The beginning had glowed, and that golden light had kept her believing long after she should have known better. Long after she really *had* known better but refused to look at it. Even now, was that initial golden glow still coloring how she thought about him? Could she help Charley bring him here under that terrible knife?

# CHAPTER 15

Cassie almost dumped the casserole into the oven when Kurt arrived, announcing from the kitchen door, "We have to talk." She'd been rehearsing these very opening words, but she hadn't worked out what should come next. When he took her opening line her first thought was that she wasn't ready yet. Her next was, Please don't tell me the woman's name. As long as I don't know who she is I won't have to see it going on in my mind's eye.

Trying to buy some time, she said, "Dinner's almost ready. Can it wait?"

He took the Merlot from the buffet as he said, "I need to get this off my chest. D'you mind?"

Cool, she told herself. Play it cool. Please, God, no tears. "Okay," she said, sliding the casserole back in the oven and leaving the door ajar. "Dinner will keep."

As he poured wine she took her seat at the table, taking a deep breath to keep her voice under control. Understanding, that's the tone. Not forgiveness—not yet—but nothing leading to an ultimatum. No burned bridges.

"I'm afraid I've gotten us into a problem," he said, setting her glass down and walking around the table to his place.

"Oh?" she said, thinking, Us? She's *our* problem?

He sat and stared into his glass as if the way to begin could be found somewhere in that red glow. She didn't help him. He looked up with that tentative smile that asked for encouragement, but she just waited.

"I have two things to tell you," he said. "Neither one is . . ."

She sipped and didn't help him.

"Neither one is easy to talk about." He looked away and sat back in the dining room chair. "First, I may have put you in some danger." Then, reacting to whatever he saw in her face, "Probably not. I mean, I don't really think so, but I can't be sure."

"Can't be sure of what?"

"I can't be sure he won't—" he took another breath and held up both palms in a "reset" gesture. "I was at my desk, working on—I'll get to that in a minute—anyway, this guy just walked in. A street guy."

"What does that mean?"

He made a groping gesture. "I mean . . . not somebody looking for a house. Just a guy off the street. What he *was* looking for was information."

"Information?"

Kurt tasted his wine. "He wanted to know who owned those houses that burned up the other day."

"Burned up—down in Huntington Station?"

He nodded. "Wallace owns the whole block, of course. Everybody knows that."

"But he didn't?"

"I mean, everybody in real estate knows. Not everybody walking down the street."

"You tell him?"

Kurt shook his head.

"Why not?"

He turned up both palms. "I don't know. Probably should have. But the guy was Latino. Not just that—this guy's a gangbanger. He showed me his tattoo."

She tried to help him. "You thought the guy—if you told

him, he might go after Wallace?"

Now he pulled a grimace as he nodded. "It sure wasn't just . . . I mean, he came in off the street looking for a name. And I didn't really—you know, it's common knowledge that Wallace owns all that ticky-tacky rental in the barrio, but I didn't know it for a fact. Not at the time."

"But you do now?"

"After he left I Googled it. One of the Wallace subsidiaries owns all that Section 8 stuff here and some more up in Owens Falls." Reacting to the question in her expression: "You know, subsidized rentals. They had a fire up there too."

"Wallace did?"

He nodded. "Their properties. Could be just a coincidence."

"But you don't think so?"

He shrugged. "I just think it's . . . interesting. And your friend's husband—Ron Langshan?—he's the Wallace spokesman."

"Ron is?"

Kurt hurried on: "What I'm trying to tell you is, this guy said something about—he was talking tough, y'know? But he said something about looking me up in the white pages. And something about you."

"Me? He knows me?"

Kurt held up a palm. "No, no. He was just talking. He said I probably have a wife."

In spite of herself, Cassie caught her breath as he went on: "So I guess I'll call him. Not him . . ." Kurt fished a card out of his shirt pocket and laid it on the table. "He's got kind of a drop box. A bodega that'll deliver a message to him. And I've decided, why not? It's public knowledge anyway."

Cassie picked up the card. One of Kurt's business cards, but on the back a telephone number tilted unevenly across the middle. "When you call this number, who answers?"

He shook his head. "I don't know. I just say I have a message for Pedro Loco."

"Pedro Loco," she repeated.

"Yeah. Crazy Peter. I just say something like, 'The name he's been asking about is Wallace.' That ought to be the end of it. But just in case, I want you to keep an eye out. If you see someone who looks like he doesn't belong around here, call me."

"How am I going to know? Ask to see his tattoo?"

"Just . . . I don't know. Just anyone that doesn't seem right." He glugged more than a sip of wine.

She thought about that. "You say that when you call, that ought to be the end of it. But we don't know that, do we?"

His eyes dropped. "I'm sorry I got us into this."

She reached over and took his hand. "By sitting at your desk? Come on, Kurt—this just walked off the street into your life. Our life. But once you call this guy, well, you're a part of whatever happens next. Which gives him kind of a hold on you. On us." When Kurt gave an acknowledging lift of his brows she went on: "Have you thought about calling the police?"

"Sure. But what am I going to tell them?" He paused a moment to let her consider that. "And suppose they find him, and roust him—which I'm pretty sure they couldn't, and wouldn't even bother to try—but suppose they do? Where does that leave *us*?" When she shrugged, he answered his own question: "Dealing with a pissed-off Pedro Loco, that's where. No. I'm going to tell this guy what he wants to know and hope that gets him off our case."

"I don't know. That doesn't . . . Is there another way?"

He turned the empty wine glass in the light, thinking about that. "Maybe I could split the difference. Give Pedro what he wants but then let Wallace know what's going on."

She stood up. "That's another way, I guess. Feels kinda sleazy, but . . . what about the people in that Owens Falls fire?"

"Article I found didn't say anything about that. It was about a hearing on some kind of a redevelopment application." Silence collected around the kitchen table. Finally, Kurt said, "It's not like I'm . . ." He tried to find the word. "I mean, Wallace is in the business."

She went to the oven. "The slumlord business."

He shook his head. "The real estate business. He has an organization. They deal with deadbeat tenants and non-performing vendors and cops on the take and all kinds of problems. He can handle this one."

Sliding out the rack, she said, "This casserole won't wait much longer."

"There's something else I have to tell you."

"It can wait," she said, thinking, I can deal with the idea of a mean Mexican but I need time to get ready for another woman.

# CHAPTER 16

*CRASH-BANG!*

Sam jerked upright in a "where-am-I?" panic. Had she actually been asleep? How long? What time was it?

Another crash. Thunder, instantly followed by the bang of lightning striking somewhere close. What if it hit this old house, started a fire? Would Charley let her out in time? She had a breath-caught mental picture of that narrow corridor outside filling with smoke. All she could do would be to stuff some wet towels along the base of the door. Delay the inevitable. By the time anyone found her . . .

She stood under the brass ear in the ceiling and yelled, "Charley! Unlock this door." She took a breath and tried to swallow the panic out of her voice. "Charley, let's make a deal. I'll promise to stay put if you just unlock the door so I'm not trapped in here." She listened, remembering that he'd said that the voice tube is in the bedroom with the lid buttoned down. The house groaned in what must be a gale. "Charley, please. Let's talk this—"

Another rattling crash. She caught a whiff of ozone, whatever that is. Ron had told her it was something that lightning does to air. At that thought, she remembered Ron standing at the bedroom window watching a storm light up the writhing oaks in a barrage of thunder. "That was a close one," he'd said with a delighted grin as he hurried to the coat closet in the hall.

Now she went back to Eric's little bed and hung onto the

edge, as if the wind might blow her away. To take her mind off
this storm, she thought about that other one. She'd called after
Ron, "Where are you going?"

"Out." He'd appeared in the bedroom door as he shrugged
on his raincoat. "I think that"—he leaned and looked out the
window again—"yeah, I think that started a fire over there."

"So where are you going?" she said again.

"Out there—where the action is."

Before she could scurry across the room he'd slammed the
front door. She went to the window and watched him plunge
into horizontal sheets of rain, oblivious to the flying leaves and
branches. He paused under a huge oak—a lightning rod, the
most dangerous place around—and then sauntered out of sight
along the sidewalk as if out for a stroll. This is part of what
makes him exciting, she'd thought. This high-wire personality.
Not just fearless, but actually drawn to danger, fire—the action—the way ordinary people are drawn to a fire on the hearth.

Now as she listened to the groans and shudders of this old
mansion, she thought that when the genes or the chromosomes
or whatever had combined to produce Ron, ordinary fear had
been left out. Like someone color blind, or tone deaf. His
normal was a higher pitch, some kind of super normal.

"He's in love with himself," Cassie had said. "So stuck on
himself that he doesn't have anything to spare for other people.
And when Amy got in the way, when you stopped feeding him
constant attention and admiration, he dumped you. Right? And
now he's taking it out on Amy."

Sam stood and went to the door. She rattled the lock and put
her ear against the wood to hear possible footsteps. Nothing.
But the sound of the door recalled something from that other
storm that she hadn't remarked at the time: when Ron had
gone out into the storm the door had rattled. Could his hand
have been shaking? Was he just courting danger, as he wanted

her to believe, or could he be a touch claustrophobic?

Now the storm didn't seem to creak the house quite so often. Could it be letting up so soon? Maybe it was just her panic attack passing. She took stock. Her knees were firm. That flutter was gone from her chest. Breath was even. She was in control. Now, keep the focus on getting out of here and protecting Amy.

She thought of Charley, standing in the door. "I want Langshan here. At Plaisance. On camera. Under the knife." Could she help him lure Ron, the beautiful man who walked like a god into the storm and who had once been able to make her glow like a candle? Could she help make him spout blood like that man on the video cassette?

A knock on the door.

# CHAPTER 17

Down the hall a floor polisher thrummed. Below the window a bus sighed to a stop at the corner. The heels of a late-departing secretary clicked over head. Behind the closed door, Walt's office held its breath. He tried to study a discounted cash flow analysis but his eyes kept sliding to the telephone on the corner of his desk.

Ten minutes ago he had checked the payroll register: 493 employees, counting part-timers. So what are the odds that one would be off-center? Pretty high. Bound to happen. But this one was his own choice. His instinct, which he trusted. From now on, follow the data. As soon as Ron's background hadn't checked out, that was when he should have backed away. But the guy was so convincing. And the big pay-offs, hadn't they always come when he'd ignored the data and followed his gut?

He was looking right at the telephone when it rang, but even so he started. He took a deep breath, waited for the third ring, picked it up and said, "Walt Wallace."

"You the landlord, right?"

"That's right. Are you Pedro?"

"Why you callin' me?"

"Kurt—the real estate man?—he gave me your contact number. I thought we ought to talk, because you maybe have the wrong idea."

"Or maybe the *right* idea. Maybe I'm gonna come lookin' for you."

"That terrible fire—we both need to know what happened there."

"Yeah? I think we both know."

"No we don't. Look, Pedro, the last thing I need—tell me, have you ever been busted?"

"What's that got to do with you?"

"Nothing. Just that, if you've ever dealt with the police, and the courts and the probation and all that, well you can understand that the last thing I need is a bunch of cops and Fire Marshall guys and insurance inspectors rooting around in my business. You understand that?"

Pause. "No. Know nothin' about insurance inspectors. So what're you sayin'?"

Wallace shifted hands on the phone and wiped the freed palm on his pants leg. "I'm saying that what happened that night sure as hell wasn't good for my business. I'm saying that I can't tell you what happened because I don't know, but I *do* know I don't want it to happen again. Ever again."

"And you know what I say about your business? Fuck it."

"I understand. This isn't about—look Pedro, I'm on your side."

Laughter, coming through the phone like a snarl.

Walt broke in: "I'm trying to give you what you want."

"What I want? Man, you gonna hand me your ass on a platter?"

"If you listen, I'm going to tell you who . . . who knows all about that fire."

Pause. "You tryin' to say that it was somebody else. I figure it's you, landlord."

"Think about it. That fire has got me into a lot of grief. Months of it. Maybe years." He waited a beat to let that register, and then: "You think I got to own a company and all this property if I'm a stupid businessman?"

Another pause, and then: "Go on, landlord."

"I'm going to give you a cell phone number. Call that and you'll be talking to the guy who knows all about it."

"Don't want no cell number. You give me a name and address."

"No." Thinking fast, Walt said, "All I have is a Social Security number and a post office box." And then, before Pedro could challenge that: "You have a pen? Here's the number."

"Wait a minute. How do I know you're not just puttin' me off onto some guy you gotta hard-on for?"

Walt was ready for that. "When you have him on the phone, say that you want to talk about seven billion minus four."

"What's that all about?"

"He'll know. And he'll know that you know. Just remember— seven billion minus four. Let me hear you say it."

When Pedro repeated it, Walt gave him the number and hung up. He folded the cash flow analysis and dropped it into the middle drawer of his desk, which closed with a reassuring bang. Speaking out loud to start the office breathing again, he said, "He'll know that you know, but he'll think of some way to handle it. He always does."

# CHAPTER 18

She jerked erect on the little bed. Had he heard her screaming a promise up the brass tube?

"Sam," he called through the door. "You decent?"

She felt under the pillow and then remembered. The blackjack was in the bathroom. The storm panic had crowded that out of her mind. Now she wasn't ready—

"Just a minute," she called, scrambling to her feet. Three steps to the bathroom. "Come on in" as she shut the door.

She grabbed the pantyhose off the towel bar as she heard him click the lock and open the outer door. The crumpled lead soldiers in the toe stretched the hose to clunk onto the floor. She wadded it into a ball, remembering the *thwunk!* against the bed, as she heard the outer door close.

"I've been thinking," he said. "Wondering, actually."

She put her ear against the bathroom door. Could she hear him sit in the chair?

"How did an attractive, savvy woman wind up with an animal?"

She swung the blackjack slightly, testing the nylon's stretch. It seemed to bounce uncertainly. Depending on the arc? Probably stretched more, the faster it traveled. How would she judge?

"A man who abuses his own daughter."

He could be standing there, not in the chair. Maybe facing this door.

135

"I've never wanted a partner, Sam. Lone hunter moves qui-etly."

Holding the blackjack behind her, she s-l-o-w-l-y twisted the doorknob.

"But you and I—I believe things happen for a reason. We came together because we're a team."

She jerked the door closed with a tiny thump. "We're a team." Just what Ron had said. Was it the memory of his smile—she'd told Cassie that Ron's smile could melt ice—that was making her knees wobbly now? Or just that she'd been surprised? Hadn't had time to think it through? Whatever, she wasn't ready for this moment.

She eased the latch close without a sound and went back to the towel bar as he said, "I have another DVD to show you."

She draped the pantyhose back with the doubled fabric of the waist covering the weight in the toe as he went on: "You're in the PR business. You know how to make a story sing."

When she opened the door, he was in the chair, with his pants on. He was facing away toward the video player he'd rolled in front of the closed door. In position. She could have clobbered him before he looked around. "I'm glad you're still up. I made a pot of tea." He gestured toward the little table, where she saw what might be a Limoges tea pot decorated with tiny pink roses and an incongruous pair of thick mugs. "Like chamomile? Thought it might help you sleep."

"Charley, I don't think I can take another TV show."

He twisted around and held up his hands. "No, no. This is just a history lesson. It's a bloody history, but the blood isn't on camera."

She went over to the little bed. "Instead of history, why don't you tell me why I'm here?"

He pointed to the dark screen. "It's . . . when you see this DVD, you'll understand." He leaned forward and filled the mugs. "I know this is a little long," he said, setting one mug in front of her on the table, "but I don't know where to cut it." He took the other mug and then clicked the remote.

After some booting-up hisses and flashes, Charley's face fills the screen. He looks away, striking a pose, and then, as he stares back into the camera he raises some kind of a homemade knife.

Charley clicked the pause button. "I forgot. There's just this little bit of blood in the beginning. Not enough to matter." He sipped as he started the DVD again.

Charley reaches his left hand into the camera and slowly brings the blade across the palm. He leaves that hand open for the camera to watch a line of blood emerge and begin to trickle toward his wrist. When he moves his hand out of frame, he says to the camera, "This blade will never be sheathed unblooded."

He steps back to reveal that he is naked, on some sort of a porch, with water behind him. "It is an instrument of honor. From a time when honor was important. More important than money, or fun or fulfillment, whatever that means.

"Imagine that this is 1907. Imagine a dusty little town called Stigler. Last year, this was Indian Territory. Now it is Oklahoma, with a new set of laws." He gestures off camera. "Over there, the general store has become a temporary courtroom. A jury sits on benches in front of the bridles, bits, hame straps, cruppers and spurs that hang from pegs on the wall. Loafers stand on the porch and in the rutted street to listen. Behind the counter a judge, who just a few weeks ago had been a saddlebag lawyer arguing cases before Hangin' Judge Parker in Little Rock, has sentenced a Cherokee man to death for murder. Down the street, behind the post office, there's a room with a good lock that serves as a jail for disorderly drunks. But the murderer isn't sent there. Instead, the judge sets a date and a time, and the murderer promises to show up for his own execution."

Sam said, "Charley, what—"

He held up one hand to silence her as his screen image goes on: "The loafers stand aside to let him pass. Someone has led his horse to the hitching rail. He mounts and rides into the Cookson Hills, where steep valleys hide the banks of spring-fed creeks that have never been marked by a boot heel. If all the white men in the entire new state of Oklahoma could be organized into a coordinated search with dogs, they could never find him in those hills.

"On the appointed date, and a few minutes ahead of the time, the murderer rides into town. He doesn't dismount. The judge watches as men tie his hands behind him and lead his horse to a spreading oak behind the blacksmith's shop. A rope is tossed across a convenient limb, a noose is tied and looped around his neck. They ask if he has any last words. He shakes his head.

"He could explain what's about to happen. He could explain that what the new law calls a murder was for him a duty. A man had killed his clansman, and so he must kill that man's clansman. But why explain? The whites *must* understand that. They took his promise to come to his own execution. Think about that. He promised to come to his own execution. He promised to come back to be hanged for doing his duty. For accepting an obligation. An obligation to family, to clan and to people. The *Principal* People. People who live by principle.

"But he has no last words for these white men who already understand. They already know that his is a culture of honor. Didn't they accept his word? They understand a culture of honor, and to show their respect for it they whip his horse and leave him twisting under the oak."

Charley smiles into the camera and opens both hands. "And this is not just the story of one man of honor. Long after Sequoyah had devised a way to read and write the Cherokee language and the people had become in so many ways just imitation whites, our Cherokee men continued to accept the sentence of death for acts of honor. They continued to give their word, and continued to return for their executions. Every one of them. Records were kept. No Cherokee failed to appear. Not ever.

"My people, I am Tsali, named for a man of honor. I knew the moment when the earth spoke to me. I fasted and meditated and studied to understand what that meant. When the truth came, I discovered what I had always known, but could not see. Now, I want to help all of us discover what we have always known. Who we are."

The image collapsed into snow and Charley clicked the screen off. "You're not drinking your tea," he said, leaning forward so that a lock of coarse black hair fell across his forehead as he picked up his mug. "That's the commercial. If we can get 'The Designer' episode to go viral, then we have an audience for this one. This one makes the pitch. How do you think it sells?"

She resisted the impulse to push that lock of hair back into place. "I don't know, Charley. I mean, that all happened a long time ago."

He sat back. "It's happening now. All over the world. What this country calls terrorism, other people see—they *understand* it as a defense of their honor culture. In Istanbul—you know, that secular city?"

She shook her head.

"Well, never mind. The point is, even there they average one honor killing a week. It's just here in love-thy-enemy land, that's where honor no longer has any meaning." He pointed a finger. "Sam, I think I know you. When you were a child on the playground and someone hit you, I'll bet you hit him back."

He waited for her to nod before he went on: "Of course you did. Honor is natural to all of us. It makes us human. It can make us the best we can be. I want my Cherokee people to rediscover their honor."

His eyes held her. Is this the way he'd looked at that computer game guy? Just before . . . On an impulse, she said, "What about you, Charley? Did someone hit you on the playground?"

His brows went up and he sat back. He sipped some tea, considering the question.

Mistake, she decided. The game is submission. Nothing to challenge or threaten.

But he answered, "Sure. But worse than that, they laughed at me. Not on the playground—when I was in high school. Did you ever think about suicide, Sam?"

She hesitated and then decided he'd smell a fake and so the truth was less risky. "No. But I know—one of my friends said she did. I don't think it's freaky. I mean, at that age."

He made that brushing-away gesture in the air. "I didn't just brood about how everybody would be sorry and what they'd say at my funeral and all that . . ." he looked away, as if back into his past. "I planned it. Every detail. I got the Greyhound schedule from Tahlequah to Joplin. Then one Saturday I bought a ticket to Grove. On the way I noticed things."

He looked back at her and flipped a dismissive gesture. "You know, just ordinary things like persimmon trees in the fence rows, and a turkey buzzard kind of fingering the air with those big feathers on the tips of his wings. Things I'd seen a thousand times but never really noticed. When I got off at the station I walked out on highway fifty-nine and got a hitch to the lake right away. They call it the Lake o' the Cherokee, but it's really all about flood control and power generation and white guys sitting up high on those bass boats. Anyway, there're lots of nice flat rocks along the shore. I had it all worked out . . ."

He looked away again, apparently remembering. The crazy idea crossed her mind that he had somehow left the room, which felt momentarily different until he went on: "I was trying to find two or three rocks that would fit in each boot—as many as I could and still get my feet in too—and then I'd double-knot the laces to make sure I didn't turn chicken when I waded out. I'd thought about it so often that I knew just what it would be like . . . the water getting colder along the bottom but warm and friendly climbing up my arms on the way out to . . . forever."

He turned slowly back to her, blinking as if waking, and smiled. "But you never had ideas like that, did you, Sam? Too well adjusted. Nothing happened when you were growing up to make you . . ." he hesitated, searching for a phrase, and then gave it up. "But what about Amy? You think she might want to put rocks in her shoes some day?"

"Amy?" Sam closed her eyes a moment, to shut out that idea. "Amy's going through a bad time, Charley. I need to be there with her."

Charley nodded. "Just as soon as we take care of business."

"This—business." Her voice sounded wobbly. "It has nothing to do with me. I mean, I'm not even a Langshan."

Another slow, considering smile. "No, you're not. We're on the same team. You and I both have an obligation of honor. Your Langshan doesn't deserve to live among the spirits on this earth, and I need to make sure that he is the last male descendent of his corrupt line."

Sam shook her head and held up both hands in a surrender gesture. "I just don't understand. Why do you have to—did this all start when you were at that lake?"

He thought about that. "No, it started a long time ago. When the Langshans were still wearing powdered wigs, and the Americans signed the first treaties with the Cherokee. The Cherokee never broke a treaty. The Americans never kept one."

"But when did it start with *you*?"

He nodded. "That day, when I was looking for the right kind

of stones, I found . . . I'm not going to be able to explain this to you."

"Try me."

When he looked away she tried to follow his eyes. Was he looking at the "my ears and whiskers" rabbit? No, he was looking through that and beyond this place. He asked, "Did you ever grab a hot wire? Electric wire?"

"I stuck my finger in a socket once. When I was little. I still remember it."

He nodded. "That surge of energy pulsing through you. Can you imagine the reverse of that? Like a big shot of calm. It takes you to a different place. Makes you into something different." He smiled at her expression. "I told you I wasn't going to be able to explain it."

"What was it? The calm thing?"

"Do you know what a talisman is?"

"I think I've heard of it. It's . . . like a lucky charm?"

He smiled as he shook his head. "Bigger than that. Anyway, when I was looking for stones I found mine."

"What is it?"

He pursed his lips, considering that, and then he asked, "Do you know what a possum is?"

"A little animal. Kind of like a raccoon?"

"About that size. But a possum . . . It's an animal that knows how to die and then come back. I was ready to die that day, but the possum called me back."

She shook her head. "I don't . . ."

"I'm not going to try to explain it. What I want you to know is that my life changed that day. I found a new path."

"You mean, all this . . . honor thing?"

"Not right away, of course. I mean, that day at the lake I just knew that everything had changed. It took a while. A lot of thinking and reading—I had to follow my path to find where it leads."

Sam shook her head and held up both hands to say that all of this was too much for her, but he went on: "I found Langshan Public Relations on the Web. When I called, I expected to get . . . you said you and your husband are separated and now you have the business. Where did he go?"

Although he hadn't moved, Charley seemed to be too close. Sam stood, legs stiff from sitting too long on the low bed. "Wallace Enterprises," she said, stretching as she walked to the bathroom door. Could she retrieve the blackjack and maybe— no, he had turned in the chair, watching her. "We both worked for a PR agency. Impact PR," she said, drifting toward the TV cart blocking the door to the hall. Could she shove it into him and get into the hall? "Wallace, they were a client."

But even if she got into the hall, then what? For some unaccountable reason she found herself distracted by the rag rug with the yellow sun. It now seemed to pulse, brightening and then dimming to some unheard beat.

"Yes?" Charley said. "So what happened?"

"You think she got that . . . I mean, that rug—it's not belle whatever-you-said, is it?"

"What are you talking about?"

Sam wrenched her eyes away from the rug and went back to the little bed, trying to bring this dream sequence into reality. "What happened? Well, I learned how to make beef Bourguignon and Amy learned to pedal her trike and I began to suspect that Ron . . . But you don't want to know about all that, do you?"

"I do, but later. Right now, tell me about—is it Collision?"

The sun in the rug was just woven rags again but she realized that she was smiling at the question, still not fully into the moment. "Should have been, at times. Lots of ego collisions in those offices. But it's Impact. Impact Public Relations. Ron really landed the account and so he managed it. In a couple of years he'd developed the account to the point where it was billing—I don't remember. Went up every month. It was enough that the Wallace people could save money by hiring Ron with a big pay increase."

"Is that ethical?"

"Happens all the time."

"So . . . Ron's a pretty savvy guy."

She nodded. "Harvard grad. Works the *New York Times* crossword puzzles."

He pursed his lips, thinking, before he said, "Not the kind of guy I could grab in the parking lot, like I did The Designer. These Long Island parking lots aren't like Vashon anyway. I went to the Walt Whitman Mall last week for a toner cartridge. While I was there I looked around. Inside the mall uniformed guys were gliding around on those two-wheelers with the fat tires, and out in the lot there was a security car. Maybe more than one, just patrolling around. So I need some way to make Ron come to me."

She shook her head. "He'll never do that. Too smart."

Charley stood. "Think about it," he said, collecting the tea pot and mugs. "We have to figure out a way to get to Ron."

She nodded. Submission is the name of the game.

He paused at the door. "The Nunnehi won't speak to you tonight. I'm going to bring you coffee around eight in the morning. And a bagel—cream cheese, okay?" When she nodded again he went on: "I hope you get some sleep. And I hope you also think about how we're going to make sure that no harm comes to Amy."

When he closed the door an echo answered. A dungeon sound. His departing footsteps were light, a hunter's tread, he'd say. But she heard them whisper to the steps. Heard the kitchen door open and click shut.

Silence.

She tested the door to be sure it was locked and went to the wing chair. His head had been right there, visible over the back. A blackjack opportunity missed. As she sat down she wondered if he was delusional or just working a scam on himself. Persuading himself he's important, a time traveler with a mission. Everything that happens gets shaped to fit into that idea. Or is that maybe what a delusion is?

She stood and moved to the other wall, just to hear her own muffled steps on the rag rug. She studied the Wonderland illustrations over the bed. Why would a mother choose that scowling Queen of Hearts for her child's wall? She imagined Countess de Dendermonde in a dinner dress, something elegantly simple set off by lustrous pearls, having slipped away from her guests to sit on the edge of this little bed and talk to her son. Perhaps she told him about the world down the rabbit hole. A world where the unexpected is ordinary. Where caterpillars smoke pipes and cats disappear and croquet mallets are live flamingos. Perhaps she told him that he had his own rabbit hole down here, where he could create his own world where autism, or whatever his problem was, didn't matter.

The way that maybe Charley was avoiding his own inadequacy in the security of a grand purpose.

Sam examined the sun woven into the rag rug under her feet, thinking about that dizzy moment when Charley had been quizzing her about Ron and Wallace Enterprises. The sun had seemed to brighten and then dim, like the Cheshire cat. A down-the-rabbit-hole rug. Unreal. This whole situation—locked in the basement of a mansion by a sexy Indian who's trying to get even for something that happened a hundred years ago—it couldn't be real.

But here she was. And she wasn't going to wake up. She

would have to get out of this bad dream on her own. Tomorrow, one way or another. No more missed opportunities.

\* \* \* \* \*

# Day Two of Captivity

\* \* \* \* \*

Men never do evil so completely and cheerfully as when they do it for religious reasons.

—Blaise Pascal

# CHAPTER 19

"Reveille!" he called from outside the door. "Bagel time."

She was dressed in the wrinkled navy suit and waiting in the chair. Somehow she had fallen asleep after the storm passed. She woke in a dream panic of embarrassment, or shame, or—what? She couldn't remember what she had been doing, or what she was about to do in the dream, but she knew the man hadn't been Ron. She said, "Just a minute" as she scrambled out of the chair and wrapped the foot of the pantyhose around her right hand with the lump of lead dangling in the toe and the excess fabric balled in her fist. Could the man in her dream have been Charley?

She took a deep breath and stood, swinging the stretched pantyhose to check the arc of the weighted toe one last time. She stepped silently to the front wall where she would be behind the door as it opened. "Okay," she said, surprised at how calm her voice sounded. "Come on in."

The door swung half open, but he didn't appear. Did he suspect something? Was he waiting in the hall as he scanned the room for her? Then the trolley cart bumped the door all the way open against her foot, blocking her view of the room. She heard the wheels trundling as he said, "You like lox? I never knew what it was until I got here in the . . ."

As she stepped around the door she caught the smell of coffee. He was in the middle of the room, hands on the TV trolley that now was loaded with dishes, looking around for her. She

149

took one step toward him, cocking the lead over her shoulder like a tennis service-stroke. The coffee aroma brought back the down-the-rabbit-hole sense of unreality. Distracted, she swung, aiming at the end of the part in that coarse black hair where the ponytail began but he leaned forward, turning to look behind him. The toe of the pantyhose glanced off his forehead.

He lurched onto his knees, upending the trolley backward. Dishes crashed. Sam bolted around him, skidding on coffee. Throwing out her arms for balance she let the pantyhose go. The lead thumped into the wall behind her as she got through the door.

A dim hall, doors on either side. Closets, she remembered—dead ends. Heels clattering along the uncarpeted floor toward the stairs at the end of the hall, dimly lit from above.

"Sam!" Muffled. From inside the room? Had she slammed the door behind her?

Up the steps two at a time into the echoing tiled kitchen, slamming this door for sure, pausing to glance around—no easy way to jam the door shut—dodging around the butcher-block cutting table into the room with the drawn drapes and portraits of stuffy guys.

Where was her phone? In the attaché case—where had he put that? Pausing under the chandelier in the entrance hall—she'd been standing right here when he took it from her. Must be through those doors. Are those footsteps on the kitchen tile? No time to make a call.

Out onto the landing between the two skinny marble dogs. Looking around. There—her Camry! Not where she'd left it, but parked in back, bumper nudging what looked like a garage.

Clattering down the steps onto the Belgian blocks—damn, there goes a heel. Hobbling along the curving driveway. He'd moved the car—could he have left the keys in it? Please, God.

"Sam! Just take it easy." His voice was close. Could he see

her? "We can talk about this."

Fumbling the car door—unlocked!—open. Leaning into the front seat to see the ignition. No key.

Kicking off the unbroken shoe and running blindly down a shaggy lawn.

"There's nothing down there, Sam. Keep going and you'll just come to water."

A brick walk. Hopping over a rose tendril escaping a weedy garden. Gasping for breath now. A hedge, taller than she could reach. Running along it. Glancing back—he wasn't in sight. Taking his time because he knew she had no escape?

An opening in the hedge. Ducking through, into another wall of green. A maze? When would she wake from this rabbit-hole dream? Following the inner wall to another turn. Listening, as she caught her breath. Damn him for moving at the last instant. But she'd still clobbered him on the forehead. Not where she was aiming, but a head shot. Why hadn't that put him down long enough for her to get away?

With his head moving, maybe it was a glancing blow. Or had she held up a little? Couldn't bring herself to really hurt him? Has he gotten to her? All that talk, and that tight butt with the Mongol stain and those hands—had something in her subconscious intervened at the last instant?

"Sam, I understand why you did that." He was close. Just outside. She followed the hedge wall deeper inside, one hobbling step at a time, twigs sharp on her bare right foot, as he continued: "Actually, I'm glad you did. Shows grit."

An interior opening leading into another aisle darkened by angular shadows. What had Alice discovered in the maze? A garden, maybe. His voice pursued her down this narrow canyon and into another. "Just put one hand out. Either left or right, it doesn't matter, but keep the same one brushing the wall of the maze, okay? Then just keep walking and you'll come out."

Maybe he wasn't coming in after her. She took the turn that seemed to be away from the voice. Storm-blown twigs and leaves crunched under foot.

"But when you do come out, I'll be here waiting for you. You see, there's only one entrance. Or exit, depending on where you are. Inside or outside. I'm outside, sitting on the grass, enjoying the sunshine and icing the knot on my forehead."

She reached another dead end. Left or right? What did it matter?

"I stopped in the kitchen to get some ice cubes and wrap them in a dish towel because I was in no hurry. I'd decided that if you ran down the driveway into the street, then you really want out and I should let you go."

She sank to her knees and said out loud, "Oh yes."

But he didn't seem to hear her because he said: "But you turned the other way. You followed your deeper self, which knows we're a team."

"I was running to the car, asshole."

If he heard, he paid no attention. "Why do you think I locked you in that little room, Sam?"

Instead of saying, Because you're a loonie, she said, "Tell me." She stood and parted the aromatic leaves. Branches as thick as her thumb. Impossible to push through to the outside.

He went on: "It was to keep you stashed away, I admit. In a safe place, until you could understand what we are going to do together. But also, it was to give you an opportunity to meet yourself. Your deeper self. Do you understand that, Sam?'

He waited. She hobbled a couple of steps along the shadowy aisle. This place was more claustrophobic than that damn room. She said, "No, I don't."

"The Cherokee understood. They sent their young men into the woods alone to fast and think deep thoughts. To meet themselves."

Another dead end. Left or right? Maybe if she kept turning the same way . . . "Did you do that, Charley?"

"I told you about me. On the lake shore, with the rocks for my shoes."

She turned left. "You found an animal skull—what was it?" Why should she keep wandering around in here?

"Possum. A little creature that survives by playing dead. Made me realize that I was playing with the idea of death. Introduced me to myself. What about you, Sam? Have you met yourself yet?"

Limping through dry leaves and twigs, left hand brushing the green wall: "If I say 'no' Charley, what happens?" She came to another dead end. If turning the same way brought her back to the entrance, then he's there waiting. Stop and think. Make some kind of a plan.

"Sam, what matters to me is Ron. Ron Langshan. The evil spawn. Now you have to decide what matters to you. You say it's Amy. The innocent victim. And you blame Ron. Do you really mean it?"

"Mean what?"

In the pause, she imagined him looking off into space, testing in his mind what he was about to say, and then: "Sam, are you sure you don't still love Ron in some way?"

That brought her to a halt. "Of course I don't love him. He's . . . How can you say that?"

"I mean at some level that you can't control. I mean, are you sure you're free of him? His magnetic field?"

"Yes. I'm sure of that." She started picking her way along the narrow aisle again. Maybe a plan was beyond her right now. A master plan. But find the first step. Shuffle the deck somehow.

"Good. Then here's the deal. You bring Ron to me, and I'll save Amy from him."

"Bring him to you? I don't know how to do that." Submission. The first step has to start with that. Then, somehow we have to get to trust, so he doesn't have to keep me stashed away in a safe place.

"That's what we have to figure out. Are you with me, Sam?"

"I'm coming out, if I can find the way. I'll walk to your voice. Just keep talking."

"When you look around, Sam, what do you see happening?"

"I see that I'm lost in this damn hedge puzzle. Keep talking so I can find my way out."

"I mean, what's going on in the world. The believers are on the move, Sam. All over the world. The God-worshipers and Allah-followers are determined to destroy each other for oil. In the process they're wrecking the environment. Are you still coming out?"

"I'm walking with my left hand on the bushes, like you said." Everything's got to be like you say.

"Eventually you'll see the entrance."

"Easy for you to say. Keep talking." Thinking, which is what you love to do. And I know what else you love. What all men love. Ron taught me that.

"Okay, here's the point. The Cherokee saw God in nature. They cherished life, and what sustains it. And they lived by a code of honor. You know who does today?"

Another dead end. His voice sounded the same, no nearer, no farther. She turned left, just to be consistent. Keep him talking. "No. Who does?"

Ron had brought the subject up with a joke. "You know what all men love but never get at home?" he'd asked with a smirk. "And it's not eggs Benedict."

"The Muslims," Charley was saying. "They don't believe in any 'love thy enemy' bullshit. They stand up for their principles. The world we live in—all of us—it's gotten more and more complicated. Don't you ever feel like it's just too much, Sam?"

A twig broke into a splinter and she jerked her hand away. "I think this is," she said. "This hedge is too much." A drop of blood welled on her thumb. She put it in her mouth, thinking, could she bring herself to do this?

"There are thousands of mosques in the west, Sam. Amsterdam and Marseille—they're already twenty-five percent Muslim. You know the most popular name for a boy? It's Mohammed. And right here—there's a mosque on Deer Park Road. Have you seen it? Everywhere, the mosques draw lots more of the faithful than the churches do. You know why?"

"Maybe because the priests, whatever they call them, they keep their hands off the altar boys." She remembered when she realized what Ron was asking her—telling her, really—to do. How shocked she was. Not disgusted, but surprised.

Charley laughed. "Yes, they're all about principle and honor. Over here, the whole notion of honor has been discredited. We can't pronounce the word without a smirk."

But in those days he was still Ron the wonderful. The next time, Ron only had to ask her, and after that he didn't even have to ask. Sure, she could do it now. For Amy.

Charley was going on: "What I mean is, how do you know what's right and wrong? You live in a two-handed culture, Sam. On the one hand this and on the other that. You see the entrance yet?"

"No. I think this spooky stuff is growing up around me." She remembered Charley standing naked in the door. He hadn't come down just to show her a birthmark and talk about his crazy mission. He had something else in mind, but at the last minute he didn't know how to get it done.

But now he chuckled a comfortable, in-control laugh. "You just stay on course and you'll come out okay. And that's the way a culture of honor works."

She would take it slow. Don't spook the macho warrior. She

turned left again and—there! Down that foreshortening alley of shiny leaves, a shaft of sunlight. The entrance. Where he's waiting.

She stood for a long moment looking at the beckoning sunshine. Then she brushed away the twigs from a place where she could sit on the ground and still see the light. Get ready for what she had to do next. This is the last chance. This time, at the crucial moment she couldn't let up. She sat cross-legged, her back against the scratchy branches, and then became aware of what he was saying: ". . . consumes everything but produces nothing. Do you know what our biggest export product is? Waste paper."

"Really?" she says. "Waste paper?" Submission. She'd get down on her knees in front of him.

"Yep. Waste paper. Trash—that's our contribution to the world economy. The end product of a consumer society. What we call progress is just the white man's superstition."

"I don't think I understand that." First get his pants down. How? He's probably new at this. Start fumbling at his fly and he'd maybe back away.

"Just look around—what do you see? Corporate greed supported by permanent war economies. The Islamic world sees that too. What we call terrorism they call the defense of their honor culture."

Maybe get him to show her the—what did he call it?—the Mongol stain again. This time move closer. Touch that sweet ravine along his spine. Pause when he shivers, and let her fingers slide down to the mark. Now she said, "And what you're doing, Charley, that's your mission, right? You've been chosen?"

"And you're my partner, Sam."

Step up against him. Put her cheek in the hollow between his shoulder blades—it will just fit—and cup those buttocks lightly, letting them tighten in her hands. "You've been chosen, and one way you know that—you're marked, right?"

"You mean the Mongol stain?"

Squeeze and spread the buttocks just a little. "Yes. The Mongol stain. I've never seen anything like that before." S-l-o-w-l-y run her hands up to that smooth-muscled waist. Turn him to face her.

A noise startled her. She looked around, feeling her face flush with embarrassment as if she'd been caught doing what she was thinking. A bird must have landed in the hedge and then fluttered away, surprised to see her in the path. "Yes, the mark . . ." she says, trying to get back on track. "That's powerful, Charley. I keep thinking about that mark." Don't turn him. Don't do anything that's not submissive. Instead, move around to face him, caressing his waist with just the tips of her fingers along the way.

"That stain," he said, "it's not so unusual."

Holding his waist, she'd lower herself to her knees, tilting her head back to keep her eyes on his face. Think about an ice cream cone, like Ron had told her. Now she said, "It is for me. I mean, that mark changes things. That changes everything for me."

For once, he is silent.

"But I was so startled. I mean, when you came in like that—I didn't know what to expect. I hardly looked . . . I mean, I didn't really see the mark." As she said this, she ran her palms up her legs inside the navy skirt.

"So what are you saying?"

"Charley, I can see the entrance now. I'm ready to come out and do whatever you say. But I need to see the Mongol stain. To really see it. Can you understand that?"

Pause, and then: "Yes. I think I understand that."

As she climbed to her feet, she tried to analyze what she's

157

feeling. Dread? No. Apprehension? A little. Excitement? Yes. You bet. Is she doing this for Amy? Yes. But now she's hurrying between the hedgerows.

# CHAPTER 20

Cassie held back her tears until Amy was inside the wrought-iron gate in the scalloped masonry wall of what had been a Gold Coast mansion that was now the home of the "Ask Me Annie" preschool. Amy wiggled her fingers over her shoulder to say "so long" as if she were just another one of the careless kids whose mother had dropped her off on the way to a pedicure. Driving back to their nondescript split-level in what Kurt called a "striver suburb," where families are on their way up, tears dripped off Cassie's chin as she repeated out loud, "I am not a weeping woman. I am not a tough broad, but I'm not a weeper. I'm an adjustment professional. I tell clients, 'Build on your strengths.' So what are mine? I know the score. I understand that male mammals are driven to spread their genes, just as the females look for strong protectors. I can deal with this." But, she was thinking, if we had a little girl like Amy, maybe Kurt wouldn't have so many bogus late nights at the office.

As she triggered the garage door opener, Cassie was thinking about the Long Island Realtors Association. They must surely have a website, and the site must surely have a calendar, and tonight's seminar on something like "Selling into a Falling Market" will surely be listed. If it's real, that is, and not just a cover story.

She slammed through the kitchen, pausing to put the kettle on, and into the third bedroom that she and Kurt had furnished as a home office. She jabbed the computer to life. Waiting to boot up, she looked at the calendar on her smartphone. Online class to teach at three. Allow ten minutes to scan the postings since the last class. Phone interview at four-thirty with the executive director of Catholic Charities for a *Social Work Today* article. Time to plan some questions after logging out of the virtual classroom. Conduct leadership training for the United Way staff tomorrow. Look over those notes tonight. Plenty of time before Kurt would show up. Damn his testosterone.

Her heels clicked angry echoes back to the kitchen. She sorted through a jumble of teabags on the window ledge next to the struggling jade plant, selected something called "Jasmine Explosion," drummed her fingers on the sink until the pot whistled, took a "Life's a Beach" mug down from the cupboard, poured and carried the steeping tea back to the office, where Google now waited.

She sipped, sat and entered, "long island realtors . . ." Fingers above the keys, she hesitated, staring at the snapshot pinned to the wall over the screen: she and Kurt smiled back at her, dancing cheek-to-cheek at a dinner for the top producers for the Hersch agency. He could light up her face. Light up any woman's, which was the problem. But was she ready to start checking on him? And ready to deal with what she might find?

Sam had waited too long to start checking on Ron. And today on the phone she'd sounded a little . . . Cassie couldn't put a name on it. But an impulsive one-nighter wasn't Sam's style. How would she define Sam's style?

Cautious? No, but definitely conservative. Raised by her father. Mom died young, or maybe bailed out of an oppressive household, Cassie wasn't sure. But she remembered that Sam had been named for Samantha Stevens, the good witch who was married to the regular fellow in the TV series *Bewitched*.

Sam had answered Cassie's Craigslist ad for a research assistant. Over Dunkin' Donuts coffee, Cassie assessed a young matron with a good figure who knew how to select a scarf and earrings to enhance her sapphire eyes and a relaxed candor that Cassie read to mean that she could handle deadline pressure. With a community college education, what she knew about research was limited to Google, but she had a good reference from Impact Public Relations. Now she was looking for an at-home job she could fit into the times when her daughter was at preschool or in bed or on a play date. Cassie hired her at twenty-five dollars an hour with the promise of a raise to thirty after three months if "we find that this arrangement is working for both of us."

After just six weeks, when her research reports began to include ideas and suggestions for other articles, Cassie raised her to thirty an hour and established a weekly coffee date to talk about work in progress. Those conversations revealed gaps in the research and new avenues with article and classroom potential. Along the way, Cassie, the social worker and professional interviewer, extracted personal information from the assistant who was becoming her colleague.

She learned that Sam's father, based on his experience with emphysema and arthritis, had decided that insurance companies rule the world and so if Sam learned medical billing she'd have as much security as he had in the postal service. But after Suffolk Community College she'd landed a job as receptionist and apprentice office manager at Impact Long Island, a startup public relations and marketing firm.

The owner, Horace Enzer, had left Edelman "the New York Difference" to import media sophistication into Long Island. But he'd found that suburban business didn't operate as a dumbed-down Manhattan. Instead, it had its own commercial language and power connections. Sam could quote him from staff meetings: "We are colonists, like the critters that float to an island on seaweed rafts or blow in on hurricanes. But this firm has landed, and we will adapt and find our niche."

He'd hired Sam for a bright smile at the front desk, but he found that she also could identify the telephone calls that should be put through to him instead of shunted off to one of the staff. Trained in medical billing, she found the time sheets and invoices simple, and she also devised a spreadsheet that revealed which accounts were high maintenance and which were high profit. Then Horace asked her to design a project control sheet that would keep track of all the assigned staff contacts—politicians, civil service, business, press, community activists, etc.—for a client who wanted to build an automobile race track in eastern Long Island. The wine-and-cheese people turned out to defeat the project, but the PR campaign had been so well managed that Wallace Enterprises kept Impact on a retainer for the next project that would require Long Island savvy.

After that, Horace increased Sam's domain from the front desk to include the computer room, which she began to make the nerve center of the business. That made her important to Ron.

Everyone in the firm knew that Ron was the closer. Horace was the rain maker. He could cultivate a prospect with grace and style at the Old Westbury Club (of course, the Shinnecock Club was out of reach for a temple-attending Manhattan colonist). He could listen—actually hear—and understand a prospect's problem. Horace could bring new business through the door, but Ron was the one who could get the signature on the bottom of the contract. Sam realized that one morning when Horace paused at her desk on his way to the conference room and said, "Buzz Ron and tell him the suckers are under the tent. Time for some Ivy League snake oil."

The conference room with the fawning interviews by *Long Island Business News* framed on the walls and the Public Relations Society Silver Anvil award statue on the credenza was out-

of-bounds for Sam when clients or prospects were in the building, but before the meetings she assembled the PowerPoint
slides and ordered the coffee and Danish for delivery warm, just
minutes before the scheduled break. "God is in the details,"
Horace said, and she was the queen of details. When they were
preparing the next pitch to Wallace Enterprises—something
about affordable housing and the Dix Hills Civic Association—
she asked Ron if she could have his slides for formatting.

"I don't have any slides," he said with a wink that made them
conspirators. "PowerPoint's for amateurs. I look into their eyes
and speak to their needs."

The Wallace pitch wound up ahead of schedule with a burst
of laughter that expelled the men into the hall. She was on the
phone to the limo service as Horace was announcing that La
Campania served the best osso bucco in seven states. In the
parade to the men's room, Ron drifted past her desk in that
walking dance, one arm swinging, head tilted and pelvis in a
modified Elvis. His wink said he'd won the business, of course.

But how that moment had led to marriage, motherhood,
divorce and ugly suspicion—Sam said it was a certainty—Cassie
didn't know. Sam had said something about the appeal of the
bad boy to the good girl. It was like dating someone who might
be connected with the Mafia. Exciting possibilities. And for a
girl who'd grown up believing in limitations, he was success-
prone. But Cassie had never probed what was obviously a tender
spot.

Privately, Cassie had wondered if Sam was one of those
women who subconsciously felt that they didn't deserve a good
man. She knew the syndrome: a distant father who left wounds
the woman tries to heal by falling into a relationship with
another distant man. Now Sam seemed to be exploring another
relationship. If she had been a counseling client, Cassie might

have asked, "Are you sure you're not just trying to get back at Ron?"

Which brought her back to Kurt. Was she getting back at Kurt? Steady, empathetic Kurt, whose feet were always so solidly on the ground that he never looked up at the clouds. All the girls signed his high school yearbook "love ya," and it was generally known that several had proved it in the back seat of his family Lincoln.

Cassie saw herself as no bargain. Named for the girl who was so beautiful she was cursed with the gift of prophesy that no one would believe, Cassie knew that she was short, square and defensive with boys. But when they were freshmen at Adelphi Kurt had searched her out. "If I buy you a Starbucks latte, will you translate this sociology book for me?"

"Why me?"

"Because you're the smartest person I know and you wouldn't want a high school pal to flunk out and spend the rest of his life digging septic tanks."

Of course this was a come-on, but she didn't get many, certainly not from guys who had their pick of girls. She coached him through Sociology 101 without ever getting into the Lincoln. To her surprise, he kept coming back. Study dates somehow turned into movie dates and dancing dates and pub-crawl dates. He stopped asking his parents to use the Lincoln when he bought a secondhand Harley, and in their sophomore year she was riding behind him and hugging her boobs, which she knew were a redeeming feature, into his back.

Eventually they parked at a Holiday Inn in Glen Cove. After all those expectations nourished in all those sleepovers and giggles, she hadn't been disappointed. Afterward, when he dropped her off at the dorm, she'd said, "Why me? Why not one of those cool girls at the Muttontown Club? Girls with daddies who could set you up on Wall Street?"

He chucked a knuckle under her chin the way he tilted her head for a kiss, but instead said, "I'm not a big-picture guy, Cassie. I'm always going to be little picture. Somebody local, doing something for local folks. And you're a girl smart enough to understand that." Then he kissed her goodnight and left her with a lot to think about.

She'd analyzed her situation as if it were a case study. Okay, he didn't make her heart pound, but she enjoyed having him around. Sure, he made her feel smart and superior, so what's wrong with that? Better than those guys who made her feel dumpy and nerdy. And afterward, at the Holiday Inn he'd said, "Cassie, you and I—we're *mated.*" After all those backseat girls, he ought to know.

But she couldn't help thinking about those girls. How did she compare? And how did it work? In the back seat, where did the girls put their feet? As she was bringing all this back, the screen dissolved to black, waiting for keystrokes.

After college she'd entered the social work master's program and he'd taken a job at Hersch Real Estate. She said, "I want to do something that makes a difference in people's lives," and he said, "What makes a better difference than finding the right home for a family?" Instead of a diamond, he proposed with a down payment on a two-bedroom ranch "fixer-upper" in Bethpage. And she accepted without ever actually admitting to herself that this was probably the best deal that was going to come along.

So, if she didn't love him in the moon-June-swoon fervor, did that make their marriage a fraud? If so, then wasn't whatever adventure was keeping Kurt out late only fair? His talent was people. Not the clinical cases in her notes, but the earnest and anxious actual people who had been transferred, promoted, kicked out, or—for one of dozens of other reasons—needed a new home. Kurt listened to each one as an individual and private package of needs, some of which could be met by the right Long Island home. And he patiently telephoned and net-worked and knocked on doors to find that right home. Cassie's idea of a salesman had been Willie Loman, frustrated and fail-ing to connect with life, but every sale expanded Kurt's reach and multiplied his connections. He exchanged Christmas cards with clients from two years ago who enclosed photos of how they had decorated the perfect house he had found for them.

No, she wasn't going to start checking up on him. She moved the mouse to bring the screen back to life and clicked on her PowerPoint slides for the United Way leadership training session tomorrow. "Lead from Strength" was the title. In her mind she rehearsed, "Have you ever called a subordinate into your office to discuss a performance problem? Did you notice defensive body language? Arms folded, maybe even fists clenched? Today, we're going to talk about another approach to leadership."

She clicked on the next slide: "Not what's wrong—what's right." And in her mind: "Leadership begins with identifying strengths and building on them." That clicked her mind back to Kurt. He was building a career on his strength. Kurt was a social intelligence genius.

# CHAPTER 21

*Okay, Cassie, I was wrong again. You're going to say I have a perfect record with men—wrong every time. So yes, I was wrong again this time. But wow!*

Sam stared at the brass ear on the ceiling. Of course he wasn't listening now in the upstairs bedroom. He was on his way to the deli. He'd flashed that little-boy grin when he said something about breakfast not working out but now he'd try for lunch. But she hadn't heard him leave. Couldn't hear much down here anyway, but did she feel his presence still in the house? But what if he was up there? What difference would it make? He couldn't hear what she was thinking. Eventually, she was going to tell Cassie what had happened. How could she not? Cassie was her best friend, a one-woman support system, and she and Kurt were taking care of Amy. Cassie was going to want to know everything. So now, while she was still . . . what . . . ? Vibrating? Well, tingling, at least. Glowing. Whatever, it was a nice feeling, and she could enjoy it by rehearsing how she would eventually tell Cassie what had happened.

*I was for-certain sure that my hybrid-beauty boy was . . . I mean, the way he ducked his head and grinned like he'd been caught showing off how smart he is. And the shy way he brought those ugly sweatpants with "Pink" across the seat, and the way he kept his distance in this damn little room—whatever. I just knew he had a woman problem. Maybe a mama-boss, or maybe even a guy that had checked out his Mongol stain and confused his hormones. Whatever. I was sure he was ready for an experienced woman. In need of that, really. You laugh, but that's how I was thinking about myself. An experienced woman. Granted, my bedroom experience was limited to Ron, but wasn't that a postgraduate course?*

She got up from the little bed and started collecting her clothes from the floor.

*I can see you're still smiling, Cassie, because you think I just projected my problem onto Charley. Or the flip side of my problem. I mean, when you told me that I'm a pushover for dominating men, I told you to stop being a nosey social worker, but I thought about that afterward. Actually, I thought about that a lot.*

How did her bra get clear under the bed? Shoes must be out there somewhere on the way to the maze.

*So before I get started and before you ask—no, it was not unprotected. Actually, that should have been my first clue. You see, when I came out of that damn maze and we were walking back up to the house . . . not touching, not even talking much, but sharing the same . . . I don't know what. The same space, somehow, if you can understand that.*

She hung the ruins of her navy suit in the bathroom and turned on the hot water tap to steam out some of the wrinkles.

*Anyway, I had this experienced-woman plan and so I asked if I could see his room. He said okay, but we were only in there long enough for him to get something out of his nighttable. But I was so clueless—what I mean is, I was so hung up on this idea of a boy with woman problems that the obvious didn't even register. He kept talking, of course. Something about the Facebook age where everyone is connected.*

She got back into the sweats and returned to the little bed. Looked like a battleground. Like somebody had put up a fight. That idea almost made her laugh.

*All I was thinking about was, well—I thought that all I had to do was get his pants down and then I'd be in control. So when we were*

*in his room I said something about the Mongol stain and he said,
don't remember just what—something about one step at a time—and
this was still in the submission phase of the plan and so, kind of
before I realized it, there we were, back down in that little down-the-
rabbit-hole room.*

She tried to straighten the sheets, decided that was hopeless
and so she stripped the bed and made it up again.

*I think I'd forgotten, or maybe I was just so locked onto one idea
that when we got to the door—it was standing open into the hall—
and looked in I was surprised by the chaos. That trolley cart was
upended on the rag rug and lox were plastered against the far wall
and the broken dishes and spilled coffee . . . well, it took us a good
twenty minutes to clean up the worst of it.*

Now she looked around, found a bagel behind the chair and
a fork in the corner by the bathroom door. Miraculously, the
chess game was still intact on the floor under the table.

*You might suppose that housekeeping would kind of break the
mood, and I guess it did, but working like that together, it kind of
changed things. The way we—our relationship, if you can understand
that. He had this lump on his forehead—honest, Cassie, it was the
size of an XL egg—and when I reached up and touched it as gently
as I could, well, when I told him I was sorry, I really meant it.*

She dropped the bagel in the wastebasket, rinsed the fork
and put it on the bathroom shelf. She fished the pantyhose out
from the corner behind the chair. The lead-soldier lump had
stretched them permanently shapeless.

*Of course, he was talking all the time, about how the Arab Spring
had no plan and Occupy Wall Street had no doctrine but it was all
just about people connecting around an idea. And that stupid movie
trailer about Muhammad, didn't that show what a film on social
media could do?*

Looking up at the shelf with the empty space left by the
French cavalry officer with his saber and the two British

infantrymen with their long rifles, she said under her breath, "Combat casualties" as she dropped the pantyhose into the wastebasket on top of the bagel.

*He was saying—I didn't follow all of it—but it was something about making the Cherokee connect around the idea of what they had been before "the trail of tears," whatever that was, while I was thinking about making a different kind of connection.*

She sat in the chair and studied the Alice pictures on the far wall.

*Cassie, I can see by the look on your face that you've guessed it didn't go according to plan. That's right—it sure didn't, but what you're thinking, you're wrong about that. It wasn't another case of getting pushed over by a dominating man. The way it developed, well, it wasn't about dominance or submission or any of that clinical stuff.*

The white rabbit studied his watch and Alice danced with the tortoise.

*It was more like dancing*

"I'm getting hungry, Charley," she said to the brass ear in the ceiling.

*I'm not going to tell you any more than that, Cassie. How I feel about him now? I wouldn't tell you if I knew. Which I don't.*

The house groaned. Was that a footstep? Overhead—everything was overhead down here—but was it approaching the stair? Was he coming back? She realized that she had folded her arms and crossed her knees. After a long silence she decided that the house was just feeling its age. Instead of rehearsing her report to Cassie she should be thinking about what she was going to say when he came back with lunch. Okay, she'd gotten him into that little bed, but it didn't go as planned.

*So what would you say about that, Cassie? With Ron, you were urging me to stand up. Go to court, get an order protection. You asked if I was still in thrall to him. In his magnetic field, that's how Char-*

*ley put it. And now, what happened this afternoon, is it just the same thing again? Sure, I started out to take control, but here I am still in this damn room.*

# CHAPTER 22

"This job supposed 2 leave time 4 reading Sartre vs texting U but luv H." Helen had just shut down her phone and found her place in "No Exit" when that to-die-for guy pushed through the door and approached her table with that Broadway smile.

"Hi, I'm Amy Langshan's dad. I need to pick her up a little early today, okay?"

"Uh . . ." automatically composing the text message in her mind: Brad Pitt with suntan and long hair. "Mrs. Spitzer always picks her up."

His smile added kilowatts. "I know. But today we have a little change of plan."

"Gee, I'm sorry, but—"

He opened both hands on her table. "You see, Cassie isn't feeling well. Probably just the flu, but she doesn't want to expose Amy. Sam—we call her that because her name's Samantha—she asked me to be ready to pick her up today. She told me to show you her driver's license to make sure I'm okay. What time does she get out?" He had a big bruise on his forehead. Probably some kind of an athlete.

"Gee, I'd like to, but I'm supposed to wait for Mrs. Spitzer."

Now he folded his hands on her table and leaned forward. "This may be an emergency" he said, his voice now with an edge of authority. "I'm her father and I don't have a lot of time." When she didn't answer, he picked up a three-fold leaflet from the tabletop. "Shall I speak to the executive director?"

She didn't answer.

He opened the leaflet. "Looks like preschool is out at three o'clock." He glanced at his watch. "I can wait until then. Thanks for your help. What's your name?"

"Helen." She was thinking that she didn't really help. Didn't tell him anything, really.

"Helen," he repeated, as if to imprint the name in memory. "When I send my check I'll put in a note saying that you do a good, conscientious job, Helen."

She leaned to watch him walking down the path toward the pavilion. Super smile. And he *is* Amy's father. Had her mom's license. But, now that she thought about it, why hadn't he just shown his own? Something didn't seem . . . She opened the school directory, found Spitzer and punched the number.

She recognized the "Hello" and said, "Hi, Mrs. Spitzer. This is Helen at preschool. Just calling to say I'm sorry you're not feeling well."

"Thank you, Helen, but I'm feeling just fine."

"Oh . . . but Amy's father was just here and he said you're coming down with the flu."

"Her father? He's there? You didn't let him take her?"

"No. I said I could only—but he said he might pick her up this afternoon."

Audible deep breath. "Helen, where is he right now?"

Helen half stood to peer out the office window. "I don't see . . . there's a car pulling out of the parking lot now. Maybe that's—"

"Helen, I'm coming to get Amy right now. Can you have her waiting for me in the office?"

"Gee, I don't know, Mrs. Spitzer. She's on a nature walk and I—"

"Do this, Helen. It's important. I'll be there in ten minutes. Do you understand?"

"I understand, but—"
The phone clicked dead.

# Chapter 23

Sam felt, rather than heard, the front door. A tremor under her feet jerked her upright in the purple wing chair and hustled her into the bathroom to check her hair. Still boring brown, but what had he said? Like a lion's mane. Dab of lipstick, wondering what he was bringing for lunch. Champagne maybe? She giggled to herself. It occurred to her that when she thought she had been initiating him he was teaching her—a married woman—a duet. Dancing. It had been her real first time. She was back in the chair when the door latch rattled.

"Can I come in without getting hit in the head?" he said.

"Only if you're bringing lunch."

He pushed the door open and paused in the hall until he could see her. Then he came in carrying a brown paper bag. "What I'm bringing is a business lunch," he said, taking a plastic clam-shell container out of the bag and opening it on the little table.

Another Caesar salad from the deli?

When he sat on the edge of the bed she noticed that the lump on his forehead had spread into a purple bruise that disappeared into the coarse black hair pulled straight into a ponytail. "Your head looks awful," she said.

He moved to touch the bruise but stopped his hand. "You gave me an upstairs Mongol stain," he said with that little-boy grin.

"I'm . . . so sorry."

Waving that away he said, "I think we had to get some preliminaries out of the way."

"I guess I don't know what you mean by preliminaries."

He raised skeptical brows. "Really?" Pause. "Well, I'd say we went through the bait and switch, the proposition, the"—now he touched the bruise—"rejection, and then the . . ." he glanced into the air for the word, "reconciliation. I'd say we're ready to talk business."

She gestured toward the deli bag. "I was hoping we could have lunch together. Maybe . . . upstairs."

He smiled. "Maybe we can. Soon, but not quite yet."

"What has to happen first?"

He leaned forward, elbows on his knees. "First, you have to deliver."

"Deliver?"

"Didn't you understand? I need Ron here. After that we can go upstairs together."

"That's what it's been about, always, isn't Charley? You never needed me for the PR stuff, did you?"

He chuckled. "Oh, that's a bonus. Sure, you can help edit the DVD and help making it go viral. But first we have to get Ron here."

"What else haven't you . . ."

"What else wasn't the truth and the whole truth and all that? Well, that stuff about day trading. Did you really think I can consistently beat the market?"

"I guess I didn't think about that."

He leaned closer, as if to confide a secret. "The whole truth about that is luck, or fate or karma—whatever you want to believe. The truth is, The Designer is underwriting our project."

"The same man that . . ."

"It's enough to make a believer of you, isn't it? Yes, the same guy. After that scene in his studio, I took my time going through that little house, and you know what? He didn't turn off his computer when he went to the Thrift Way, just put it to sleep, so I could rummage through his life. He had a 'lists' file with phone numbers, wine labels, Christmas card and birthday names and addresses—he must have emailed birthday cards to a couple of dozen people. And PIN numbers. His bank statement was in the desk drawer and ATM card was in his wallet. The card and PIN worked at the Bank of America ATM in downtown Vashon and in O'Hare where I changed planes. I waited a couple of days and drove into La Guardia—well, you get the idea. I guess The Designer often holed up there in the woods on his own, because nobody seemed to miss him for a long time. What else is on your mind? Let's get it all out of the way."

She reached to the end table and picked up the picture of the man in the turban with the long skinny pipe. "What about this guy? You said something about people not understanding him."

He smiled, looking past her as if listening to something in the distance. "Can you imagine that you never learned to read and write? And then, starting absolutely from scratch, you worked out a way to do it. A system so efficient that kids don't have to spend years learning how to master it. A Cherokee child can learn to read and write his own language in about three days."

"But you said they didn't understand him."

"He had to show them. They thought it was some kind of a trick until his daughter showed them that she could read. Like we have to show them honor. That's what we'll use The Designer for. And Ron. When you bring him here."

"But I can't . . . I don't know how to do that."

He sat back and pointed a finger at her. "Oh, I think you do. You may not realize it, but somewhere in your memory bank is the way to call Ron."

She shook her head. "I couldn't get him to do anything when

". . . when we were together. Now . . . we're not even speaking."

"You're not working on the problem, Sam. You keep trying to work on me, but Ron is the problem. *Our* problem."

"I don't know what you want me to do."

"I don't know either, yet. But I'll know it when I hear it. So talk to me about Ron. I want to know everything about him. I want to *understand* him."

He sat forward on the edge of the bed again, all business. What had happened to the gentle lover who hadn't let her get to her knees before he'd led her to that bed? "Here's the deal, Sam. If you lie to me or withhold information at any time in this conversation and I find out about it—and I *will* find out about it, because you see, I now hold all the cards in this game. You made your play, Sam. It was gutsy, and it might have worked. But now if you try the smallest—if you even fudge a little fact—then you bring trouble to Amy."

She heard herself repeat, "Amy?" in a strangled voice.

He nodded. "It would be so easy. Cassie said on the phone yesterday that she's at preschool. Your cell had a number. Cross directory took me to "Ask Me Annie." They told me that Mrs. Spitzer—that's Cassie, isn't it?—she picks Amy up. You want me to bring Amy here to show you how serious I am?"

Staring into those black eyes, she knew he could do it. Would do it. Something about the confident way he slouched back against the wall, those gentle hands now loose on his knees, brows up in a question and that smile that said—what? Certainty. He was going to do what he believed he had to do. Whatever or whoever got in the way. No one he could use was safe. Including Amy.

"I don't . . ." she groped "he's smart. Went to Harvard. You won't trick him into coming here."

He hitched forward on the edge of the bed. "Go on. Tell me about him."

"So you can . . . what?"

"Make things right."

"Right? You mean murder him. My own husband. Father of my child."

"Abuser. Spawn of corrupt seed."

"How can I—do you realize what you're asking?"

"Yes. Of course I do. Did you think life is a free ride? Well, here's the toll booth. Have you got the price now, or do you have to have Amy here?"

She sank her face into her hands. Through her fingers she said, "What is it you're looking for?"

"I don't know. But I'll know it when I see it. When you tell me."

Silence thickened. Finally, he prompted: "You say he's smart. What else?"

Face still in her hands, she shook her head. "I don't know."

"Brave? Would you say he's brave?"

She looked up, thinking about that. "No. But he's fearless. I think that's different, don't you?"

"I don't know. Maybe. Tell me what you mean."

"He talks about his father. A pilot. He said that if you have any doubt that you can land your airplane on a ship—he was a navy pilot—then you can't do it. Ron thinks it's all about self-confidence."

"What is?"

She shrugged. "I don't know. Most everything, it seemed."

Charley pursed his lips and nodded. "That's interesting. Tell me some more."

"If I do this . . ."

He nodded and roiled a little "go on" gesture.

"If I help you get . . . to reach him. Is that the end of it?"

"Sure. Then it's up to me."

"I mean, for me. Can I—" she circled a finger in the air "—get out of this little room? This place?"

"Of course."

But there had been a hesitation, a flicker of something in the eyes that told her he was lying.

He went on: "This has never been about you. This is bigger than you, or me. I explained that. This is about justice. And inspiration for the People."

But she knew this was also about control, which was about having her here. And getting him into that bed hadn't changed anything. Probably made it worse.

He said, "So tell me some more about Ron. What does he believe in?"

"Believe in? I told you. He believes in Ron."

He shook his head. "Nothing else? Give me an example."

"Well . . . one night when there was a big storm with lightning, Ron had to go outside. To see if maybe there was a fire."

"What did that have to do with confidence?"

She raised her palms. "I don't know. Maybe nothing."

"No, go on." He made that little rolling gesture again. "You say he *had* to go out."

"I just mean that was so . . . just like Ron. Something was going on, even something a little scary, and he had to go out and meet it."

Charley looked away, holding that idea. "You say he's too smart for a trick but he's so confident . . ." he looked back, eyebrows up, "maybe he couldn't resist a dare?" When she didn't answer he made that rolling gesture again. "Tell me some more. What about his evil side. You know, with Amy—what kind of a man can do that?"

"Evil? I never thought Ron was . . ." she closed her eyes for a moment, trying to find a way to say it. "He could be so sweet. And understanding—he knows how to read people. Play back what they want to see. But there was always something . . ." she shook her head.

"Give me an example."

"Well, when we were first married we rented a little house in Bethpage. It had a sunny kitchen window, and I started spreading bird seed on the ledge. I got sparrows and finches and— Ron called them 'titsmice.' " She paused, smiling at the memory.

"Go on."

"Well, one day I looked out the kitchen window and there was Ron, out in the backyard with . . ." she held up her fists and pulled one back. "It was some kind of a high-tech slingshot that he'd bought on the Internet. I couldn't believe it—he'd spread some seed on the driveway and he was shooting pellets at my birds."

Charley stood and walked across the room, releasing energy as he sputtered, "That's . . . that's . . . what kind of a . . ." As he came back to the bed she noticed that he took five paces. It was six for her, she remembered. "Go on," he said, sitting down again.

"You don't understand," she said. "He wasn't . . . it wasn't something to hurt me. He didn't think of things like that. He just doesn't."

"Doesn't what?"

She shifted in the chair, realizing that he was asking her to explain something she didn't understand herself. Hadn't thought about. Hadn't wanted to think about. "He didn't consider those birds anything but—they were targets, that's all. He was like a bomber who drops on targets, not cities."

"I can kind of understand that. Lots of Cherokee are hunters, but they kill for the table. This was just . . . you'd been *feeding* those birds. Outside your window. Didn't you say something to him?"

"Of course I did. And he said he was sorry. That he didn't realize how I felt. And . . ." She leaned forward a little. "I believed him." She sat back again. "What's more, Charley, I still do."

"Believe him?"

She nodded.

"I don't understand," he said.

She started to say that she didn't understand either. Which was true, but an evasion. Groping for a way to think about it, she looked at the lead soldiers on the shelf above his head. Dozens of figures out of the same mold. "Can you imagine some kind of a factory for making people?" she said. "Maybe one person goes by on the assembly line with a part missing. Not a thumb or a foot—not something that shows. Something like . . . an ear for music. Or fear. Or . . . empathy. The worker doesn't want to stop the line to put that in. He's got a quota to meet. And so out comes Ron. Finished goods, but missing a part."

She paused, but Charley shook his head.

"Trying to explain my birds to Ron was like trying to teach someone who's tone deaf how to sing harmony. There was just no . . . connection."

Charley reset his feet, about to get up again, but then he leaned back. "Who did it?"

"Did what?"

"Whatever it was. Turned off the controls. People don't come off some kind of assembly line, Sam. You think Ron is the only incomplete person walking around today?"

She thought about that. "No. I think . . ." She gave up because she didn't know what she thought.

"We're all incomplete," he said.

"You too?" she asked

"Of course. That's what life is all about. Getting there. Or going toward it."

"I guess. But Ron is different. He's incomplete in a different way."

"What did it to him? His father?"

"I don't know. His father is a big deal. All that stuff about landing on the carrier and confidence . . . but what does it matter?"

Charley pursed his lips and nodded. "It does matter. It's the way we can get to him. Get him here."

"I don't—can't you understand? You're not going to get him here. Inside a place like this? I told you—he goes outside to find the lightning."

Charley stood again and walked around behind her chair to the door. "I hadn't thought of it like that. You mean, maybe someplace outside?"

"Where are you going?"

"Nowhere. I'm not going anywhere."

"Why are you standing back there behind me?"

"I thought maybe it would be easier for you. I mean, if you didn't have to keep looking at me, maybe it would be easier to talk."

"Well, it's not. Charley, don't psychoanalyze me." As he came back to the bed she went on: "When I can't see you it's like that creepy ear in the ceiling—" she jerked her thumb up "—where you eavesdropped on me."

He held up both hands as he sat on the edge of the bed. "Aren't you going to have some lunch?"

Sam looked at the paper sack on the table, thinking about her champagne fantasy when she'd heard him at the door. "Maybe later. Right now I'm having too much fun."

"Sam, I don't want to make this . . . look, do this in your own way. Just tell me some more about Ron. Like, how the two of you get a business started? And what happened to it?"

She realized that now that she could see him she didn't want to look at him. "Well, we were both working at this PR agency when Ron landed a big client. A real estate company." She forced herself to look into his eyes. "You know, this morning, after . . . the maze, I felt like I could trust you. Now when you're behind me I get the creeps."

He touched the bruise on his forehead. "I feel like I have to keep you in sight too, Sam. But we're getting there. Building trust. We're going to be a team. We just have to learn how to work together. So tell me . . . what happened at the agency?"

She took a breath, putting herself back into that time. "The boss, a guy named Wallace, took a shine to Ron and hired him. By that time we were married, and so I had to leave too."

"But I thought you had your own agency."

"You don't understand. You see, hiring Ron was a two-step dance. Wallace couldn't just hire him away from the agency."

"Why not?"

"Well, I guess he could, but it wouldn't look right. Not . . . ethical. And so Ron and I resigned and set up shop. And then— big surprise, the Wallace account moved to us."

"Was it a surprise?"

"Are you kidding? Like I say, the whole thing was a dance. But as long as we took the proper steps . . ." she shrugged. "Where is this . . . why do you want to know all this stuff?"

"Because you know how to get to him."

"I keep telling you—I don't."

"You don't realize it, but you do. It's there," he pointed to her head, "but you have to discover it. We have to discover it, together." He looked at his watch. "But first we'd better call your friend Cassie. You promised, remember? And you'll need an explanation for another day or two."

"What can I say?"

"You'll have to think of something." She noticed how gracefully his hand waved a little gesture. "Let's leave that to cook a while. Let your subconscious work on it. Remember the video I showed you?"

She looked away. "Yes, I remember."

"We talked about putting it on YouTube, remember?"

Looking at the White Rabbit, she nodded.

"Well, I'm counting on you to help me get that ready for prime time."

"What do you mean?"

He leaned toward her. "I mean, it has to be edited. It's too long, and too . . ."

"Gory. It's way too gory."

He nodded. "What we have to find is the footage where he reveals himself. Where he's the arrogant, heedless . . . where he's just another Langshan. You see, everything's connected. We're all connected to the earth, and to the animals and each other. You and me, Sam. A connection brought us together. And these Langshans, they're all connected, clear back to the guy who ordered that firing squad."

She thought of the way they had been connected earlier. Shoving that idea away, she said, "All right, say we can find footage like that. I don't remember it, in all that blood, but say it's there. Then what?"

"We need a strategy, don't we? A marketing plan. Once we have our show—I think we should think of it as a show, don't you?—once we have it on YouTube, what will make Cherokee people pass it around? Link it to Facebook. Make it go viral."

"You need a selling proposition."

"What's that?"

"That's marketing-speak. You're making a pitch for action. What you're asking is low cost." She waggled a forefinger in the air. "Just press a key and send the—the YouTube show along to your Facebook list. But what's the reward? Say I'm on your target list. When I get it, why should I pass it along?"

He nodded understanding and looked away, eyes narrowed, considering. "I think . . . Sam, I think there's a huge reward." He looked back, brows arched. "If we do it right, when you pass it on, *you're* connecting. Making yourself part of something great. Doing something about a terrible wrong to your people. Discovering who you are." He flashed a smile. "How's that for reward?"

She felt herself flinch from the voltage in his eyes, but she didn't look away. "Okay, that works. Self-esteem is a reward. You want me to start editing?"

He shook his head, smiling. "Not yet. One episode, that's just . . . an incident. We're selling a campaign. We need at least one more for our launch. We need Ron. But first, what are you going to tell Cassie?"

"I guess I'll tell her the truth."

"The truth?"

"I'll tell her I'm working on a project."

He nodded. "That's it. A PR and marketing project."

# CHAPTER 24

As soon as she recognized Sam's voice, Cassie said, "Ron came looking for her. Looking for Amy. You've got to do something about that guy, Sam. He's dangerous."

Holding the cell phone away from her ear so that they both could hear her, Sam said, "Came looking for her? Where?" She could feel the warmth of his face close to hers.

"At the camp. He tried to pick her up at the camp."

Sam leaned away to look at Charley. He nodded and pointed to himself. Sam went back to the phone. "What happened? Is she okay?"

"She's fine. The kid at the desk called me and I came and got her. But next time—"

"How do you know it was Ron?"

"Because that's what he said. He's her father—that's what he told the kid. Besides, who else could it be?" Without waiting for an answer, Cassie plunged on: "And Ron had better look out. You know that fire? Where Mexicans or Salvadorans or whoever they are—where they got burned up? Well there's a guy looking for the owner of that property. And guess who's their spokesman?"

"The Mexicans?"

"No, the owners. The spokesman is Ron."

"You mean, the owner—it's Wallace? How do you know all this, Cassie?"

"Because we're—that guy, his name is Pedro, he called Kurt.

187

Where are you, anyway? What's going on, Sam?"

Charley rolled a "keep it going" gesture. Sam said, "I'm—out of town, off the island. I'll explain it all when I see you, but I have to ask you to take care of Amy another day or two."

"Out of town where? Look, Amy's no problem. We love having her. But I'm worried about Ron."

"So am I," Sam said, letting the story spin itself. "That's what I'm working on. This isn't a big romantic adventure, Cassie. This is about finding a way to keep Ron . . ." she pulled away to glance at Charley, who nodded and stabbed a "thumbs-up" gesture, "to keep him away from Amy. And from me."

Cassie chuckled. "You putting out a hit on him?"

Sam didn't look at Charley. "Don't I wish," managing a little laugh. "Matter of fact, I am working with a guy and . . . we're collecting some electrons. That's easy to do, these days, and what we're getting, it's telling us an interesting story."

"You've got him under surveillance?"

"Look, Cassie, this is all going to end up in court. You know, when I tell the judge why we need an order of protection. So it's best for you if you can say you don't know anything about it, okay?"

Charley leaned away, smiling and nodding. He mouthed "The fire!"

"Okay, sure," Cassie said. "I'm glad you're working on the problem. And don't worry about Amy."

"Can I talk to her?"

"I put her down for a nap after lunch. Want me to wake her?"

"No, just tell her I called and I love her. Tell her I'll be home in a day or two." Charley held up three fingers and she added: "Three days at the outside."

Charley touched her shoulder and shouted a silent, "The fire!" again. But without prompting Cassie said, "If your surveillance connects Ron to that Depot Road fire . . . but you just

188

started it, right? The surveillance, I mean."

"I didn't say surveillance, Cassie."

Cassie's voice smiled across the wire. "No, your honor, she said nothing about surveillance. But Sam, this guy Pedro sounds like a mean dude."

Charley made the rolling gesture again.

"Tell me what happened. Why did this, Pedro? . . . Why did he call Kurt."

"Didn't call him. Walked in off the street. Kurt thinks it was kind of an impulse, the guy was walking by and saw the sign, and Kurt alone in the office and thought, 'I'll bet that guy knows who owns that house.' Which, of course, Kurt does."

"He thought Kurt owns it?"

"No, but he thought Kurt knows who does. And he's right. Everybody in the business knows who owns it."

Sam leaned away again to glance at Charley, who nodded and gestured thumbs-up, before she asked, "Did Kurt tell him?"

"It's public record, you know. Common knowledge around town. The guy is going to find out one way or another. And rather than bring him to us—he made a threat, Sam. Against me and Amy. So yes, Kurt told him. But first he warned Wallace."

"What kind of a threat?"

"The kind you have to take seriously. This guy Pedro, he's scary. When do you think you'll have the goods on Ron, or whatever it is you're doing?"

"I don't know exactly, but I'll keep you posted," Sam said. "I don't know how to thank you for taking care of Amy, Cassie. You're a special friend."

"Just get that guy out of her life, Sam. And yours."

# CHAPTER 25

When the phone chimed Ron pulled it off his belt without look-ing away from the Long Island section of the *Times*. He let it chime again in his hand as he finished the paragraph, ". . . retrofitted for empty-nesters. Buyers are attracted to traditional outside but modern inside." He glanced at the screen, which only showed "Private Caller."

When he answered, a quiet voice said, "Hey, man. We gotta talk." Something in the tone suggested a man speaking into his cupped hand.

Ron said, "Who is this?"

"Friend of a friend, man."

"What friend?"

"Tell you all about it when we talk."

"I don't know you and I'm turning you off."

"Yeah, you do that. Then I'll hafta come see you?" Making it a question.

"See me about what?"

"Depot Road. Man says you know about that?"

Ron sat up in the faux Eames chair and let the paper slide to the floor. "I know it's a street in Huntington Station."

"Bad fire on Depot Road? People burned up. One of 'em was a little girl, four years old. You know?"

"Just what I saw in *Newsday*."

"Not what the man says."

"What man?"

"The man that knows. The man that owns is the man that knows, right?"

Ron switched off the lamp, stood and walked to the window as he said, "This man, does he have a name?" The street in front of his Cape Cod rental was shaded by the double row of sycamores that had been planted by town fathers now long forgotten. A man leaning against one of the peeling trunks holding a cell to his ear would be invisible.

"Oh, you know the name. Everybody knows the name."

Two cars were parked at the curb across the street, interiors dark in the night. Automatically, his mind recorded: light-color, maybe gray, SUV, probably a Lexus, and a dark four-door sedan. "Maybe everybody does, but I don't."

"No? How 'bout Wallace. That a name you know?"

Ron glanced around the apartment as he walked back to the chair. Nothing to grab but a kitchen knife. "Well, you're right about that. That's a name everybody knows. You trying to tell me he gave you my name?"

"Loaded you into the gun, man. Hey, what're friends for?

"I don't think you know Mr. Wallace."

"Oh no? I'll tell you how good I know him, man—I know about seven billion minus four."

For a moment Ron didn't make the connection. And then he couldn't believe it. The son of a bitch. Couldn't wait twenty-four hours to give me up. He cleared his throat to be sure of his voice. "I don't know what you're talking about."

"We get together and I'll explain it to you, man."

"Explain it to me now."

"Can't do that. But look, man, I'm not sayin' you had something to do with it yourself. The man just said you know something. Maybe you can point me in the right direction. Somebody I ought to talk to, y'know?"

Ron nodded to himself. Starting a wild goose chase might be

the way to deal with this. But first, talk to Wallace, see what he says about this guy. "Okay. I'll listen to what you have to say, but that doesn't mean I have—there's anything I can tell you."

"Understand. Just give me a time and I'll pick the place?"

"Going to have to wait a little. I'm leaving town tomorrow. Little business trip. But I could call you when I get back and we could set something up."

"How long you gonna be gone?"

"Just a few days. I don't know exactly. Depends on how things go."

"Where you gonna be?"

"Look, if you want to meet, give me a contact number. If you don't want to meet, that's just fine with me."

Pause, and then: "Gonna give you a number. Public place, right? You ask for Pedro Loco. Got that? Guy on the phone won't know anybody that name. You say, sorry, wrong number. Then you wait for me to call, okay? Won't be long. Now, you got a pen?"

After he clicked off, Ron went to the window again. Nothing moved under the sycamores, and the dark cars were still parked at the curb. Pedro Loco. Obviously a street name. So Walt was spooked by a street kid. What, exactly, had he told this guy? What *could* he tell? All he really knew was that he'd talked about how many people there are on the earth and what a nice place Huntington Station was before all the tamales moved in.

Ron scooped the newspaper off the floor and went back to the Eames chair. He tried to get back into the article about houses that are traditional outside but modern inside. If this place was his he'd knock out that wall—who needs a dining room these days?—and open up this claustrophobic living room. Create some breathing room.

He stood again, replaying the night of the fire. Vinyl gloves over powdered hands. Gibbous moon. An old drunk on the curb at the deserted hiring site. Could he have seen something?

Ron shrugged into his jacket and escaped for a long walk down the dark streets.

★ ★ ★ ★ ★

# Day Three of Captivity

★ ★ ★ ★ ★

In all some 90 thousand Indians were relocated. The Cherokee were among the last to go. Some reluctantly agreed to move. Others were driven from their homes at bayonet point. Almost two thousand of them died along the route they remembered as the Trail of Tears.

—Documentary: *The West,* by Ken Burns and Stephen Ives

# CHAPTER 26

"Brought you news of the outside world," Charley said the next morning, backing into the room and raising an elbow to let the newspapers under his arm drop onto the rag rug.

"Outside world?" she said. "What's that?"

He set paper bags on the little table. "I'm sure you're getting tired of deli meals."

"No," she said, gathering up the newspapers. "I'm getting sick of them."

"Okay, how about Chinese for lunch?"

She shook her head. "I'm sick of the whole thing. This place—I have to get out of here." She sat in the chair, scanning the *Newsday* headlines. "Foreclosures Down, Short Sales Up."

As he distributed bagels, cream cheese and lox around the little table, he said, "Soon. We'll get you out soon. I've been thinking about what Cassie said. About the fire. I think she told us how to get you out of here."

"Oh? So what did she tell the warden?"

Instead of answering, he sat on the edge of the bed, spread cheese on half a poppy-seed bagel, forked a slice of lox on top and held it out to her. When she didn't reach for it he lifted his brows and nodded toward the bagel to say that he wouldn't answer until she took it. When she gave in, he selected a sesame-seed, spread a perfect eighth-inch of cheese, found the right slice of lox and popped the lid on one of the coffees. She waited.

"That guy Pedro, he's going to spring me?" she finally prompted.

He sat back, tasted the bagel and sipped the coffee. "Have some breakfast," he said.

When she took a bite he handed her the other coffee. "Yes," he said. "Pedro's our guy. He's going to bring Ron here. Then you're sprung."

She faked a sip of coffee before she said, "Never happen."

He crossed his legs, making a show of getting comfortable. "You don't believe me?"

Instead of answering, she said, "How're you going to—look, you don't really know there's a connection to this Pedro guy. That's just Cassie's idea."

He nodded agreement, chewing the bagel.

"And even if you did find a connection, Ron's never going to come here."

He put down the cup and opened a "why not?" gesture.

"Ron's . . ." trying to find a way to say what she felt, she looked down at the bright center of the rug, the sunshine of this basement cell. "This place is claustrophobic for me. For Ron . . . well, he's just not going to do it."

"I don't have to bring him down here."

"Okay, then where?"

"All I need is someplace—" he shrugged "—private."

She shook her head. "Ron isn't going to walk into some place he doesn't know."

"Too smart?"

"He *is* smart, yes. But also . . . remember what I told you about the night of the big storm?"

Charley nodded. "He went out in the rain."

"And the lightning. Outside."

"Outside," he repeated, thinking about that. "You think he was more comfortable outside?"

"I've given up trying to understand Ron."

He licked cream cheese off a finger. "Tell me, Sam, do you think Ron did it?"

"Did it? You mean . . ."

"Set that fire."

This time, when she shook her head she realized that she had closed her eyes, shutting everything out. "Of course not."

"Why not? Didn't he shoot the birds off your feeder with a slingshot?"

"No. They were in the driveway. And anyway . . . they were birds."

"What about Amy? She's not just a bird."

Sam didn't answer.

Charley drained his cup and set it on the table between them. "What kind of a man can abuse his own daughter?" When she didn't answer, he said, "The same kind of a man who could order exhausted and helpless men to stand in a firing squad to execute one of their own. That's the wisdom of blood revenge. Don't you see, Sam?"

She didn't answer.

"The old people didn't know anything about DNA, but they understood retribution. Cleansing the bloodline. And not just the Cherokee—there's something in the bible about guilt down to the seventh generation." He hitched forward onto the edge of the little bed. "Here we have it right in front of us. One of the Langshans is murdering brown-skinned people right now. A hundred and seventy-five years later. Seven generations." He balled his right fist into his left palm. "Stamping out this murder gene, that's what blood revenge is all about." He took a deep breath and sat back again. "What I'm all about."

"But not me, Charley. This isn't about me."

He took a breath with a glance at the ceiling, gathering patience. "It's not your *fault*, Sam. Bad things happen to good

199

people. But you have a stake in this. Your stake is Amy."

"Because she's his? She's got his . . . his gene?"

He raised both hands. "Oh no. The People didn't—the murder gene goes down from male to male. Amy is your stake because she's a victim too. *His* victim." He dropped his hands to his lap. "If he's not going to come here, then we'll have to think of some other place. But first, have some breakfast."

She took a real bite of the bagel and discovered that she was hungry. The coffee was still warm enough to be palatable. The surreal was beginning to seem ordinary.

Looking off into the distance, Charley said, "When you were talking to Cassie, where did you come up with that idea of surveillance?"

She laughed, trying to remember. As she spread cream cheese on another bagel she said, "I don't know. I had to say *something.*"

"That was a great choice. You said something about electronic surveillance being easy. That's what made the idea go down. Cassie bought right into it."

"Too bad it's not true."

Charley sat back against the wall and bumped his head on the shelf of lead soldiers. He waved an acknowledging gesture—I understand what you mean about this room—as he asked, "Do you think Ron would buy into it too?"

"Not a chance."

Rubbing his head, he said, "What if I said I had proof?"

"He wouldn't believe you."

"What if you said it?"

Sam put the remains of her bagel on the table. "You want me to . . ."

Charley nodded.

She thought of the DVD, The Designer spouting blood and gurgling incomprehensible last words. Charley wanted to do that to Ron. The beautiful, confident man who had given her joy, and Amy. "It wouldn't work," she said.

"Why not?"

She hesitated, picturing Ron bopping past her desk after he'd closed the Wallace deal. "Because he doesn't get pushed around. He does the pushing."

"Okay, no pushing. What if we're offering a deal? Suppose we know about that fire. About Ron and the fire."

"What's to know? That Cassie thinks he had something to do with it?"

"We'd have to come up with something better than that. But suppose we can."

"Something like blackmail? Ron would never give in to that. I told you—he's not going to get pushed around."

Charley thought about that. "And he needs to be out in the open. Someplace where he feels in control. What else? What turns him on?"

"Challenge. Excitement. Ron likes the rush."

Charley nodded. "So we need to make it like a dare. A challenge, but under his control."

"Charley, what you're asking me—I can't help you do this."

He smiled and sat forward, careful of his head. "Do you think Ron started the fire that killed those people?"

"No. Of course not."

"Then he won't go for it, will he?"

"Go for what?"

"What we're planning." He waited, watching until she looked away, and then to make sure, he went on: "Look, let's say Ron didn't start that fire. You believe that, right?"

She nodded.

"Then if I claim to know that he did, whatever I say, he's not going to listen, right?"

She nodded again.

"Then let's figure out what I'm going to say. You can help

with that, can't you? I mean, not to worry—you know that whatever we come up with, it's not going to work."

She considered that. "If it doesn't work, then what?"

He raised his brows to acknowledge a new idea. "Okay, then all bets are off."

"You mean, I'm out of here?"

He smiled, nodding. "After you talk to Ron, you're outta here. Either way."

She knew he was lying, but what choice did she have? "All right, that's a deal," she said.

# CHAPTER 27

Ron cruised the Nissequogue mall parking lot, where the few cars were parked close to the big-box stores. Bobbing his head to Madonna's "Frozen" on WBAB, he noted his odometer readings as he passed the huddle of parked cars and again at the end of the lot. Then he turned and drove the entire length of the lot, noted the reading and turned again to measure the width. Now he could calculate how much of the lot was empty, which would only confirm what everyone knew: there were too many malls on Long Island. But Wallace loved data.

He knew that vacancy rates were now north of seven percent and malls that once were anchored by Lord & Taylor and Bonwits were now renting to dance studios, clinics and even grocery stores. An idea occurred to him: why not a community college? That's a growth industry. But Wallace had his own ideas. Probably had a banker's tip that Consolidated Properties was behind on some payments and ready to unload this loser.

Ron had finished collecting the parking lot numbers and was pulling into an empty slot so that he could do a walk-through and take some notes inside when his cell chimed. "Unknown Caller." He punched Madonna off and answered.

"Hey Ron, you heard from Pedro?"

"Who is this?"

"I'm your new friend."

"You got a name, friend?"

"Sure thing. But you already know the name Pedro, right?"

"I don't know what you're talking about."

"Oh, I think you do. Pedro, that's the name of trouble."

"Doesn't trouble *me.*"

"Look, man, I'm trying to explain. You got a problem with Pedro. You don't know it? You will. But I got a problem too. We're in this together, man."

Ron twisted in the seat to look around the parking lot. Nothing but parked cars and acres of empty concrete. "Just what is that? What is it we're in together?"

"I want to talk about that. Tell you all about it. But not on the phone. Understand?"

Something about the phrasing or the intonation didn't sound like the Hispanics Ron knew, but Huntington had enough wetbacks to organize their own OAS. Mex, Salvadoran, Honduran, who knows what else? He said, "I don't need to talk about a problem I don't have."

"You telling me you haven't heard from Pedro yet?"

"I'm telling you I'm ringing off."

"Okay, you do that, and your wife, Sam, she'll make sure you hear from Pedro."

Ron felt himself stiffen. He took a moment to make sure his voice was still in the casual middle range. "My wife? What's she got to do with . . . what we're talking about?"

"Why don't you ask her? Here she is . . ."

"Hello Ron." No mistaking the voice.

"What's going on, Sam?"

"You tell *me*, Ron. This guy showed me a CD that sure looks like you. I mean, if they put me on the stand and made me swear—could they make me testify against my husband, Ron? Even if we're separated and I've asked for an order of protection?"

"What kind of a CD? What's this all about, Sam?"

"It's all about you, Ron. You're going to want to see this CD.

204

Believe me, you really are."

*Bang!*

Ron jerked around to see a broad-beamed skirt climbing into a Lexus SUV parked in the lot behind and downstream from him. Had that been her trunk lid? "I don't know what you're talking about, Sam," he said, noticing that his voice had climbed out of midrange.

"That's good. I've been telling the guy with the CD that you can't know anything about it. Now you tell him."

"Hey Ron, you really look pretty good on my CD. Walkin' that little strut of yours. Like a guy afraid of nothing. You're gonna like it."

"Walking where?"

"Oh man, you're okay. You got it right—that's the question. I know where because I set up the camera. But without me that CD is just a guy walking down a street at night. So the CD is interesting, but me—I'm your problem. No, actually, Ron, I'm the *solution* to your problem."

"I don't know what you're talking about. What is this CD? And who're you?"

"I'm just a homesick Mexican. All I want is to get back to Oaxaca. There's no work up here, man. Not enough for what it costs just to get by. I gotta get home, somehow."

"What's this CD you keep talking about?"

"I told you. This guy Pedro? I got problems with him too."

"What kind of problems? He's a Crip and you're a Blood?"

"No, but something like that. You ever hear about a neighborhood watch?"

Ron glanced around the parking lot again. Deserted, as best he could see. "Kind of a vigilante thing?"

"Dunno what that means."

"Volunteers?"

"Yeah, man, that's it. My job was running a camera looking

out of a bedroom window most of the night. It was running the night of the fire. I've got the CD, but nobody else has seen it. Except your loving wife."

Ron moved the cell to wipe his left hand across his upper lip. He remembered walking toward the house with the missing siding strip, the bottle in his right hand, checking the street both ways. Salsa music coming from somewhere. A bedroom window with a camera? "Look, I'm sitting here in a parking lot. Give me a number and I'll call you back. Ten minutes, okay?"

"No. We don't finish this now, then I'll have to find somebody else to help me get to Oaxaca."

"What d'you mean, somebody else?"

The little chuckle in the phone made Ron ball his left fist as the smug voice went on: "Your wife says that landlord guy, Wallace, he could take nine thousand out of his walking-around money."

Ron mopped his mouth again. "Nine thousand, is that what we're talking about?"

"That's all. Just enough for the ticket to San Antonio and then the coyote to get me over the border. Little left for the bus. I don't want to make anything on this, man. Just get home."

"I don't have nine thousand dollars of walking-around money."

"Not walking around, but sitting there in the Bethpage Federal Credit Union, man. Ron's rainy day fund. I'm talking to your wife, remember?"

"How did she get in this?"

"I'll explain all that, man. You wanna know the whole story, just pay attention. You afraid to meet an unarmed man in a big empty public place, then I'll just have to get my ticket home somewhere else . . . You ready to listen?"

Ron took a breath. "I'm listening. That doesn't mean I'm ready to pay blackmail."

Another annoying chuckle. "Who said anything about blackmail? This is civic service, man. You Huntington folks want me outta town, but you won't give me a passport or enough work to earn the price to get over the border without one. This is how you solve the problem for everybody."

"Yeah, sure."

"If this was blackmail, you think I'd be asking for a—a diminuto nine bills? Look, I'll send you a post card when I get down there and you'll know that's the end of it."

"I said I'm listening. What's the proposition?"

"We're going to meet in a big open parking lot. Middle of the day. Okay?"

"Keep talking."

"When you go home today, you're gonna make a round-trip reservation on U.S. Air from Islip to Syracuse with a change in Philadelphia for day after tomorrow."

"I can't just hop off to Syracuse. I've got a job."

"Come on, man, you can work that out. Your aunt died. Shit happens. Now, you got something to write this down with?"

"Just a minute." Ron took a ballpoint and a credit card receipt out of the glove box. Writing on the back of the receipt against the center of the steering wheel, he repeated, "U.S. Air. Syracuse w/chng in Philly."

"Right. Flight leaves at eleven fifty-four in the morning. Tomorrow you go to the Credit Union and draw nine thousand dollars in cash. No bill higher than a hundred."

"Won't I have to make some kind of a . . . I don't know, a declaration?"

"I don't think so—it's less than ten thousand. If you do, say you're buying a boat or something. Put the cash in an overnight bag with your cell and whatever you want to read on the airplane. You're not going to need a toothbrush. Got all that?"

"Why Syracuse?"

"Got a nice big public parking lot. So has the Philadelphia airport. When we're in the air I'll pick one of them for our conversation. We'll have both gone through security, and so we won't feel . . . you know, *uneasy* with each other. Be sure and have your cell with you."

"What if they open my carry-on? Why am I carrying all that cash?"

"You're going to the Turning Stone Casino. High-stakes Texas Hold 'Em game, and the fellas don't like checks."

As Ron wrote "Turning Stone" he said, "I don't know. Seems complicated. If you've got the price to Syracuse, why don't you just go on home?"

"Come on, man, I told you. Airfare is the little part of my problem. Getting across the border, that's where the money goes. Now, I'll be watching to see that you arrive at Islip around ten forty-five. Leave your car at long-term parking. Long term, got that?"

"Why long term?"

"Because that's a big lot. Good place for me to hang out. Park somewhere I can see you, okay? Keep your cell turned on until you board. If I call you in the departure lounge, don't look around to spot me. If I don't call you then, turn your cell off until they make that announcement about portable devices, and then turn it on again. One way or another, I'll call before we land in Philly and tell you what to do."

Watching a car back out two aisles away on his left, Ron wondered if this parking lot also was a good hangout and if perhaps this guy was watching him now from behind some tinted windows nearby. "Why does this have to be so complicated? Just pick a Seven-Eleven somewhere and I'll meet you tomorrow in the parking lot."

Another smug chuckle in the earpiece. "This *has* to be complicated, my friend. You're a complicated guy. I can't take any chances with you. I've learned that from your loving wife."

Before he could control it, Ron's fist banged the steering wheel. "You're going to tell me what she's got to do with this?"

"Absolutely, Ron. Gonna tell you the whole story. Just gonna cost you nine bills. Little piece of your rainy-day fund. But you also get a bonus award. You also get a CD. Picture of an arsonist walking down Depot Road . . . That is, unless you're afraid to meet an unarmed man in an open parking lot in the middle of the day."

# CHAPTER 28

*CLANG-CLANG-CLANG-CLANG!*

The *New York Times* spilled out of Sam's lap.

"Hear that?" Charley called from outside the locked door.

She said, "What's that, the jail break alarm?" The din stopped and she bent down to gather up the scattered pages.

"That is the voice of a Seth Thomas alarm clock. That's one of our historical artifacts, along with a signed first edition of *The Good Earth.*"

"And why should Seth speak to me?"

"Because this clock was on Countess de Dendermonde's bedside table. Which made it handy." Hammer blows shook the door. What was he doing? "And because when the alarm rings, it unwinds a spring, which turns the little wind-up twister on the back of the clock." More hammer blows. "Did you ever try to buy a handgun in New York? You read all the editorial writers waving their arms about how easy it is—all the weapons coming up from Virginia—but just try it. Unless you've got connections on the street . . ."

He rattled the door. "Now I'm installing a simple drop-latch lock. Then I'll tie a string to an empty thread-spool wedged over the wind-up twister. If the alarm goes off, the twister rotates and the string winds around the spool, which lifts the latch."

"Charley, are you serious? That sounds like a junior high school project."

"This is just for your peace of mind. Tomorrow I'll set the

clock for three-thirty. Long before then Ron will be an inspiration for the Cherokee. You and I, we'll be talking about the end game."

"Let's talk about that now."

"We're not quite ready." More door rattling. "The latch holds. Now I'll put an eye-screw in the ceiling so the string can lift it straight up. What I was saying about hand guns . . . if you don't have a street connection, forget it. But pellet guns . . . you can buy them on the Web. And some of them . . . they look just like . . . the real thing. Like a Beretta. Okay, now I just have to thread the string through there and hook it up."

"Tell me about the end game."

"Well, first I have a date with Ron. Me and my toy gun . . . You know, when The Designer realized that he'd been captured by a toy, that oh-shit! look in his eyes, that was a real rush."

"You were talking about the end game."

More door rattling. "Well, tomorrow I'm going to have that oh-shit! moment with Ron . . . Then you and I, we have a YouTube show to edit. And then we need a YouTube promotion plan and an exit strategy."

"An exit strategy?"

"Just for me. For you, it's a reunion. You and Amy . . . there . . . that should work. I'm going to set the alarm for almost now. Don't worry, I have the end game worked out in my head. Just some details to tie up."

"What kind of details?"

"We'll talk about that tomorrow. Right now, you need to take it easy for another few hours. I know you think that your guy Ron is smart, and dangerous . . ."

"He is. I don't just think so. He really is."

"Okay, I understand. He's a worthy adversary. Otherwise, this wouldn't have any meaning. Because he *is* worthy, I have to recognize the outside chance that—"

*CLANG-CLANG-CLANG-CLANG!*

Longer this time. A scrape. The room seemed to exhale as the door opened and stood ajar. Sam put the paper aside and stood. The clanging stopped.

Charley pulled the door open and stood in the entrance, grinning. "I was a junior high school science ace. Now, just on the outside chance that justice is not served tomorrow, old Seth here will let you out."

# CHAPTER 29

Ron glanced in the mirrors at every intersection on the way home from the mall. No one followed. When he pulled into his garage and closed the door behind him with the remote he took a deep breath. He looked around in the familiar half-darkness.

The milk crate held some cans and half a dozen bottles and jars for recycling. He'd used an empty with a Taylor label that night in Depot Road. What was it? Didn't matter. It had burned up, along with the purple spray can and the butane lighter with the rubber band. Also the gasoline can. In the corner by the track for the garage door was the driveway salt with the box of vinyl gloves on top. The unused butterfly knife was in the street near the old drunk, with no fingerprints through the gloves he'd worn. He'd been so careful.

But shit! Yes, a camera in one of those dark windows . . . that was possible. How could he have anticipated that? No way. And even then, a CD didn't mean anything. Not without Sam. "It's all about you, Ron." God damn that woman!

The garage began to shrink. He got out of the car and went through the connecting door into the kitchen. He took a glass out of the dishwasher and punched ice water from the refrigerator. Something made him look around. The house was silent. The window above the sink framed gray sky with scudding clouds. No camera.

Don't get paranoid.

Upstairs, in the office he'd converted from an extra bedroom, he logged on and Googled his calendar. Realtors Association Legislative Committee at Bon Appétit tonight at seven. He pulled up his phone book, found the number of Dianne Browne, called and told the recording, "Hello Di, this is Ron. I've gotten caught up in a family flap and will have to miss the meeting tonight. Sorry. Di, if this is helpful, I was prepared to weigh in on the curfew proposition. I'd say move the time up to one o'clock. Some bars will lose some business but we'd be better off not attracting all the kids chased out from the rest of the Island after last call. Talk to you later."

Then he fished the credit card receipt out of his pocket and smoothed it on the desk. "US Air . . . Syracuse w/chng in Philly . . . 11:54 . . . $9K . . . Turning Stone." He leaned back in his ergonomic chair. The guy had said something about going through security and feeling okay with each other. Meaning they'd both know they weren't armed. Screw that.

What would get through security? Unless Islip had installed one of those undressing machines since he'd last flown out of there, security meant walking through a metal detector and sending the carry-on through an X-ray scanner. So he had one day to make a weapon that wouldn't set off a metal detector or show on an X-ray. Probably impossible. But start with something plastic or wood to go through the metal detector, then figure out how to make it look innocuous in an X-ray scan.

Maybe a crossbow.

He punched his PC on. While it was booting up he called Timothy's Pizza on Little Neck and ordered a sausage, pepper and onion. Google listed pages of crossbow information, most of it describing modern hunting equipment with rifle mounts and telescopic sights. The Wikipedia drawings of medieval bows were too complicated for a one-day project, and probably too bulky to conceal even if he could build one.

When the doorbell chimed he went down for his pizza, thinking about how to define a search for what he needed. Plastic or wood, something to pass through x-ray and be concealed from the guy he would be meeting on the plane. As he tipped the delivery kid two bucks—Sam always said he undertipped, which took his thoughts back to Sam. She was the problem. Pedro and this new guy, they were just bouncing around out there without Sam. She tied it all up into a problem. Bitch.

Thinking about Sam on the way back up to his office with the pizza reminded him of her stupid bird feeder and his slingshot. Maybe some kind of a slingshot. Wooden, to go through everything. He could keep the rubber pulls in his pocket and then assemble the slingshot in the airplane lavatory. For ammo, do they still sell glass marbles at toy stores? If not, driveway gravel would work. He'd only need a couple.

Back at his desk with a slice in one hand and a bite in his mouth, he Googled "slingshot" with his free hand. Scrolling through the pictures of tubular steel frames and wrist-brace designs, he noticed that even the high-tech models with lead buckshot seemed limited to small game. Not what he had in mind. Maybe a head shot at close range would work, but how could he be sure of that?

Scrolling down he found "Slingshot to hunt big game." He clicked on a YouTube video that provided a view over the shoulder of a brush-cut guy in camouflage. As a four-point buck stepped into frame, the voiceover, hushed as if not to spook the deer, said, "At ten yards, a cedar arrow with a hunting head will drop a deer as fast as a thirty-ought-six."

If he had an arrow, he wouldn't need a head shot.

At the bottom of the article was a list of hot links:

Hawaiian sling

Polespear

Stone bow

He clicked on "Hawaiian sling," which turned out to be a spear-fishing weapon like a cross between a slingshot and a bow and arrow. Rubber tubing was attached to a wooden handle. Hook an arrow onto the tubing, pull it back, aim and let it go.

As he munched another slice he studied the article. Simple wooden parts. He could make an arrow out of a dowel pin. The guy said ten yards was close enough for an arrow to bring down a deer. His arrow wouldn't have a steel head, although maybe he could think of something. If not, just a sharp wooden point would probably do. He'd surely be closer than ten yards. But how about the rubber tubing? That was critical.

He Googled "Huntington, New York, fishing equipment" and up came eight listings. Three of them listed "spearfishing guns." Tomorrow he could surely find one with the kind of rubber tubing he could cannibalize for his Hawaiian sling. Maybe some other components too.

"An unarmed man," the guy had said. In an open parking lot in the middle of the day. The smug son of a bitch. He was in for a surprise. But Sam, she's the wild card. When he dealt with the guy he'd have to find out how she played into all this.

Thinking about the confrontation seemed to suck the air out of this little room. He shut down the computer, closed the box on the remains of his pizza, turned off the puddle of light on his desk and took the pizza box downstairs. Rain rattled the kitchen window as he stuck the box into the refrigerator, and so he grabbed a jacket from the front closet. Out in the open he could relax, walk his gold card to Starbucks for a grande and breathe the misting rain while he thought through all the things he had to do tomorrow.

★ ★ ★ ★ ★

# Day Four of Captivity

★ ★ ★ ★ ★

I wonder if I've been changed in the night? Let me think. Was I the same when I got up this morning? I almost think I can remember feeling a little different. But if I'm not the same, the next question is "Who in the world *am I*?" Ah, that's the great puzzle!

—Lewis Carroll, *Alice in Wonderland*

# Chapter 30

Sam stared at the brass funnel in the ceiling. She knew Charley was out of the house. "Going to find another real-looking pellet gun," he'd said. "And then something different for lunch." She'd felt, rather than heard, the heavy front door slam. But that brass ear seemed to be still listening, even to her thoughts.

Faintly, through thick masonry, she heard something. She climbed onto the bed and leaned close to the wall below the drawing of Alice dancing with a weeping tortoise. Holding her breath, she listened. A bird. Somewhere outside, in a world with a real sun, a mockingbird practiced his repertoire. She imagined leaf shadows and an occasional breeze bringing scents of turned earth and the tickle of ragweed. How many songs was the mockingbird imitating? He slid in and out of refrains—or melodies?—so smoothly that she lost count. What time was it? Was he singing to a setting sun in a billow of saffron cloud? How long had Charley been gone? Did she miss him?

That idea startled her. But yes, in this isolation even the jailer was welcome. Was that all? Just a break in the monotony? No, she had to admit. Just thinking of him gave her a little buzz. Did that make her a slut? She smiled at the thought. Ron had told her she carried a whole convent-load of inhibitions, and even after Amy was born he'd called her "Mother Superior." So maybe Charley had activated her inner slut. So what? Maybe that wasn't all bad.

She'd been closed up here now, how many days? Three? Four?

Days that spilled into each other with no boundaries and no change. But actually, there *had* been change. This prison cell, with its pathetic sunshine rug, had shrunk. And those pictures, Alice dancing with the weeping tortoise and the white rabbit in formalwear, were nightmare images now. The disappearing Cheshire cat watched in the same way that the copper ear in the ceiling listened. Crowding her, like the walls.

She stood and went into the little bathroom to study her face in the mirror.

Who was that haggard woman with the stringy hair and the gray pallor? And those scared eyes? They seemed to be peering into . . . what? She scrubbed her face, tied her hair into a ponytail and went back to the chair.

Was she actually becoming an accomplice to murder? No question about that. The murder of a man who had given her black despair, but had also given her singing joy. But a man she had never known, even in those singing times. What had there been about Ron that had drawn her to him? He wasn't one of those moody, vulnerable guys that women want to mother. Not vulnerable at all. Armor plated, in fact. Always in control. He walked with that hint of a swagger, head tilted and one arm swinging. Cool. His characteristic expression was a half smile, and he seemed to look at everything through binoculars. Seeing things up close, observing every detail, but from far away.

Once, trying some pillow talk to prolong an intimate moment, she'd asked him to remember his happiest time. He turned onto his back with his hands behind his head and thought about the question, but what he remembered was a time when he was very young and his father locked him in the car. It was probably only five minutes or so while his father went into a drug store for cigarettes, but at that age it seemed a long time. Thinking about it that night, he closed his eyes and shook his head on the pillow. She said that it must have been terrifyingly long, but he didn't answer.

She'd persisted: that was a bad memory; what about a happy one? She'd hoped he might think of some moment they'd had together, but instead he came up with a time when he was in the fifth grade. (Why was his childhood was so much with him?) One of Ron's classmates—"His prissy name was Arthur"— didn't show off in class, rarely raised his hand, but when the teacher called on him he always had the answer. The girls giggled when he walked by. On the softball field, even when he made an out it was always a deep fly to centerfield.

Arthur had a wooden pencil box. All the other guys carried their pencils loose, or maybe in some plastic gizmo, but he had a wooden box that was painted, or maybe even inlaid. Probably the loving gift of an aunt, or maybe his grampa.

The guys found little ringneck snakes in the weeds alongside the railroad tracks behind the soccer field. They smuggled the little dry wigglers into school in their pants pockets and played with them under the desks when the teacher was at the blackboard. One day Ron slipped a ringneck into Arthur's fancy pencil box. When Arthur opened the box in social studies the snake slithered out and across his wrist. He screamed and ran to the door. All the guys got a great laugh. Arthur was scared of snakes. Somehow, Ron had managed to hit him right where it hurt.

Staring into the night, Ron had laughed out loud at the thought.

Trying to go along with him, Sam had said, "You must have been a playground hero that day."

Ron shook his head and, still not looking at her, said, "Oh, I didn't tell anybody. All the guys were talking about it, of course, but I never let on. If everybody knew, that would spoil it."

"Spoil it? Spoil what?"

Ron stared into the dark, thinking about that. "Don't you

understand? I'd found the . . . the key to him. His combination." He turned to face her. "I didn't need anybody else."

Maybe it was that night when she gave up trying to understand her husband.

Now she looked away from the staring face in the mirror and went back to the chair, wondering how she had gotten to this point. The big seduction, that was part of it, no question. Getting Charley into that little bed had been supposed to put her in control. Had she really thought that? Sam could hear Cassie's analytic, social-worker voice, saying "Grow up, Sam. You never believed that. You've gone from your father to Ron and now to this guy. One controlling man after another. You tell yourself you're trying to take charge, but what you're actually doing is reinforcing his upper hand. Deep down, isn't that what you've wanted all along?"

She stood and walked the circuit of her cell, six paces long and four wide. Twenty paces around, back to the bed, where she had listened to the mockingbird. And where she had discovered her inner slut. But now she and Charley were planning Amy's father's murder. Step by practical step, as if it were a fundraiser.

When she got to the chair she sat down and closed her eyes to shut out the four-wall limits. Charley kept trying to sell the idea that they were cooperating for a grand cause. Was she beginning to buy that? Okay, she was cooperating, no denying that. Did that mean she had bought the proposition?

Face it, Charley's crazy. Those gentle hands that had caressed her breasts and belly were the same hands that cut the throat on camera. If he succeeds in murdering Ron, if he could possibly succeed . . .

And he could. When she'd dangled the bait, Ron had taken it. That possibility had never taken form in her mind until now. Ron was so much brighter, so much more competent, more *practical* than this . . . this beautiful dreamer. But it could happen.

And if it did happen, then she wouldn't be a partner. She'd be in the way.

She looked up at the brass horn in the ceiling. He'd conned her from the get-go. Charley was more Internet savvy than he claimed. Hadn't she always realized that? Okay, at least suspected it. He didn't really need her to put something on YouTube. Any computer klutz can do that. Millions do. What he needed her for was to hook Ron. Which, maybe, he had done, with her help. She was going to have to live with that.

If she had any more life to live.

It was possible that she was never going to get out of this room. Entirely possible. Likely, even. She considered that idea for the first time. Held it at arm's length and examined it, as if she were considering a site for an event. What difference did it make, either way?

She remembered the miracle in the hospital bed: ten perfect tiny fingers, each with its perfect little pink fingernail. Those little hands discovering the touch of her breast. That surprisingly aggressive little mouth on her nipple. Those first stumbling steps. And "George." She didn't know a George, were certain Amy had never heard the name, but "George" was her first word. Not just spoken once but a riff that she repeated for days. Later in the park, waiting for Amy to examine the veins of an oak leaf and the creeping progress of a ladybug across the path and then the texture of lichen on a boulder.

Sam closed her eyes and took a breath to stop the memories crowding into her mind. Getting out of here was important. No more missed opportunities.

She stood and began to walk the perimeter again. Charley's crazy idea was that he was history's man. Settling an old score. Making himself a hero. And, it occurred to her now, Ron was his own man. Only that. Not a thought for anyone else. What did that mean for her? Those scared eyes in the mirror knew the answer to that.

As she walked around the tight little room she began looking under the bed and the chair and into the corners. She remembered swinging the pantyhose blackjack at Charley. Letting up at the last instant, but still bringing him to his knees. The trolley capsizing, dishes crashing. What had she done with the blackjack? It was nowhere in sight. Had he taken it? She dropped onto her knees—not under the bed. As she stood she saw it—under the bagel in the wastebasket.

"No," Sam said out loud to Cassie. Deep down, another controlling man is *not* what she's wanted all along. Maybe the inner slut needed him, but the slut's not in charge now. She fished out the blackjack and swung it—*thwack!*—against the mattress. Then she draped it back over the towel bar in the bathroom.

★ ★ ★ ★ ★

# Day Five of Captivity

★ ★ ★ ★ ★

Who controls the past controls the future. Who controls the present controls the past.

—George Orwell

# CHAPTER 31

When Ron slowed to navigate dead-man's curve next to the marina, he lost his train of thought. This damn 25A. Just asphalt laid down over the wagon tracks the British made on the way to Fort Salonga. Since then dozens—shit, probably hundreds—of mayors and commissioners of all these little burgs have preserved all these kinks and turns to protect the owners of the cookie-cutter ranches and splits built where the road ought to go.

He shook his head to bring himself back to the problem. What the Scuba Shop called a Hawaiian sling and sold for thirty-nine bucks was just a slingshot without a fork. A piece of hardwood shaped for a grip with a loop of surgical tubing secured to the end. In the middle of the loop was a little socket for the end of a spear. So now he didn't have to make something from scratch, but the thing was designed to shoot a spear, which meant the tubing was too long for the dart he had in mind. He needed to shorten the tubing but still keep the socket in the center. When he got home he'd examine how the tubing was secured to the end of the wood. Probably easy enough to unfasten it, cut a piece off both ends and then hook it back up.

On the way he'd stop at the lumber yard and get an eighth-inch dowel for the dart. Easy to whittle one end to fit into the spear socket in the tubing. How to make a point? Plastic, maybe, but think about first things first. The Hawaiian sling wouldn't set off a metal detector. But how could he be sure they hadn't installed one of those stand-up machines that undressed you?

The last time he'd flown out of Islip he'd just walked through a metal detector, but that was when? Maybe four months ago. Phone call? Might be able to think of a story . . . "I'm in a wheelchair and need to know what kind of security . . ." No. That might just open a file on his call. The only sure way to know would be to drive out there and check. He glanced at his watch: eleven fourteen. No time. Everything had to be ready and tested today. And besides, the sling was a little bulky for a pocket. Better packed in the carry-on, but then it would show on the X-ray.

He slapped the steering wheel when an answer came. He'd have to take tubing off the sling to shorten it. He could wait to put it back after he got through security. He nodded as the idea took shape. When he got home, he'd break the lock on his bag and use the tubing like a bungee to hold it closed. Perfect. Then the handle and dowel can go inside, and no rent-a-cop would associate them with what looks like a bungee holding his carry-on shut. And even if someone did ask about the pieces of wood, he could think of something. A toy he was making for a nephew, or a gadget he was designing to keep the lid of his barbecue propped open while he was smoking fish.

As he went over the mill dam in Centerport he said under his breath, " 'Carpe diem.' Seize the day. It never comes around again."

★ ★ ★ ★ ★

# DAY SIX OF CAPTIVITY

★ ★ ★ ★ ★

What matters is not the idea a man holds, but the depth at which he holds it.

—Ezra Pound

# CHAPTER 32

Ron didn't cruise the long-term parking lot, just pulled into the first open slot, which was way the hell out in left field. He kept forgetting that Islip no longer served just short-haul passengers, but he'd allowed extra time. He locked the car with the remote and, carrying his sausage bag that was tied with the rubber tubing, he walked toward the control tower, not glancing into any of the cars he passed. The guy was probably a hundred yards away somewhere, maybe in the terminal, watching with binoculars. He thought about a little gesture, maybe a "hi there" wave, but decided against it. Stick with the script.

Inside, he couldn't resist a quick look around. Suits with briefcases, a mom with a fold-up stroller, a young clinging couple. How about that dark guy in the denim jacket sitting alone in the food court? No, this was just what he'd told himself not to do. Don't look for a greaser. Guy could look like Mr. Suburb. Could even be in disguise. Anyway, he's not going to be obviously hanging around. Stick with the script.

Just as he'd expected, he only had to walk through metal detectors. Loafers and jacket with the wooden dart in the sleeve went in the tray, along with his pocket stuff, including the ball-point with the sharpened nail. They all went through the X-ray tunnel ahead of the carry-on with hardly a pause. On the way to the gate he stopped at the men's, waited at the urinal to be sure no one had followed him and then locked himself into a stall. When he released the tubing around his carry-on, it gaped

231

open a little, but the other lock held it enough to carry. He found the Hawaiian sling handle, snapped the tubing back onto it and tested the pull. Stiff, but when the time came he'd be powered with adrenalin.

As he groped in the bag past the money in manila envelopes to find the Wallace Enterprises ballpoint pen, he heard two guys come into the men's room. With the pen in his hand, Ron paused to listen: ". . . the Meadowlands? So why aren't they the New *Jersey* Giants for Christ sake? Or how about the New Jersey *Jets*?" Ron unscrewed the barrel of the pen. Where the ink cartridge had been, he had substituted a finishing nail with the head filed down to a point. "Sounds kinda down-market, right?" the guy was saying. "Which we know is exactly the problem." Careful not to drop it, Ron slid the nail out and tested both ends against his thumb. "But that's the fact of the matter, right? I mean, you're going to play it, then say it." Ron felt nothing, but the sharpened point produced a drop of blood.

He fished the dowel out of his bag and had just jammed the nail into the hole he'd drilled in the end when his cell pinged. He pushed the door open to make sure the two guys had gone before he answered.

"You at the airport yet?" the voice on the phone said.

Ron started to say, "You know damn well I am" but decided to stick to the script and answered, "Yeah. Just went through security."

"Got the money?"

"In my hand."

"Hang onto it. There's a change of plan. Something's come up. I'll contact you tomorrow."

"What do you mean, tomorrow? I've got my ticket and—"

"What I mean is, stand by for a call tomorrow." Click.

He stared at the dead phone. Bullshit. This is no change of plan, this *is* the plan. Use the airport metal detector as a pat-down, make sure I don't have a weapon. Sure as hell the guy's waiting somewhere. Probably in the long-term lot.

Smart thing to do would be to leave the car and grab a cab home. Come back tonight for the car. But what if the guy didn't call? Probably mean that there wasn't anything *to* this. No CD, nothing. But what was Sam up to? Something was going on. Only way to find out is to stick to the script.

Ron threaded the dowel up his sleeve and poked the sharpened nail into the lining at the cuff. He flexed his arm to be sure it stayed in place. The sling slipped into the inside jacket pocket. Not even a bulge as long as he didn't button the jacket.

As he walked through the terminal he looked around. No one seemed to pay any attention to him. Outside, he paused at the taxi line. Last chance to play it safe. He touched the lump of the sling through his jacket pocket and walked across the street toward the long-term lot, savoring the little bounce in his step. What Uncle Apple had called his testosterone strut.

He was just one aisle away from his VW when he heard, "Just keep walking."

He looked over his shoulder. A little guy, black hair down to his shoulders like fairy Alan's, back in Custis. But this guy was holding a blue-barreled nine millimeter. "Shit," Ron said, waving a gesture with his free hand. "I knew it. I should have taken a cab."

"But that would have taken all the sport out of it, right?" the guy said.

Ron craned another glance over his shoulder. Guy was dark, with that kind of flat, Mex-looking face. He said, "When we get to your car, put your carry-on in the back seat and get in front."

Ron raised the carry-on. "The money's right here. Give me the CD and we have a deal, okay?"

"First we go for a ride."

"You said the parking lot. Do the deal out in the open, in the parking lot." Guy was wearing a yellow cotton sweater with the sleeves pulled up to his elbows and pre-faded jeans that looked like they'd been pressed. What kind of guy wears pressed jeans?

"I lied. Here we are." The guy stopped about five feet away from Ron's Jetta. "This would be easier if you had a four-door. Put the bag in back and get behind the wheel."

Ron tossed the carry-on into the back and slid into the driver's seat.

"Now lean all the way forward. Right up against the wheel. Put your hands on the top of the dash. Now reach your left hand down and release the catch on your seat back." Ron felt it snap forward against his shoulders.

"Good. Both hands on the dash now." The guy shoved the seat back tight against Ron as he climbed into the back seat. "Okay, now you can sit back again. Remember that pretty pistol I showed you? It's pointed at your seat back, just about the middle, where your heart and lungs are. Remember?"

"I remember," Ron said into the rearview mirror. Guy's face was smooth as a girl's. Maybe a little beard shadow on his chin and upper lip. But he handled that nine like he knew how to use it.

"So let's go. Get back on Vets Highway. Take it all the way to the Sunken Meadow. Then I'll tell you the turns to make."

Backing out, Ron asked, "Is Sam going to be waiting for us?"

"Sam will be there. You miss her?"

Ron managed a laugh. "I sure do. Like a case of poison ivy." He swung out of the airport north onto Macarthur Boulevard. "You've got the money in that bag. Check it out."

After a while the guy said, "Looks like it's all there. Thanks a lot."

"Any time. Now where's this CD you told me about?"

The guy had a fairyland giggle. "You didn't believe that, did you?"

"Not really. But when you put Sam on . . . I kinda had to know what she's up to."

"When you get on Vets just hold it at sixty. Along the way I have a little history lesson for you."

"History?"

"You ever hear of the Trail of Tears, Ron?"

# CHAPTER 33

Cruising along Vet's, the guy talked about the Cherokee, their early treaties with the English and then the Americans. "Cherokee never broke a treaty," he said, "and the whites never kept one." Ron listened the way he listened to talk radio in the car, keeping it in the background while he was inside his own thoughts. Guy's not about to shoot while we're doing sixty and my hand's on the wheel. How do I get an edge?

While the guy talked about honor and values and responsibility to the clan, something about a network of obligations and collective identity, Ron was trying to remember if he'd passed a police station on the way to the airport. The only one he could think of was way the hell over on Deer Park Road. And even if he got to it and pulled into the parking lot, the guy wouldn't just let him get out and walk inside. Fire station might be better. He called up a mental picture of the one in Centerport. Maybe he could swerve in and crash through those big doors . . . but then what? Didn't matter. They probably weren't going past there anyway.

Sunken Meadow Parkway had grassy shoulders sloping up to oak and maple thickets. As the guy was talking about whites finding gold along the creeks in the land of the Cherokee—he called them the Principal People, which made Ron think of a bunch of school principals, which reminded him of Uncle Apple back in Custis—Ron was thinking about slowing down and then jerking the car into a stand of saplings. There would be a hell of a lot of bumping and crashing and he could maybe get out and away before the guy realized what was happening. But get away where? Play hide and seek with a nutcase Indian and his nine millimeter?

They drove all the way to the end of Sunken Meadow with the guy talking about Jackson selling out the Principal People and soldiers rounding them up into stockades. The guy told him to take the exit west on 25A and then started talking about some kind of a long march to Oklahoma with a couple of thousand graves along the way. Ron's hands were getting slick on the wheel. Fort Salonga's maybe five minutes ahead, and then Northport, he thought. After that, Huntington. Wherever we're going, we're getting there.

The guy prattled on about Sequoyah and a written language and a newspaper and a legislature—who gives a shit?—as an unfamiliar bubble grew in Ron's chest. Acid taste. Fear. He'd been cocky. Put himself into a situation he couldn't control.

He took his right hand off the wheel to locate the dart in his left sleeve as he swallowed the bubble. Just a little edge, that's all he needed. Don't panic into something stupid.

The guy turned them down Little Neck Road talking about a firing squad, but now Ron was not even paying background attention. When they turned at those two stumpy pillars Ron knew where he was: a big old down-at-the-heels north shore mansion. Wasn't the place standing empty? As he pulled up the drive he recognized Sam's Camry in front of the garage. "Okay," the guy said, "you remember the drill. Lean all the way forward, release the seat catch and put your hands on the dashboard."

As the guy climbed past the seatback that he pressed against Ron's shoulders, Ron slipped his hand into his jacket. Sling was there, loose and ready.

When they were out of the car, the guy covering him with the nine from four or five feet away, Ron swallowed the fear bubble and nudged the sling with his elbow to make sure it was still handy. "We're almost there now," the guy said. "See that path going down the hill?" As they walked past a big pile of what looked like hedge trimmings the guy started talking about Redbird Smith and some guy named Hogshooter.

"Hogshooter?" Ron said, trying to get the guy to lighten up. Anything to change the tempo. "That a family name?"

"Like yours is Langshan. Difference is, Hogshooter is an honorable name. He and Redbird Smith went to Washington, but President Wilson rebuffed them." Ron caught a glimpse of water through the trees. He flashed a mental image of diving off a high bank and swimming under water until he was out of pistol range. Forget it. Movie idea.

"After that," the guy was saying, "the Principal People discovered their clans again. They restarted the ceremonial fires and the sacrifices and the stomp dances. It was a time of rebirth."

"That what you're up to?" Ron said. Keep him talking. Find some way to distract him, just long enough. Passing an unruly stand of bamboo, Ron thought he heard some kind of a moan, as if these old people were still hanging around.

"Something like that," the guy said, hanging back a little farther as the trail grew steeper. Ron could see an overgrown little house with a porch perched on stilts. As he went down, skidding a little on matted oak leaves, he could see water between the roof posts and then, past a fleet of boats swinging at mooring buoys, he recognized the municipal pier of Northport Harbor.

"Here we are," the guy said. He gestured toward the porch with the gun barrel. "This is the studio."

"Studio?" Ron repeated, stepping onto the porch and looking around. A narrow, gravelly beach below, a line of wrack left by high tide and patches of spartina marking mussel beds. With his back to the guy, Ron shook the dart down his sleeve until he felt the sharpened nail cupped in his left hand.

When Ron turned around the guy had followed him onto the porch, still keeping his distance. To change the tempo, stop dancing to the guy's tune, he said, "You remind me of a kid I knew in prep school. His name was Alan." Ron twisted his shoulders in a mincing, feminine gesture. "All the guys bullied him."

The eyes in that dark face widened momentarily. Got to him. Ron pressed: "This your way of getting even? Proving you can be one of the guys?"

"I told you. This *is* getting even. For my clansman on the Trail of Tears."

"You're really working at that idea, aren't you? Trying to sell yourself that you're this big man doing this big thing for other people. But you know better, don't you? It's men, isn't it? Men make you uncomfortable, don't they, fellow?"

The guy raised the nine millimeter to point at the raftered ceiling, as if inviting Ron to make a move. "You're making this easy, *fellow*. You're beginning to annoy me. But don't worry about which side of the plate I bat from. You could ask your wife about that."

Ron tried to make his laugh unforced. Keeping this going, he said, "I've been wondering about that. You have our girl up there somewhere in the big house?"

"She's up there. But down here, this is where the action is." He pointed upward, drawing Ron's eyes to a red light under the eaves. "Are you ready for your close-up, Ron?"

Ron asked, "What is that, some kind of a camera? Those spiffy pressed jeans of yours, is this all about some kind of a show?"

"This is all about your big moment. Maybe the first thing you've ever done for someone else. All the Cherokee are going to know you, Ron. Just like they know Sequoyah."

"That's some kind of a tree, isn't it?"

He laughed. "Yes, it's a tree. A great, beautiful tree named after a great man. Nobody would ever call you a great man, Ron, but you're going to be famous. The star of the show. So stand tall and show the camera your best side."

Still holding the nine millimeter up as if to shoot out the ceiling, the guy side-stepped over to the wall. "The whole Cherokee nation is going to know you, Ron." He bent down and picked up some kind of a leather pouch from under the window. "They're going to know you as the Langshan who gave in to a toy." He held out the gun. "It's a toy, Ron." He tossed it to Ron, "Just a pellet gun."

Ron took an involuntary step back to catch it as the guy thrust his hand into the pouch. Looking up at the camera, the guy announced, "This is justice time for Ronald Langshan." He drew out a heavy, homemade-looking knife.

In a disconnected adrenalin flash, Ron thought of the butterfly knife he'd tossed into the street the night of the fire. He stared at the gun he was holding in both hands against his stomach. Looked lethal. He squeezed the trigger twice—just puny clicks—and tossed it against the wall. Guy wanted him to feel foolish. Gesturing toward the knife in the guy's hand: "That's a fake too?" Keep him talking, keep his distance. He gripped the dart with the nail between his first and second fingers but left it in his sleeve. Open up just a little more distance.

The guy hefted the knife loosely, as if weighing it. "No. This is tradition. Its edge was ground by a blacksmith. A craftsman, like Sequoyah. It came down to me from the time when you Langshans created this moment. Created this obligation."

Ron spread his jacket open on the way to a "hands-up" gesture. "You think that blade is big enough to go against my bare hands? That your idea of fair?"

"You still don't get it, do you? I explained all that, Ron Lang-shan. For once, this isn't just about you. This is about something bigger than another self-centered Langshan." He tossed the knife to his left hand and took a half-step forward. He wasn't going to give up any more distance.

Ron stepped back again and slipped his right hand into the front of his jacket and gathered the tubing around the sling before he drew it out. "It's really all about making you into a big man, isn't it?" Still seeing everything from that super-charged distance, he watched the guy's answering step as if from the eye of the camera in the eaves: a slow dance. The guy thought *he* was leading.

The guy tossed the knife back to his right hand without look-ing. A demonstration. "No, it's about evil genes. The sins of the fathers going down to the seventh generation."

"This is really about the buzz, isn't it?" Watching the guy, so caught up in his big act that he didn't even notice that Ron was sliding the dart out of his left sleeve and fitting it onto the tub-ing. "You and I, we know about life on the edge. Like this, right now. That's really why you brought me here, isn't it?"

The guy was so in love with the lines he'd memorized that he just kept reciting: "For thousands of years people have understood how this works. Now your time has come."

He swiped the knife toward Ron's belly. Easy to avoid. Just a step in the dance for the camera. The guy took his own step, but his eyes widened when Ron extended his left arm with the sling and drew back the rubber tubing. "Actually," Ron said, "it's your time. Smile for the camera."

The guy stared, rooted with surprise. Ron had time to aim, holding the tubing under his chin with the sharpened nail head of the dart almost on his thumb knuckle. The release sounded like an exhaled breath.

The guy just stood there. No expression. For a moment Ron thought he'd somehow missed, but then the point of that big knife wavered, sagged, and the knife clattered onto the deck. Slowly, the guy looked down, and then Ron saw what looked like a pencil stub sticking out of his shirt.

The guy raised both hands to the dart as if to pull it out. He took a step back and then another before his right knee buckled. Still looking at the end of the dart he toppled onto his right side. A driblet of blood sprouted from the corner of his mouth and ran down his cheek. His hands still cupped the end of the dart and his right foot scraped, searching for a purchase on the planks.

Ron stepped forward and picked up the knife with his right hand. He reached down and grabbed a handful of that black fairyland hair. "You want to talk about history?" He lifted and the guy's searching foot gave it up. "What you just learned—it's written by the winners." He put the blade on the stretched throat. "And you're a loser."

The guy actually smiled. "No," he said. "I believe."

"Believe what?" Ron leaned forward, trying to see into the black eyes, but they looked past him, at something over his head. "Doesn't matter. You don't matter. Never did. Just another speck of protoplasm trying to make itself the center of the universe."

Ron drew the heavy blade across the stretched throat. Blood spurted, gushed and then pulsed onto the deck. He stepped back, but not before it soaked the left leg of his khakis. He remembered the homeless man on the curb that night of the fire. Lots of blood, just as he thought.

The camera under the eaves. Ron realized that when the guy had felt the blade on his throat, he'd looked up at the camera. Still into that crazy game. Standing on tiptoe, Ron could just reach the camera with the knife. After half a dozen whacks the camera broke out of the brackets and spilled a disc onto the deck. Ron sailed the disc into the harbor. "There goes your immortality, man of destiny. Memento mori." He threw the camera after it. Turning back, he noticed the toy nine millimeter against the wall. Looked real, but when he picked it up it was obviously plastic. Guy had been cute. Captured him with a toy. But the last surprise is the one that counts. When he tossed the toy into the harbor it bobbed up and drifted into the spartina along the water's edge.

He stretched the tubing, shot the Hawaiian sling far out and watched the tide catch it. He considered the knife, thinking about what he had to do next. Knife might still come in handy. The guy was still twitching and seeping. He sure had a lot of blood.

On his way to the house past the bedraggled rose garden, Ron remembered the carry-on with the cash. The guy must have left it in the car to keep his hands free. Thoughtful of him. Now it was there waiting. Ron listened in his mind to the guy's last words. "I believe."

"So do I," Ron said as he climbed the hill past the weedy roses. "I believe in me."

# CHAPTER 34

"Helloooo Sam!"

She jumped out of the chair and stood in the middle of the room, fists clenched and training her head left and right like an antenna, trying to locate the sound of his voice.

"Reunion time, Sam." Coming closer. Thump. Footsteps overhead. The kitchen.

"I know you're in here, Sam. I saw your car outside in the driveway. You and your terrorist boyfriend, you were ready for a quick getaway?"

In the driveway? Charley must have moved it. What happened to Charley?

A door opened. Back stairs. She caught her breath. More footsteps. Walking back across the kitchen. Must have seen the door to the back steps. Didn't come down here. Doesn't like basements. Did he leave the door standing open?

"Let's not play games, Sam." His voice was fainter. Going upstairs? "You know I'm not going to leave until I find you." She looked up at the brass horn in the ceiling. If he was searching the bedroom, would she hear him down the tube? Charley must have brought him here. How else could he find the place? So the connection at the airport, that must have worked. But then . . . she could think of only one possibility.

"Your friend and I came to an understanding, Sam." Voice still distant. "Met at the airport and talked about what he needed. Turns out I just had to look into that camera he's got down there in the boat house and say what a shitty deal the Cherokee got." Closer again. Coming back downstairs. "Now he's got the disc to show the people back home, and he's on his way to his next gig. Told me to come up here and explain things to you."

Deep breaths. Keep grounded. She stared at the Queen of Hearts, glowering from the wall.

"Your friend, he said you and I can come to an understanding too. He gave me a message for you. Don't you want to hear it, Sam?"

If he came in here he wouldn't be pushing a cart like Charley had been. He'd probably stand in the hall, shove the door wide open and look around first.

"I guess you could be hiding out in the woods somewhere."

YES! She almost said it out loud. Lots of places to hide out there. Go check out that boxwood labyrinth.

"Doesn't seem likely. Why would you hide when your car is right there in the driveway?"

Not right overhead in the kitchen. Maybe in that dark room with all the bearded guys in the gilt frames.

"I think you're here somewhere. Within the sound of my beloved voice."

A scrape across the floor. He moved a chair? He's sitting down?

"This old house doesn't have many closets to hide in, but it has a lot of rooms. If you make me find you, Sam, I'm going to be pissed. We'd both be better off if you just come out now so we can have a little talk."

Floorboard creak. Walking around, looking?

"Is this hide and seek, Sam? Like you used to play with Amy? Look, Sam, I know that Amy's your hangup. Your idea about me is all wrong, but never mind. Let's talk about what you want. If supervised visitation has to be the deal, well, I could accept that. So just come out and let's talk."

Long silence. Maybe he's out in the foyer where his steps wouldn't sound on the terrazzo.

"Come on, Sam, let's be grownups." Closer now. "I'm going to find you, so let's not play games."

Back in the kitchen?

"You wouldn't try to sneak out on me, would you Sam? Make a run for it? I guess what I have to do is figure out how to search the rooms and still keep an eye on the doors."

Not down here. No way to see the doors from down here. Please God, or Charley's Nunnehi or anybody else up there who's listening: please don't let him come down here.

"Maybe I can lock the doors from the inside. I suppose you could—"

*CLANG-CLANG-CLANG-CLANG!*

Without consciously moving she found herself crouched in the corner, staring around with trapped-animal eyes. The clamor was everywhere. She raised her hands to her ears. Then she remembered: Seth. The alarm clock. Charley's time lock. She heard the latch scrape as it lifted. The door exhaled open and drifted ajar.

Knees wobbling, she stood and stumbled to the door. Peered out. Dark hall, with a rectangle of light spilling down the steps at the far end. The *CLANG-CLANG-CLANG-CLANG!* bounced around the bare walls like an echo chamber. A rickety end table outside the door. She edged out as if onto quicksand, grabbed the clock off the table and snapped the twine running up to some kind of an eye-screw in the ceiling as she jammed the alarm button down.

Sudden silence, as loud as the alarm had been.

"Is that you, Sam? Your alarm clock? You just waking up down there?"

Four doors along the hall, all closed. What had Charley said?

Closets. And one for something else, she couldn't remember what. Footsteps. She saw his feet coming down the steps at the end of the hall. Without thinking she backed into her cell— familiar territory—and pulled the door closed.

"If you've set off some kind of an alarm to draw me down here while you get away . . ."

So this is it. In a moment he'd kick open the door. Check out the room and then step inside. He'd expect her to be scared and helpless. Stepping carefully, as if he might hear her, she went into the bathroom.

"These doors seem to be locked. You wouldn't have a key, would you Sam?"

There it was. The pantyhose was stretched, but the lump of lead was still in the toe. She wadded up a grip and let the rest trail behind as she went back into the bedroom.

"Furnace room is open. You couldn't climb up that coal chute, could you? Maybe, but I doubt it."

She looked up at the light bulb in the ceiling. Unscrew it? No time. Hide behind the door? No. Face him. She planted her feet on the sun in the rag rug with her hands behind her, pantyhose puddling out of the way at her feet. She thought of Charley discovering the skull of the raccoon or whatever it was. A shot of calm that makes you into something different.

Something scraped outside the door. "What's this little antique table doing down here in the basement? And what's— oh, I see. This must be the alarm clock I heard . . . Light's coming from under the door, Sam. Game's up. You going to come out so we can talk?"

She actually felt a smile. He didn't want to come into this claustrophobic little room.

"You going to make me come in after you?"

She hefted the pantyhose behind her, testing the stretch.

*CRASH!*

The door slammed open against the wall. He was a murky silhouette in the dark hall until he stepped into the doorframe. She recognized that cool smile, and then she saw the bloody khakis—and the big knife.

"Oh Ron, what have you done?"

"Me? I've been dealing with a terrorist. But Sam, what"—as she swung the pantyhose his eyes widened—"have you—?" raising his left arm. But too late. The weighted toe crunched into his temple. His eyes rolled up and he buckled onto his knees and then into a fetal lump. The knife bounced on the rag rug and clattered into the corner.

She took time for a calm look around the little room. When she tossed the pantyhose blackjack back onto the bed she considered taking one of the lead soldiers as a memento. Instead, she nodded to the Queen of Hearts. Still moving in slow motion, she stepped over Ron's bloody leg and through the door. In the hall she pushed the door closed, dropped the latch into its socket and checked to be sure it held. Then, thinking of Amy, she began to hurry toward the light spilling down the stairs at the end of the hall.

# CHAPTER 35

Pain. Throbbing behind his eyes. The mother of all hangovers.

Ron tried to sit up. The floor tilted and the walls moved. Floor? What was he doing on the floor? And those walls, so close . . . where was he? He touched his head: a tender lump alongside his left eye.

Memory seeped back. Sam. He'd found her. An alarm clock in the basement. And then she must have hit him with something. Sam? Not the Sam he knew. She would have begged, maybe whimpered a little. What's happened to her?

And how long had he been down here on the floor?

He looked at his watch: three twenty-seven. He managed to sit up. Time . . . Groping for a point of reference, he remembered the eleven fifty-four flight to Syracuse. Then the guy in the parking lot and the drive back to Huntington. Now it was coming back: the walk down to that little porch on the water, the Hawaiian sling and the knife and the blood running across the stained planks like spilled paint—he remembered it all now. A lot had happened in what? . . . three and a half hours? So he couldn't have been out long. Maybe just a few seconds.

Carefully, like a drunk, he pushed off the rug onto his knees and then his feet, arms out for balance. Catch up with Sam before she called the cops. He lurched to the door, twisted the knob and pulled. Jerked. Kicked it. Pulled with both hands. Not even a rattle.

Locked in.

What's this room? Toy soldiers on the shelf and picture-book drawings framed on the walls. Except for that chair, kid's furniture that made the room feel smaller. Some kind of a nursery? And that smell? Not sweet but . . . some kind of cosmetic? Female, somehow. Just his imagination? How long had Sam been hiding in this room? And now that she'd locked him in here, where was she going? The police? That nosey broad she worked for? The woman who had some kind of a business messing with other people's business. Careful not to look around at the shrinking walls, he jerked his cell out of the leather case on his belt. Call her cell and try to find out what she's up to? He hesitated. Waste of time, and didn't matter anyway. Whatever she's up to, it's bad news.

He stared at the cell, trying to think of someone to call. Wallace? He could say he somehow got locked into this broken-down gold coast mansion . . . Maybe looking into a property that . . . How could he finish that sentence? He could think of something, but it wouldn't matter. Wallace wouldn't buy it. Wallace would just call the cops. Hadn't he already given him up to Pedro?

The thought of cops brought to mind that guy gushing blood onto the wooden deck of the boathouse. He hadn't taken care of that. Need to do . . . what? Weight him down and sink him in the harbor maybe. Have to think about that. But first things first. Get out of here. Then Sam. Then the guy.

What's that strange noise? This little room is as sound-dead as a studio. His own breath? Like he'd been running. A bubble pressing his chest. Taste of acid. Heart attack? No, panic. Like the first night aboard ship, trying to sleep in the third rack of a stack of four. He walked around the room that tilted underfoot as if this crummy old place were under way, noticing the armies of lead soldiers on the shelf over the bed and the line drawings framed on the wall. He looked into the little bathroom. Again, the hint of a flowery, female scent. Either his imagination or his senses were amped up to the max. She'd been in here but now she was on the loose.

Where was she going? And what had she been doing here in the first place? There was too much going on, too much he didn't know. "Three-quarters of the universe is dark energy, and most of the rest is dark matter," he recited out loud in a wobbly, uncertain voice, to stir up this dead air. "Which means we know nothing about almost everything, Thanks, Uncle Apple. That's a big help."

On his next trip around he put the cell carefully on the little table and sat in the one adult-size chair. Deep breaths. Plenty of air in here. Hang onto that idea. And the walls aren't really closing in. Stop looking at them. Control. He cleared his throat.

Try something else. Lists. Harvard houses: Elliott, Lowell, Adams, Winthrop, Dunster—what a comical name. Wonder what it looks like. A dome like a dunce cap? Think about some other list. Navy ratings. Because of his yeoman's patch they called him "Quills." Electrician's mate was "Sparky"; carpenter's mate, "Chips"; signalman, "Flags." Breathing almost normal now.

How to get out of here? NOW. Before Sam does whatever payback thing she has in mind. First thing she's going to do is run to Amy, wherever she has the kid stashed. Maybe that gives him a little time. But not much.

Looking around the room for an idea, Ron saw the big homemade knife where it had skidded into the corner. Maybe he could hack his way out of here somehow. He stood—now the floor was steadier under his feet—and took the two steps to pick up the knife. Seemed heavier now. He touched the edge above the sticky brown stain. Not razor sharp. What had the guy said? Ground by a blacksmith. That smithy better stick to horseshoes.

He tried the blade between the door frame and the jamb, but it was too thick. Too thick even to start whittling the frame. He tapped the door with the handle of the knife. Solid. He'd be old and gray before he could even chop a hole in it. He went back to the chair and sat with the knife across his knees, eyes closed to shut out those enclosing walls, and picked up the cell from the end table. Had to call somebody. Somebody who'd come right now, and not call the cops.

"Hey man." He heard the Mex-feminine voice, as if Pedro had answered his thought. As if the street punk was sitting right here in the room, or maybe on the phone. Ron punched the air.

"Of course." Now he really did hear a voice, his own, still wobbly against the pressing silence. "You just want to talk, don't you, Pedro? And the last thing you're going to think of is a call to the cops, right?" Pedro's going to have to be dealt with eventually. Sooner or later he'd have to set up some kind of a meet where the situation's under control. Why not this little room?

He looked around, hefting the knife to get comfortable with its tip-heavy feel. No room to maneuver. Whatever weapon Pedro brought—it probably would just be some spic switch blade—but it wouldn't matter. Surprise got him into this fix, and surprise would get him out. Without giving himself time for second thoughts, he flipped open the cell, found the number in the directory and pressed in the call. Get out of here. Now.

As it rang he looked around. Kids' book illustrations. Reminded him of the toy gun. Should have kept that to bluff Pedro. But how could he have known that he'd need it? He touched the tender lump next to his eye. He didn't have much experience with pain. Unpleasant. And what was the deal with that alarm clock? Who'd have expected Sam to—

"Yeah?" the phone said. Nothing feminine about that rumble.

"I'm a friend of Pedro's. Would you take a message for him?"

"Don't know any Pedro."

"Pedro Loco. Just give him this phone number, okay? Tell

him Ron is waiting for his call."

"Don't know any Pedro. Or any Ron." But the guy took the number.

Up on his feet again, now with something to do. Something that kept these walls from closing in. He walked the edges of the room like a dog claiming territory, planning his meeting with Pedro. Expect a knife. A street blade, like the butterfly knife Ron had tossed out the car window that night on Depot Road. He hefted the big homemade knife. Greaser wouldn't be carrying anything with that kind of reach. Thinking about knives brought up an adrenalin buzz that replaced the shut-in panic. On the edge. Where he lived at his best.

Pedro would be coming out of the hall. Dim light. He'd lift the latch and open the door. Might not step inside until he saw Ron empty-handed, so the big knife had to be out of sight.

Ron tucked the knife under the blanket on the bed with the butt end of the handle sticking out just enough. He went into the little bathroom. Toothbrush and toothpaste, hair brush, a scatter of hair pins, dispenser of liquid soap, towels, a water glass. Toss a glass of water into Pedro's face? No, too risky. A woman's blue suit that must be Sam's hanging behind the door. What was she wearing when he came in? He couldn't remember.

As he went back into the other room the rag rug rumpled under his foot. He stepped back, bent down and tugged at it. The rug slid toward him. Moving quickly now, he went back to the bathroom and jerked a towel off the rack.

His phone chimed. He cleared his throat to steady his voice before he answered, "Hello?"

"Yeah."

"This Pedro?"

"Who wants to know?"

Ron wiped his upper lip with the towel before he answered: "Friend of a friend, like you said. You still want to talk?"

"Talk about what?"

"Seven billion minus four. Depot Road, and Wallace."

"Thought you was on some kinda trip."

"It got cancelled. Now I'm ready to tell you what I know."

Pause. "Okay. Here's where you go."

"No, that won't work. You're going to have to come to me."

"Bullshit, man."

Ron used the towel again. "That's the only way this is going to work. You'll understand when you get here. It's a nice private place where nobody's going to bother us. Nobody'll even see us."

"Where's that?"

"You know that big old house on Littleneck Road? Big stone pillars?"

"Saggy old iron gate? Yeah, I know the place."

"That's where I am. Place is empty. You can come right in. Door's open. We can have a nice private talk."

"Where you gonna be waiting for me?"

"Go on back to the kitchen and you'll see the stairs down to the basement. That's where I am."

"Basement? What you doing down there?"

"I'm in the real estate business, you know? I was checking out this property—the owner, he's not just a friend. He wants us to put this place on the market for him. Anyway, when I was checking it out I managed to get myself locked in down here."

"Locked in? What kinda real estate man is that?"

Deep breath. Patience. "Stupid mistake, I agree. But shit happens, y'know? Anyway, I realized this is a nice place for a private talk and so I thought of you."

"Thought of me? Ain't that sweet."

Ron licked his lips. "Hey, you want to talk or not?"

Pause. Ron held his breath, "Happens I gotta a crew in that neighborhood today. Let's see, maybe I could . . . Yeah, okay. I can come by there for a little while."

"Good. Come quick as you can."

A little chuckle. "Sounds like you gonna be there whenever." The phone went dead.

Ron picked up the knife, grabbed the edge of the rug and pulled it into his lap as he sat in the big chair. He sliced a hand's-width slit along the edge of the rug, twisted the towel into a rope, slipped it through the slit and knotted it. As he worked he was replaying in his mind's ear what Pedro had said. Something about a crew in the neighborhood. Probably a lawn crew. Pedro must be some kind of a lawn service foreman. He spread the rug out on the floor and jerked the towel. The rug slid easily, especially when he stooped and jerked close to the floor. He scooted the rug up to the door, got down on his hands and knees and sighted along the top of the rug to make sure that when the door was unlocked it could swing open over the rug.

Hurrying—Pedro was in the neighborhood—he filled the glass with water, grabbed the soap dispenser and went out to the hall door. He dribbled soap around the floor in front of the door and poured the glassful of water over it. Had Pedro's English been a little better now, in the role of crew chief, than when he was playing the street thug? Ron spread the rug carefully over the soapy floor and then went back and forth to the bathroom with four glasses of water to soak the rug. He jerked the towel, and the rug slid like a toboggan.

Bending over to hold the towel close to the floor, he backed toward the center of the little room until the towel was almost taut. He visualized Pedro opening the door and looking in from the hall. Not a big guy. His voice didn't sound big, but that didn't mean anything. We know nothing about almost everything. Never mind—he could be big as a moose and it wouldn't matter. But if he had a gun . . .

Even if he did, he wouldn't come in shooting. He wants to talk, find out about Depot Road. Wait until he steps onto the rug, then give it a jerk and go for the big knife on the bed. Seeing it happen as if on stage, he felt the buzz of adrenalin. The room even grew a little.

# CHAPTER 36

When she went across the terrazzo foyer, past the stone dogs and across the Belgian blocks onto the driveway, she remembered her abandoned shoes as the gravel spoke to bare feet. She looked around. Camry wasn't in front, where she'd parked it. Then she remembered: when she'd been running toward the maze she'd seen her car in front of the garage.

Hobbling along the driveway she got to the bend and—yes! Right there beyond the propane tanks at the kitchen window was her freshly washed but street-weary Camry. Ron had said the keys were in the ignition. Could that be possible?

Running on her complaining feet—could Charley have left her a just-in-case gift?—she got to the door and looked in. God bless you, Charley. Whatever god is yours, in whatever time or place you are now, bless you Charley for thinking of me and my Amy.

# CHAPTER 37

"Hey man. You got a nice house."

Ron pressed the cell to his ear with his left hand and squeezed the other into a sweaty fist. He swallowed to calm his voice. "Glad you like it. Belongs to a friend. You inside?"

"No. Just looking around. Your friend needs some hard-working Mexicans, mowing and trimming and stuff."

Ron wiped his upper lip and took a moment to keep his voice casual. "Just come on in and we'll talk about what that Depot Road . . . incident. Everything I know about it."

Pause, and then: "Yeah. Bet you would."

"What is that supposed to mean?"

"Supposed to mean I've been taking a little look around."

Ron stood and moved the phone away from his mouth, telling himself not to answer without knowing where this was going. Pedro let the silence grow. Finally, Ron asked, "So what did you see?"

"Interesting old place. Old gardens. Some kinda funny hedges, like making little paths. You didn't think I was just going to walk in there without looking around, did you?"

Ron was pacing the squeezing perimeter of the room. "Okay, you checked it out. Now, if you want to talk, this is the time. I don't have all day."

The phone chuckled. "You're right about that, man. Time is limited."

"Hey look, Pedro. I was up front with you, so what's going on here?"

"What's going on is, I asked myself: why would this guy who's supposed to know something about that fire—why would he bring me to a place like this for a meeting? And the basement—what kind of a place is that for a meeting?"

"It's where I am. I explained that."

"You didn't explain it all."

"What else do you need to know?"

"Well, that little house down by the water. You didn't explain that."

Ron stopped his trip around the perimeter. The air emptied out of this cell. He could hear his own rapid breathing. "All right. I can tell you about that. Just come in so we can talk."

"Lotta blood down there. You know about that?"

"I told you . . ."

"Guy down there with his throat cut. Mexican guy."

"Not a Mexican. A terrorist. He was trying to—"

"Looked like a Mexican to me. And think I oughta know."

"He's a Cherokee. An Oklahoma Indian. And he's a killer."

"Don't look like a killer to me. Look like a dead Mexican. Y'know, I never supposed you—that guy, he said you knew something about that fire. I thought maybe you knew somebody that hates Mexicans."

"Look, you don't understand. That guy—"

"I didn't suppose it was you. What'd we ever do to you?"

"Nothing. I've got nothing against Mexicans. You don't understand. If you come—"

"Maybe you oughta listen a little. Don't know how much time we have left."

"Time? What have you done?"

"When you called I ask myself, why would you bring me to this old place for a meeting? And down in the basement? So, first thing I do, I walk around outside. Very carefully, in case you hiding somewhere. I see a woman's shoe in the driveway. Down the lawn there's a big pile of brush. Someone has been trimming all those hedges. And then I go down to that little house by the water, and that's where I find him. The Mexican you killed."

"Wait. You don't—" A strange smell. Does fear have an odor?

"The last Mexican you killed. Those folks on Depot Road weren't enough? And what did you have planned for me? Don't answer. Just listen. Don't have a lot of time. After I find the Mexican I look around the house. You told me it's just you here, and you're down in the basement, but I look around to make sure. Propane tanks outside the kitchen, a busted-up little chair stacked by the back door, a woman's shoe in the driveway and the front door standing open. So I go in and look around inside."

"Please, Pedro. Just let me—"

"Didn't I say listen? You want to know what's going to happen to you, I'll tell you. Just listen. All the time I'm looking around this big old empty house I'm thinking about those folks on Depot Road. Working people, take care of lawns and carry out the dirty dishes and mop the floors. One night their house catches on fire and they can't get out. So that makes me think about those propane tanks outside the kitchen."

"Oh God. Please, Pedro."

"First I go out to that pile of hedge trimmings and break up a few of the dry ones. On the way in I pick up the pieces of that busted chair. Then I find some matches in the kitchen and a roll of shelf paper. You know that big fireplace in the front room? 'Bout the size of my kitchen. I stepped clear inside and arranged the paper and the hedge wood under the pieces of the busted chair to start a nice little fire. Those chairs around the dining room table? Some kinda dark wood that looks like it's going to burn nice and slow. Fireplace is so big I could stack three of those chairs in there. You know what I did then? Bet you can guess."

"Just let me explain," Ron's voice collapsing into sobs. "Please, please, please."

"Too late for that, Mr. Mexican killer. 'Cause what I did next, I went back to the kitchen and snuffed out the pilot light in that big old stove. Then I turned on all the burners. Then I got the hell out of there."

That odor. Not exactly sweet. A chemical smell. "There's still time. You could let me out and I'll explain everything."

"No, I can't do that. Even if I wanted to. I'm back in downtown Huntington now. I'm not going to be anywhere around when that place blows. But you probably got a little time to think about it. And think about those folks on Depot Road."

The phone went dead.

★ ★ ★ ★ ★

# Two Days Later

★ ★ ★ ★ ★

Man is a credulous animal, and must believe something; in the absence of good grounds for belief, he will be satisfied with bad ones.

—Bertrand Russell

# CHAPTER 38

"The police didn't buy her story right away," Cassie said. "Especially that part about spending two hours with Amy before she got around to calling them. They had trouble understanding that."

Kurt raised his eyebrows and nodded. "Yeah, that could be a problem. What'd she say?"

"Just that—" Cassie smiled and shrugged "—at the time Amy seemed more important. Eventually, they let it go and went on to the rest of her story. Everything checked out. Charley was, I've forgotten his name—Ben Russell? Russ Bennett? Something like that. Not Bear Paw, or . . . anything that *sounds* Indian. Graduated from high school in someplace called . . ." she hesitated. "Tallequah. In Oklahoma."

Cassie held up a finger. "First, there was an unsolved murder on Vashon Island, in Washington, just like she said. A computer game designer. And when the mansion caught fire and blew up, she'd been here—" she turned the finger onto the table "—reconnecting with Amy for two hours. They have our word for that. So how could she have caused it? Or why?" She sipped coffee. "They say that propane is heavier than air, and so the explosion probably went all the way up from the basement. Or down. Whatever, the fire was so hot that nothing is left."

He pushed his mug onto the invisible line that would complete the right triangle of the kitchen table corner. She recognized the unconscious move to create order and braced herself: Here it comes. "Cass, there's something I have to talk to you about."

"Okay," she said, thinking: Please don't tell me her name. I can handle this, but I really don't want to know who she is.

"You must have wondered why I've been getting home late recently."

"Well, I know the housing market's lousy. I figured . . ." she shrugged. "Yeah, I wondered."

"I could tell. I should have talked to you sooner, but I was—" he pulled a face "—embarrassed."

"You thought I might go . . . out of control?"

He shook his head. "No, not that. Not at all. You can handle anything. In a way," he moved the mug into more perfect alignment, "that's kind of the problem."

"*I'm* the problem?"

He took a deep breath. "No, but you're always so . . . on top of things. And I can't seem to get anything together."

"What do you mean?"

"Well, I haven't closed a deal in . . ." he raised both hands in a surrender gesture. "You write the checks. You know."

"But that's not your problem, Kurt. You can't control the worst housing market collapse in what? Sixty years? Seventy-five?"

Kurt stood and walked around the table to the sink. With his back to her, he rearranged the glasses on the drain board: tumblers on the back, juice glasses in front. "I know you want a baby, Cass. But do you know what college costs today?"

"College?"

He came back to his chair at the table. "Well, yes. You can't start something like a baby without thinking about what that means."

Cassie leaned across the table to him. "You've been thinking about a baby?"

"You have to figure on thirty thousand a year. If he gets into Harvard or Yale—God, I don't know what that costs."

"So you've been working overtime?"

He leaned back, away from her. "Overtime is just shoveling sand against the tide. No, I had a big plan. You ever hear of a vulture fund, Cass?"

She shook her head. "Sounds gross."

"Not as bad as it sounds. The way it's supposed to work . . ." he glanced up at the fluorescent fixture to find the words, "an investor—that's the vulture fund—buys a mortgage in default."

"Buys it from who?"

"The bank. Rather than foreclose and write off a big loss, the bank sells the mortgage to the vulture for a smaller loss. The vulture then sells the house back to the owner at a higher price but one that the owner can afford. Everybody wins."

She stood and filled both mugs. "Somehow, I don't think it works out that way."

"I think it probably does. At least it can. But it's not working out for me. For us."

She sat and took a reflective sip. Coffee was getting old. "You bought the wrong mortgage?"

"Cass, I'm not quite that stupid. No, I didn't buy a mortgage. I bought into a fund that's supposed to be picking up these distressed properties and selling them back. They said they're interested in the Huntington area, where I think I understand the values. Plenty of underwater properties now, but a growth market long term."

"Let me guess. Wallace?"

"How did you know?"

"I didn't. But somehow . . . go on."

"What I've been trying to tell you is, our savings—what you call the baby account—that's now the vulture fund account."

"All of it?"

He closed his eyes and nodded his head. "Telling you about it, this is embarrassing. I can't believe I bought that proposition."

"You lost all of our savings?"

"Not quite. But too much."

In the silence, she decided not to press that point. "You said you bought some kind of a proposition?"

He turned his hands palms up and stared at them, rather than look at her. "The way it works, there's a general partner, that's Wallace Enterprises, and there are limited partners. Investors, like me. Us. The income is divided among the partners."

"But the general partner gets his share first?"

"You got it. How'd you know?"

She resisted the impulse to reach across the table to clasp those turned-up hands. "Well, the way you're not looking at me—that's a clue."

Kurt raised his head and struggled up a smile. "What made me buy the deal is a finder's bonus. I earn a bonus for every mortgage I bring in that results in a refinance deal."

"Sounds reasonable," Cassie said. "Lousy market, so make lemonade out of the lemons. Did you bring in some deals?"

He nodded. "Several. Three just last week."

"Great. So what's in the bonus account?"

He held up thumb and forefinger to shape a zero. "Nothing ever gets through the review committee."

"The what?"

"Investment review committee. General partner and his advisors." Kurt shrugged. "Has to be some kind of a process to decide how to spend other people's money, right? It's in the prospectus and the contract."

"So why don't they okay your deals?"

"Took me a while to figure that out." He twisted a self-deprecating smile. "They have the limited partners' money, right? So why risk it on mortgages?"

She sat back, taking that in. "But that's . . . that's a Ponzi scheme."

"Something like that. But their ass is covered. I've read the papers thirty times. Plenty of disclaimers. And they're actually turning a few mortgages around in other markets."

"Where they don't have to pay a finder's fee?"

"Hard to tell from what they publish, but"—he shrugged— "that would be my guess."

"I suppose a lawsuit would just be good money after bad."

He nodded. "And I want to keep selling real estate here. That kind of a lawsuit wouldn't help my reputation."

"All these late nights," she said, making sure she understood, "you've been working?"

"You have to catch people in the evening to pitch refinancing. Talk to them in the home they're about to lose." He waggled his elbows like wings. "Every vulture knows that."

"So the Wallace crowd, they're not just taking your money— they're raising the hopes of all those people and then turning them down."

"The Wallace guys don't have to tell them. I get to make that phone call."

She closed her eyes and shook her head, thinking about Kurt, the guy with the emotional intelligence that had produced a scrapbook of cards and notes from clients happy in their new homes. "And you got into this because I . . . make you feel inadequate?"

His smile brought tears to her eyes. "And just in case there was any doubt, meet Kurt the vulture fund loser."

Cassie stood and dragged her chair around to his side of the table. "You know, Kurt, deciding to have a baby is not about having money for college."

"What do you mean?"

"It's all about having faith."

"Faith in the future?"

"Yes, I suppose. But that's not what I mean."

"Faith in each other?"

"That too."

"But that's not what you mean?"

"No. I mean just . . . faith in life."

He thought about that. After a while she said, "When you were coming home late, I got to thinking about all those girls in the back seat of your Lincoln."

"Oh, come on Cassie. That doesn't—"

"Let me finish. I've always felt like I didn't . . . I couldn't, well, measure up. No, don't say anything. That's the way I felt. The way I've always felt. So let me ask you: would the back seat of your Honda . . . it's not the Lincoln, but would it do?" She laughed at his expression. "And do you still know a private place to park?"

Laughing with her, he said, "I can probably think of a place."

She stood and took his hand. "But I've always wondered about the feet. You'll have to show me where to put my feet."

★ ★ ★ ★ ★

# HALLOWEEN MORNING

★ ★ ★ ★ ★

**And the end of our exploring,**
**Will be to arrive where we started,**
**And know the place for the first time.**

**—T.S. Eliot**

# CHAPTER 39

Sam's Camry skidded on the sodden oak leaves as she approached the stop sign on Depot Road. She threw an instinctive arm in front of Amy, who was belted into the front seat beside her. But Amy just kept chattering about the "parade of horrors" coming up in preschool this morning and why she had vetoed all her mother's costume suggestions. "*Every*body will be a witch" and "Ghosts are corny" and finally just "Come on, Mom."

A few blocks farther, past a billboard that announced "Nine Luxury Townhouses Coming Soon" above the Wallace Enterprises logo, Sam edged into the line of cars in front of the wrought-iron "Ask Me Annie" gate. Amy unbuckled as they slowed and when the Camry stopped she was out, scrambling to join the other costumed preschoolers on the sidewalk. But just as she reached the gate she turned and flashed a quick wave.

Sam waved good-bye to the Queen of Hearts.

# ABOUT THE AUTHOR

A son of Oklahoma, **Weyman Jones** first wrote about the Cherokee in an undergraduate honors thesis at Harvard. Later, he published two historical novels for young readers about Sequoya, who created a written language for the Cherokee. *The Edge of Two Worlds* went to seven printings and earned the Lewis Carroll Shelf and the Western Heritage Awards. His non-fiction book on computers was republished in several languages.

After serving as an enlisted man and then a junior officer in the U.S. Navy, Jones had a career in corporate communications. Now he writes mystery thrillers that draw on his experience. His fifth brings the ancient Cherokee culture of honor into conflict with contemporary values.

Weyman Jones lives with his wife in Santa Barbara, California.